❋   ❋   ❋

CHARLOTTE VALE ALLEN

ACTS
OF
KINDNESS

*Island
Nation
Press* LLC

◆144 ROWAYTON WOODS DRIVE ◆ NORWALK, CT ◆ 06854 ◆

❅ ❅ ❅ ❅ ❅ ❅

Acts of Kindness
ISBN 1-892738-03-1

First Published in the USA in 1979
by New American Library, Inc
Berkley Edition 1987

Cover & book design by deLancey Funsten.

This edition published 1998 by
Island Nation Books LLC
144 Rowayton Woods Drive
Norwalk, CT 06854 USA

Printed in U.S.A.

❅ ❅ ❅ ❅ ❅

Visit the author's website at:
http://www.charlottevaleallen.com

ACTS
OF
KINDNESS

❄   ❄   ❄   ❄   ❄

AUTHOR'S NOTE

One of the earliest books I wrote was published under the title *Gentle Stranger*. I had wanted to call it *Acts of Kindness*, a title that had genuine relevance to the story. The publisher insisted. The book was called *Gentle Stranger*.

Then, some time later, when I wrote this book, my title for it was *The Gatehouse*. My publisher at that time didn't like the title.   Feeling a little wicked, I suggested calling the book *Acts of Kindness*. The new publisher loved the title. But in my mind, this book will always be *The Gatehouse*.

Also, in the twenty years since this book was written, pregnant women are now actively discouraged from smoking. The author is well aware of this and does *not* advocate either smoking or drinking alcoholic beverages during pregnancy.

PART ONE

✳   ✳   ✳   ✳   ✳

One

HE GOT UP SO ABRUPTLY SHE WAS STARTLED. WAS IT A JOKE? HE GOT up, made a strange, awful sound. And then there was motion, falling. He threw out his hands, falling; his body hitting the mike, the boom swinging, catching her in the throat. An instant of blinding pain. And then she was falling, too.

For weeks after, lying in the hospital bed, she kept remembering over and over thinking it had been a joke. Clowning around. But no joke. It had all been real. Not a joke, a nightmare. And everything, everything was ended in just thirty or forty seconds. She couldn't seem to make herself accept that fact, kept turning her head as best she could every time someone came into the room. Expecting it to be him. It never was. It was never going to be. He was dead. But still her eyes kept searching the empty doorway. As if he might be there but her vision had, in some way, been impaired and she simply wasn't able to see him. But he *was* there.

People from the film company came, with stricken eyes and ineptly articulated expressions of sympathy. Appearing embarrassed. And Leonard came and sat down in the chair beside the bed, held her hand. He looked as if someone had struck him between the eyes some time before and the pain of the blow was just now beginning to register. He said, "Gene, I know it really isn't the time to talk about this. But it has to be talked about sometime. Just so ... We've had people from the insurance company all over us. And Workmens' Compensation people. Claims people. Investigators. The press. There's no question it was an on-the-job accident. So, the thing is, you'll be compensated. Probably for life. It seems so goddamned *crass*, having to talk about this to you now. But it's got to be done. I thought you should know."

She watched his face, his mouth; hearing his words, finding what he had to say quite incredible. Like some incomprehensible foreign science fiction film. Like something she might have been dubbing. Putting dialogue to some lunatic space scene. Putting her voice into the mouth of some foreign actress whose gestures, face, and body were in no way related to the voice Gene was giving her.

Leonard went on at some length about the settlement, the compensation, the probable lifetime income she'd receive for having been rendered permanently unfit to pursue her profession. And she lay watching him, waiting for him to talk about Bill. Waiting tensely, knowing that would be next. He and Leonard had been best friends. Leonard had been there, in the booth, seen it all. She wondered how Leonard viewed it when he reran it all in his mind. Did he see it the same way she did? With Bill struggling up out of the chair, throwing out his hands, falling. And the boom whipping around through the air like a sword, or a club.

"I still don't believe it," Leonard said, looking down at his hands. "The whole thing … Who knew?" he said, looking up at her. His expression so pained she felt very sorry for him. "Did *you* know?" he went on, not expecting an answer, knowing she couldn't give one. He wouldn't have waited in any case. Bent on delivering his particular perspective. "Forty-two years old. There wasn't a damned thing wrong with the man!"

No, that was true. She turned her eyes away, staring at the wall. Thinking, There wasn't a thing wrong with him. Nothing. He was so good it had to have been something I dreamed. People like that don't live, don't keep on living. Of course not.

"I'm sorry," Leonard said helplessly. "I'm so goddamned sorry! If you need anything, anything I can do for you, let me know." He reached over to place his hand on hers. She looked down at his hand. She could see he was touching her, but she couldn't feel it. Her eyes felt so dry. Too dry. They moved with difficulty, watching him. "I'll be back," he said, getting up, buttoning his overcoat. "I wish I could say something that would make this better," he said, feeling monstrously frustrated, inadequate. "Or do something. I'll be back," he said again, helplessly. And bent to kiss her forehead before going away. She didn't feel the kiss either. She was only aware of his aftershave and his lapel brushing against her cheek. And then she was aware of his absence.

She had far too much time for thinking, lying there in that hospital bed. Weeks. Night and day. The silence, the thinking, broken by the intermittent arrivals and departures of specialists, nurses, technicians. People coming and going, serious faces always intact. Even their professional, intended-to-be-heartening smiles serious. They scarcely interfered with her thinking. There wasn't anything they could do, in any case. They made that clear in their apologetic fashion.

In a matter of minutes losing someone she'd loved, a career she'd worked hard to build and the ability ever to speak above a whisper. Irreparable damage to the larynx. And scars on her throat. From the tracheotomy and the surgery, the failed attempt to reconstruct her larynx. Reduced now to a peach pit in her throat. A peach pit that, when she first tried, produced a hissing whisper and felt as if it was scratching the interior of her throat.

"You're just out of practice," they told her. "It's been a while since you've used those muscles. Keep talking, the pain'll go away."

She didn't think she cared. Bill was dead. And gone. Buried. He might have been someone she'd dreamed one night. Dreamed over a course of nights for over three years.

"But you're very lucky," the doctor assured her. "The baby's fine."

She just stared at him, wondering if he realized how much of a fool he was. She knew precisely how the baby was. That quiet lump of tissues sitting up there in between her pelvic bones. Safely protected by her body. And surely they didn't think she'd let absolutely everything be taken away? Did they think she'd lost her reason along with her ability to speak audibly? Nothing was going to happen to the baby. Unless she had to die. And there seemed no possibility of that happening, they told her.

"You're just fine," the doctor said. "You'll be able to leave here next week."

She thought about her apartment. About Bill's things in the apartment. And was suddenly panic-stricken. Knowing she couldn't possibly go back there and face Bill's clothes, his books, his cologne and his luggage, his shoes, his razor. She couldn't. And used that hurtful peach pit to catch the nurse's attention, to ask for pencil and paper. Writing down the number, asking the nurse to call Leonard. Who came very quickly, looking frightened as if there was something terminal she planned to say to him. He sat in the chair beside the bed and watched her hand moving over the page, nervously waiting to see what she was writing. She tore the page off the notepad and thrust it at him. She'd written, "Take my keys. Go to the apartment. Bill's things. *Please*. Take them away!"

Her eyes were round, apprehensive as she watched him read. He folded the page in half, pushed it into his coat pocket, asking, "Where are your keys? I'll take care of it."

She didn't want him to hear how she sounded, so pointed at the bedside table and he opened the drawer, removed her bag, and handed it to her. She fished around inside, found the keys, and gave them to him.

"I've got to be out of town for a few days," he said, holding her hand. "I'll be back next week to take you home."

She forgot herself and started to cry, even the crying possessed of a frighteningly mechanical sound. Like a toy might sound weeping. Leonard moved to the side of the bed and put his arms around her, stroking her, saying, "I know, I know. Don't worry. I'll take care of everything. And I'll be back next week to take you out of here."

He moved to go and she clung to him, needing him there for just a few more moments. Terrified of facing the future that would begin next week. A future so empty it was like gazing into a mirror and finding no reflection there. Nothing. Blank glass.

She cried long after he'd gone. With her hand wedged into her mouth, her teeth biting down. Feeling the pain. Wanting for a few minutes to close her eyes and find herself gone as Bill was gone, as her voice was gone, her life. Was gone.

She sat down in the living room after Leonard had left and tried to think. Tried to think in spite of the flow of images parading past her eyes. Bill sitting over there on the arm of the chair with a cup of coffee, reading the *Times* from front to back. Bill in the kitchen mixing drinks, talking to her from one room to the next. The place was tainted, crawling with memories. Just as this mass of assembling tissues would soon begin crawling inside her.

I've got to get out of here! she thought, frightened by the oppressive images, by her sudden powerlessness. Too vulnerable. Something might happen. A mugger. Someone. And she couldn't scream, couldn't speak above a whisper. New York wasn't a place for someone like her to live now. Not someone who couldn't scream.

She felt like screaming. Sat there, closed her eyes, and tried to scream. Blood vessels in her head feeling on the verge of bursting, trying so hard to scream. Nothing. A wheezing animal sound when she wanted to shatter the windows, the mirror with the scream she could feel inside her.

Get out! Got to got out! Get away, right away, all the way away! Where? How?

Go home? To what? To her father, her sister and brother-in-law, the farm. No! That was gone. She couldn't go back to that. Not now. Away, yes. Somewhere. Where?

Oh God! How had all this happened? Why? They'd been so happy. Too happy. Dangerous to be that happy, to have everything going so well, so successfully, so happily. Dangerous. She got up and went into the bedroom. Stopped. A steel fist pounding her in the belly, seeing the bed, hearing nighttime whispers, laughter. Got to get out of here! She threw open the closet door, dragged out her bags, placed them open on the bed. No wait! The furniture, the paintings and photographs, the books, the stereo. Madness to leave all these things, simply walk away. Think!

She sat down on the end of the bed, fists clenched, looking around slowly. There must be a plan, logic. You can't just fly out of here, run away. Think! Where to go? Somewhere new, somewhere clean and utterly free of familiar signs, memories. It came to her. Of course. Bill's home town. Three-plus years of hearing him talk about it. And visits there. To go see the house he'd grown up in. And the cemetery where his parents were buried. Far enough away. Yet close somehow. She'd go there, find a place.

A place to hide. A place where she could have this baby, live with this baby, Bill's baby. How could you *die*? She burned holes in his pillow with her eyes. How could you die and leave me? Pregnant, without a voice. And scars. She fingered the bright red scar tissue on her throat. How could you die and let all this happen to me?

Angry and hurt and horribly scared. Thirty-three years old, pregnant with no career. The dubious comfort of a lifetime compensatory income. And Bill's money in their joint bank accounts. Very little else. No insurable interest the salesman had told him. "You can't make her a beneficiary. You're not related. Now, if you were married ..." And Bill patiently explaining, "But the minute the divorce becomes final, I'm going to marry her. I've already got a wife. Isn't there *some* way?"

No way.

Perhaps the first thing she should do is go to the bank, withdraw the money. Yes. That's a good idea. Before someone—his elusive wife, perhaps—came along and tried staking claims on what was hers, Gene's, what Bill had given to her. She jumped up off the bed, grabbed her bag, her coat, her scarf. Went out.

To walk the two blocks over to the bank on Third Avenue and present the teller with a withdrawal slip for the entire balance in the savings account, a check for the balance in the checking account.

"How do you want this?" the teller asked her.

Gene opened her mouth. "Cashier's check," she whispered.

"Pardon?"

"Cashier's check?"

"Sorry, I can't hear you. *How* do you want this?"

The look on the teller's face one that said, "This chick's a nut. Why the hell's she whispering?"

She'd cry, start crying. Please, don't let me cry in this place in front of all these people. Forming the words slowly, carefully, everything inside her straining. "Cashier's check."

"Oh! You want a cashier's check!" Smiling brightly, as if she was as pleased Gene was able to get the words out intelligibly as Gene might have been had this been some sort of bizarre contest for defectives. As it was, she lit a cigarette—what further damage could she possibly do?—and nervously tapped her fingers on the counter while the teller checked the balances, did addition, subtraction; canceled the passbook, ascertained there were no outstanding checks on the checking account. Then she got a check, went to the typewriter, and slowly typed it out. Disappeared somewhere to have a bank officer sign it. Then at last passed the check over the counter with a smile, saying, "Have a good day, now."

I should smile, Gene thought, but I can't. I'm sorry. I can't.

She left the bank thinking about the car. That was hers.

"If I can't make you my damned beneficiary," he'd said, "at least I'll put everything I can in your name."

"You don't have to do that," she'd protested. "You really don't."

"Hey, listen," he'd said, softly, in that gently persuasive way she'd never been able to argue with, "just in case something happens. *Just in case.* You have to have something to go on with."

"I won't listen!"

"You'll listen! Don't be stupid, Gene! There's the baby to consider here, too, if we go ahead with it. And if worse comes to worst, you can always get twelve or fourteen thousand for the car. Then there's the money in the accounts. She'll come popping out of the wood-work if she ever hears I've kicked off. And she'll make goddamned sure she gets everything she can. So I want to make sure there are a few things she can't get. So just shut up and go along with it! Okay?"

Miserable irony. He was always so stinking right about everything. And it was the wife who'd turned up to claim his body, to grieve pub-licly, to arrange services and the burial.

If she dwelled on the thought, it'd kill her. She wouldn't think about it. She returned to the apartment to write a letter to Leonard, asking him, as one last, very large favor, to dispose of the co-op—also in her name—put everything into storage, and she'd be in touch with him as soon as she found out where she wanted to be.

She couldn't use the intercom to speak with the doorman. He couldn't hear her, kept switching off. So, finally, she went down in the elevator and as slowly and clearly as she could, made him under-stand that she needed help with her bags; needed the car up from the garage. The relief doorman took over and the regular doorman rode back up to the apartment with her. Sympathizing, saying, "Sure was a nice man. Can't tell you how sorry I am. Won't be the same with-out him." She wished he'd shut up. Turned to look at him, her eyes telling him to Shut up, shut up! He saw and did.

He helped her load the bags into the car, then closed the trunk and even locked it for her, asking, "Going away for a while, huh?"

She nodded, pressing a twenty-dollar bill into his hand. Amazingly, he didn't want to take it. But she pushed at his hands, shaking her head.

"Not coming back are you?" he said sadly, looking down at the bill, then up at her, watching her shake her head again. "You take good care of yourself," he said. "Okay getting out of here?"

She nodded.

He tipped his hat to her and went to the service elevator.

She got into the car, started it. Quiet hum of the engine. Telemann oozing from the rear-window speakers. WNCN. She raised the vol-ume, put the car into Drive, drove up the ramp, out into the street. Heading for FDR Drive. Heading eventually for the New York State

Thruway. Heading out. Her throat throbbing. As if the sutures were still in place. Touching her throat, fingering the raised ridges of scar tissue. Then readjusting her scarf, covering it all.

✳   ✳   ✳

She checked into a downtown hotel, looked up a real estate agency in the yellow pages, made a note of the address, checked the location on the map of the city shed bought in a gas station just outside of town, then sat down with a wild thumping in her chest. As if someone or something was chasing after her. As if she'd been running for a long, long time and simply had to stop for a moment, rest, before getting up to start running again.

That was the feeling: flight. And she wasn't at all sure what she was running from. Except perhaps familiar places evoking too many dangerous recollections. She'd violated every rule, everything they'd brought her up to believe. Living with a man who was already married to someone else. Living with him, pregnant with his child. Voluntarily, gladly impregnated. Left now to continue on alone. Old rules of morality circling her head like screeching birds of prey, waiting to swoop down on her, take chunks of her flesh.

But I don't believe any of that, she told herself, looking around the room; looking through the open doorway at the old-fashioned bathroom. I don't believe that. I never did. It didn't work for me. But still. To be single and pregnant. Single with a child who will grow up and have to go to school with other children. Other children with full sets of parents. No.

No. For the sake of this child, I'll be a widow. I *am* a widow. Legalities, words on paper, mean nothing. Words mumbled over two people, meaning nothing. A widow. Mrs. Elliott. Eugenie Elliott. Place "Mrs." in front of my name and I am, all at once, a socially acceptable commodity.

She wished it were possible for her to take Bill's name. To somehow legally change her name to his. But, thinking about it, it didn't seem worth the trouble involved. And who was there to know her? Who was there to care if her name was simply Gene Elliott, or *Mrs.* Eugenie Elliott? There was no one to care. Except this child. This child would care. And would someday ask. And she'd answer.

She rested her head against the back of the armchair, thinking about how she might answer. Your father. Your father died. It was an accident He went away one afternoon and took my voice with him. I am thirty-three. In twenty years when you are twenty, I will be fifty-three. In twenty years it will be 1995.

She couldn't imagine it. Not being fifty-three and not having a twenty-year-old child. So far off into the future it scarcely seemed worth considering. The past, though, seemed infinitely worthier of contemplation. A total of three years, four months, and some days. The four months and some days she'd spent falling in love. Being pursued. Adoring every moment of it. So easily persuaded into a "sensible arrangement." All the sense of the arrangement of no consequence because she'd wanted to be with him and everything else was unimportant. Just to be there with him. Awed by him, by his features, his talent and his success, too.

He'd been so high, once upon a time. A star. Of the theater, of films. And slowly on his way down when they'd met. Gradually coming down, aware of it, uncaring. "Less money I have to pay that miserable woman," he'd said, without rancor. The wife received a percentage of his income. It was all written down, documented, filed in some place of authority. Because she'd taken him all the way up there to the top, pushed him up there where he'd thought he wanted to be. And he'd gratefully signed over that lifetime percentage of his earnings. Believing to the last that she'd earned it, deserved it. Then.

Fifteen years later, he'd minded very much and occasionally cursed his generosity, his overblown sense of responsibility. "She's got me locked up, tied down, on ice for the duration. It isn't fair. But at the time, it seemed fair. Part of me still thinks it's fair, in a way. I'm sorry, Gene. But I didn't know I was going to find you."

She hadn't cared about the finances. Didn't care all that much even now. Except that he was gone and never coming back and she was going to have his child. And she'd never be able to tell this child the whole truth about its father. Because everything in print about him included mention of that wife. And that wife wasn't her. What fiction she was going to have to create around the bones of reality. She felt too tired even to think. And her throat ached. She wondered if the pain would ever go away. Closing her eyes, imagining the doctors laying open her throat, playing with the shattered mechanism in there that had been her security, her hoped-for future, her pride.

A farmer's daughter from central Illinois. With a mother frail and filled with limitless, fond aspirations—if not for herself, then for her two daughters. Endowing them with elegant names, filling their heads—trying to—with dreams of magnificent possibilities. A small, dreaming woman with distances in her eyes.

Amelia had, in her teens, taken to ridiculing their mother, forcibly putting down her dreams and fantasies. Amelia waving her big, capable hands, the corners of her mouth tight, saying, "You're living in a dream world and I don't have the time to sit around with you, dreaming. I've got work to do. Somebody around here has got to." Amelia working the farm with the strength and commitment of any man. More. Dismissing her mother and sister and their gentle dreaming with the wave of a roughened, unpretty hand.

But Eugenie ate it with every meal, breathed it with every conversation, grew a hearty distaste for the dirt, the deprivation, the stench of animals and manure. And finally, after her mother died, got to Chicago. To work in the book department, a salesgirl, at Marshall Field's. Reading her way through everything available. Saving her money to go to New York. And in New York, shared an apartment with an on-the-rise actress who one afternoon said, "With your voice you could get into dubbing, voice-overs; make a fortune." And, pure luck, everything clicked. The time right, the place right, all the opportunities failing into line. Within three years establishing herself. Radio commercials, TV. Dubbing. Dubbing an Italian film Bill had made. He was overdubbing himself, all the while smiling across at her. Then he took her to dinner. And then for a drive in the country. After that, he began telephoning at odd hours. To talk. Telling her, "The sound of your voice makes everything mellow, brings me into a quiet place inside me. Something I've been needing so badly."

Flying off to California or to Spain. Every time he came home, the first thing he did was telephone her. Until she knew his schedules, waited for his calls. And, finally, gave herself up to all the feeling he'd generated inside her with his truthfulness and crazy laughter and whimsical observations. Until he dropped dead of a coronary one afternoon and left her broken in too many ways.

✳   ✳   ✳

She went out to look at houses with Mrs. Whitney, the real estate agent. And looked at the houses, moving back and forth inside herself between anger and despair. At some moments hating Bill for causing all this to happen to her. At other moments, longing for him, missing him so much the ache extended into her elbows, her knees; every joint in her body seized up with grief.

Mrs. Whitney was kind, patient. Lent her full attention to Gene's whispered comments about the houses, and kept finding more and more and more places to look at until weeks had gone by and Gene felt she'd go mad if she had to stay in that stark hotel room very much longer. And Mrs. Whitney said, "I've got a gatehouse. It's really about the last listing I've got to show you. It's a lovely place. The only problem is, there isn't any real property, landwise, that goes with the house. It belongs to an estate and it's on the estate property. And everybody so far has been crazy about the house but not crazy about Mrs. Prewitt who owns it. You'll see what I'm talking about for yourself."

It was a lovely place. A gray stone gatehouse. With two spacious bedrooms. A high-ceilinged living room. A large kitchen, a dining room. Fireplaces in the living room, dining room. Flower beds either side of the front door. The entire place secure behind ten-foot-high wrought-iron gates.

"I want to buy this one," Gene said.

"Everybody does," Mrs. Whitney said tiredly. "Until they get a list of some of the snags."

"Tell me."

"You get the sum total of forty-five feet in every direction. To meet the zoning requirements. But the entire property belonging to the gatehouse is on an easement. Which means Mrs. Prewitt can come marching through here any time she likes. You can't put up anything on the property lines. Like fences or bushes. None of that. We've been through this at least twenty times with her. The bottom line is, if she doesn't like you, she won't sell. So far, she isn't selling. But it's worth a try. Are you willing?"

"Yes."

"Okay. I'll call and try to make an appointment to see her. She may be in a good mood and see us right away. She may be in a snit and make us wait three weeks. Keep your fingers crossed she's in a good mood."

They returned to the hotel and Mrs. Whitney called from there while Gene watched her facial expressions. Sitting in the armchair, smoking a cigarette, suddenly needing to have that gatehouse, having to have it. Mrs. Whitney hung up and smiled. "She'll see us at two-thirty. Come on, let me buy you lunch."

Mrs. Whitney was a nice woman, a caring person. Beyond the call of professionalism. Over lunch, asking, "May I call you by your first name?"

"Gene."

"Jean?"

"No. Eugenie. Gene." Why did it still hurt to shape the words, push them out?

"Oh, *Gene*! My name is Marie. I hate to be inquisitive, but was it an accident?"

Gene nodded.

"That's really too bad," Marie sympathized. Then deftly switched subjects. "I cant imagine anyone choosing to live here after New York. I think living there would be great. Still, each to his own." She chattered on, studying Gene. Wondering about her. Such a potent aura of sadness, it seemed to encase her. A pretty woman. With very long, very thick-looking hair of a rich, chocolate-brown color. Skin too pale. Brown eyes, almost black. A pretty mouth, but uncertain. Her throat always wrapped in a scarf. Marie speculated on what might lie beneath that scarf and decided she didn't want to see or know. But wasn't it a shame?

Mrs. Prewitt.

She looked to be in her early forties but could have been older or younger. A large-eyed blonde. Tall and thin and intense. Possessed of a low, whiskey voice and a surprisingly full mouth that drew Gene's eyes. The shape of her mouth a message, somehow, in itself. And the gray-green eyes. A woman who, but for the intensity and expression, might have been beautiful. Formidable. Yet from moment to moment appearing to waver, as if acting out a role, but unsure of all the dialogue. Gene accepted her invitation to be seated, silently suffering Mrs. Prewitt's intense stare. Wondering what on earth this was all about.

Marie Whitney passed over a sheet of paper upon which was written Gene's offer for the gatehouse. Mrs. Prewitt looked at the paper, then at Gene, asking, "Would you intend to live alone in the gatehouse?"

Gene answered, "Eventually, no."

Sharply, angrily, Mrs. Prewitt said, "Speak up!"

Mrs. Whitney, embarrassed, started to explain, but Mrs. Prewitt shushed her, saying, "Let the woman speak for herself!"

"But she …"

Mrs. Prewitt glared at her and Marie closed her mouth.

There was a long, heavy silence. Adele Prewitt looked at the woman sitting opposite, wondering why she had the feeling she was going to sell her the house. A feeling of something close to desolation. What was there about her?

Gene wanted the house. And looked back into the gray-green eyes seeing something there it would have been impossible to define. But something. And the shape of her mouth. Gene reached up and unwound her scarf. Mrs. Prewitt's eyes moved to Gene's throat, flickered back to Gene's eyes, the gray-green undergoing the subtlest of changes. A minuscule dilation of the pupils, perhaps.

Marie didn't want to look, did, and felt a sudden dizziness. The scars looked very new, raw. She looked down at her handbag. A terrible moment. Awful. She shouldn't have brought Gene here, inflicted this on her. The silence held. She risked looking up to see the two women staring at each other.

Adele couldn't seem to think for a moment. She had an impulse to get up, cross the room and place her hand on Gene's throat. Touch her. She felt so ashamed of having forced this moment into being she couldn't, for a moment, think of any way out of it. Then, the training falling back into place, said, "Well have tea," and got up, went out to tell Sally to put on the kettle. And stood for a moment, bracing herself on the counter in the kitchen with her eyes closed.

"You okay?" Sally asked.

Adele shook her head, waving Sally away. God! How could I do that? I didn't mean to do that. How did I come to be someone who could be so cruel?

In the living room, Gene readjusted her scarf, crossed her legs, and lit a cigarette,

"You didn't have to do that" Marie Whitney said in an angry undertone. "She's an *impossible* woman!"

"I want the house," Gene said. Thinking, She isn't at all impossible. "It doesn't matter," she reassured Marie. What the hell matters? she wondered, looking around the vast living room. The only thing that matters is that I can't spend any more time in that hotel room. I'll go insane if I have to.

Mrs. Prewitt returned, sat down, lit a cigarette, crossed very long, slender legs, and stated, "I accept your offer, Mrs. Elliott. I'm sure Mrs. Whitney has told you the terms."

Gene nodded.

"Good. That's settled. Now tell me something," she said cannily, unable to stop herself. "When are you expecting this child?"

"Four and a half months," Gene answered, regarding her with growing interest.

"That's wonderful," Mrs. Prewitt said. And smiled. The smile astonishing.

So that both Gene and Marie Whitney automatically smiled back, at her. Gene wondered for a moment if Mrs. Prewitt wasn't perhaps a little mad. And, being mad, was able to detect it in others. Had, in fact, recognized the madness in Gene herself. Whatever it was, she wanted to spend the entire afternoon here watching this woman change from one face to the next to the next.

The housekeeper brought in a tray with a silver tea service and Mrs. Prewitt busied herself pouring out the tea, her cigarette incongruously bobbing in the corner of her mouth. Squinting against the smoke.

Gene wondered why she had her hair pulled back so severely. It actually looked as if it might be painful. Small ears lying flatly neat against her head. Not a speck of makeup. Her skin absolutely perfect but without any color. As if she was in shock. Or ill.

"Do you work, Mrs. Elliott?" Adele asked, handing across a cup of tea, offering a plate of *petits fours*. Gene wanted to laugh at the sight of the small, iced cakes. They seemed pathetic. But she took one. She could tell this woman wanted her to. A peace offering?

"No," she answered.

"I see." Adele nodded and sat back, removing the cigarette from her mouth, setting it down on the lip of the ashtray. She'd poured a third cup of tea, but made no move to touch it. "You'll send for your things now. From New York? Is that right?"

"Yes."

"Well, good," Adele said, mystifyingly. She wanted desperately to talk to this woman but felt hampered by the agent's presence. I'm behaving like a fool, she told herself. Noticing a slight tremor in her hands as she retrieved her cigarette from the ashtray and took a hard drag on it.

Marie Whitney couldn't make sense of any of it and wanted to get right to work on the papers before anyone could do any mind-changing. "We really should be getting back now," she said to Gene. "We've kept Mrs. Prewitt quite some time."

"Don't rush us," Adele said quietly. "You're not going to lose your sale. Give the woman a chance to relax, drink her tea. All you people live strung out on such high-tension wires. The rest of us haven't quite your urgency about paperwork and commissions. If you're in a desperate hurry to rush away and start getting it all done, go ahead. I'll see to returning Mrs. Elliott to her hotel. Does that suit you, Mrs. Elliott?" Please understand what I'm saying. I need you to stay. Just for a little while. You're someone … someone …

Gene didn't know really what she was doing, but nodded in assent. She didn't really feel like leaving. The thought occurring to her that her mother would have loved this house. It was, in all likelihood, probably the house of all her mother's dreams. Gene suddenly felt comfortable for the first time in months. And was filled with curiosity about this odd woman.

Uncertainly, Marie Whitney got up, saying, "I'll speak to you later then, Gene."

And Gene nodded. Then Mrs. Prewitt got up to see Mrs. Whitney out.

Adele stood a moment after closing the front door, very aware of her heartbeat. The pulses throughout her body. She returned to the living room, at once lit a fresh cigarette and sat down, crossed her legs, and looked again at Gene.

To Gene, it felt as if this woman was studying her inch by inch. Performing a visual dissection. Gene didn't care. The baby shifted. She sat drinking her tea, looking at the room. Not in the least uncomfortable under Mrs. Prewitt's eyes.

"I've gained a reputation with those people for being peculiar, difficult. Probably even crazy. But any behavior that falls outside the normal range of acceptability is suspect. I'm not crazy. Or especially difficult. I'd simply prefer to have the gatehouse go empty than suffer the presence on my property of people I don't care for. To me, that's simply good sense. To the real estate people, it's just short of demented." She picked up the cup of now-cold tea. I'm making myself look worse and worse, she thought. She isn't interested in my philosophical viewpoints. But she stayed. You did stay. It changes the feeling of the entire house, having someone here with me. Someone else other than Sally. Or Lawrence. "Were you a singer or performer of some sort?" she asked incautiously. "I get the feeling that you were."

"No."

"Something. You can still speak, make yourself understood. But it seems—devastating to you. It seems evident you required your voice more than most of us."

"You're playing at clairvoyance," Gene said, very relaxed.

"Who knows?" I don't know *what* I'm doing, Adele thought. Babbling.

"I had a career," Gene admitted. "Doing voice-overs, dubbing." She hadn't spoken this much since the surgery. She was beginning to feel the strain in her throat.

"Oh God!" Adele said softly.

Gene's eyes widened in surprise. The woman looked as if she might actually begin to cry.

"Don't worry about the paperwork," Adele said quickly, doing battle with strange emotions. "Move into the house whenever you want to. It's all newly painted, clean. You saw that. Perhaps," she said, a little breathlessly, "you wouldn't mind if I dropped by from time to time to chat?"

"I won't mind."

"I'll have Elton drive you back to your hotel now, if you're ready."

At the door, they shook hands. Something more about this woman's eyes and the shape of her mouth and the contact of her hand.

"I hope you'll be happy with the house," Adele said.

"Thank you."

❋   ❋   ❋

Elton was big and black and silent. Gene sat in the rear of the old Rolls Royce feeling caught up in what felt like one of her mother's fantasies. What a strange woman! But it didn't matter. She was tired. And wanted to sleep now.

✳ ✳ ✳ ✳ ✳

Two

SHE MOVED IN WITH A RENTED COT, A CHAIR AND TABLE FOUND IN THE gatehouse cellar, and a radio she bought on impulse in the hotel gift shop as she was waiting for her bill to be tallied. Rather than feeling elated, she felt bewildered. As if there should have been an instruction booklet that went along with the balance of her life and it was missing.

Mrs. Prewitt sent Elton down to ask if she needed anything. Gene wrote a note saying, "Thank you, no." And then, her bags unpacked as best as possible, she decided it would be sensible to stock the kitchen. She got into the car and drove until she found a shopping area, made her purchases, returned to the gatehouse, put everything away, and then sat down on the chair in the near-empty living room with her hand on her belly, distractedly aware of the baby.

She ate some beans directly from the can and went to sleep.

The next day, she thought more realistically about the baby. She needed a doctor. And a telephone. A telephone in order to contact the doctor, should the need arise. The new logistics of this life enervating, exhausting. She got up, went out, and walked up the long driveway to the main house. The housekeeper came to the door, nodded at Gene as if she had built-in radar that determined, without telling, the purpose of the visit, and said, "Come inside. I'll get Miz Prewitt."

Gene stepped into the black-and-white-marble-floored foyer and stood gazing down at the floor, looking up when she heard Mrs. Prewitt's heels come clicking down the hallway. Looking up to find Mrs. Prewitt's face familiar now. Very familiar. And thought it odd. And somewhat depressing. Because she had a dependency—however transitory—on this woman, and suddenly wished not to be dependent upon anyone, for anything.

Adele was unreasonably excited, glad of another opportunity to see and talk to this small, dark woman.

"Come in," she said, waving Gene into the living room. "We'll have some tea. How are you getting on? Will you have some tea?"

Her eagerness cutting through any reservations Gene might have had.

Gene nodded. Then said, "I need a telephone. And a doctor."

"Of course!" Adele, on the verge of sitting down, got up, walked to the desk in the corner, flipped through her address book. Saying, "I have a doctor. I'll make an appointment for you?"

"Thank you."

Adele made the call, jotted down the date and time of the appointment, the doctor's name, address, and number; handed the paper to Gene. Then said, "Now for a telephone."

And arranged that, too.

"All right," she said, very efficient, an interesting flush of color riding her cheeks. "Anything else?"

"No."

"Please sit down," Adele said, sitting down and offering Gene a cigarette from a lacquered box on the coffee table, taking one herself. "My name is Adele," she said. "Call me Del."

"Gene."

"Yes, I know. Come for dinner this evening," Adele said. "There'll just be the three of us. Lawrence, you, and me." Is this a mistake? Maybe I shouldn't.

"Lawrence?"

"My husband. You assumed I was divorced, that I live here alone, didn't you?"

"Yes."

"I know," Adele said, looking suddenly on edge. "Everyone does. But we are well and truly married." I'll die being married, go into a grave married. Or an institution.

Gene couldn't think of any suitable response.

"Would you like to see the house?" Del offered, crushing out her cigarette.

"Yes."

The two women walked from room to room with Del saying very little. She was intent on watching Gene's face, her reactions. Wondering, What happened to you? You come and go, present, not present. A small, very pretty woman. The pregnancy scarcely visible.

Unless you looked for that sort of thing.

"This is Lawrence's room," she said, opening the door. Not a flicker of response on Gene's face as they continued on, through the dressing room and bathroom, to the next room. "And this is mine." Stating the obvious: We do not sleep in the same bed, don't ever share a room. We do, however, do battle midway. I have battle scars.

"Beautiful house," Gene said, feeling tired again. Adele's room very pretty, very comfortable. Far more feminine than the woman, from externals, led the observer to expect. The only hint that she might be someone possessed of this sort of taste in the shape and mobility of her mouth. And her eyes.

"You're surprised, aren't you?" Del said. What am I telling you?

Leave me alone, Gene thought, finding Adele's application of pressure suddenly unbearable. She wanted to return to the gatehouse, to lie down on her rented cot and sleep. Just sleep. Not see or hear or feel or think. She followed Del through the rest of the rooms, nodding in approval, grateful when they at last returned downstairs. Adele saying, "Come at seven. All right?"

"Yes."

Del put out her hand, stopping Gene in the doorway. Venturing to put her hand on this small woman's arm. It felt too bold a gesture. "Rest," she said, her voice and manner suddenly soft, caring. "You're worn out."

Gene shook her head, confused, And stepped out, away, walked down the steps, and returned along the driveway to the gatehouse. Thinking, It was a mistake. A dreadful error. To have grown such an immediate, passionate attachment to a house. Just a house. Having to have it, when having it meant interference in her life. This woman telling her to "come at seven." And, "Rest. You're worn out."

❋   ❋   ❋

Del watched her walk away, then closed the door and went through to the kitchen to advise Sally there'd be one more for dinner. Then, suddenly restless, went upstairs to her room. To pace back and forth, energy surging through her system; no outlet. She sat down finally in the chair by the window with a cigarette, gazing out the window. Seeing only her own thoughts. Wondering, Could anyone possibly understand when she had never been able to understand it herself?

It was Lawrence who'd insisted on the separate bedrooms. It had never been her plan. But she'd accepted his preferences. Initially. Innocently. And it was Lawrence who instituted the games. Incomprehensible games. Some she was equipped to comprehend. Others that remained totally outside the sphere of her understanding. How had she come to be married to someone who cultivated what had once been her love and had since become her obsession; cultivated it carefully, like hothouse orchids; kept her on a light leash, dangling the bait in front of her nose? Or was it bait? You lie to yourself. On and on and on. Knowing what all of it is. Refusing to acknowledge it. And Lawrence saying, "Do whatever you like. You should see someone else." Knowing full well she couldn't. All her wonderful so-called intelligence of no use whatsoever. Because the one thing she wanted to do, wished to God she could do, was escape Lawrence and her continuing despicable need to win. She'd loved him, married him, and at the end found herself trapped—by fears by need, by desperation—in a life with someone she frequently, silently, prayed would die. Thereby freeing her.

Trapped. God! Get me out of this! Give me the strength to put an end to it before it puts an end to me!

That small, pretty woman baring her ravaged throat in order to convince me of her need to possess the gatehouse. Courage. I haven't any. I'm so drawn to you by your courage. Wish I could be you. Pregnant. Even voiceless. Lawrence refusing even to allow me that. And I went ahead, did as I was told. A fool. A terrible fool. To believe surrendering the baby would make him more sympathetic, more caring; return him into love with me. He didn't care. And I gave it up out of me, wanting to believe.

I would give anything I possess—doubtful possessions—to be a small pretty woman sleeping on a cot in the gatehouse with a child growing in me, voice or no voice, to be free in the world without an obsessive need to prove myself right or to prove myself at all; where is my courage, my convictions, my once-proud intelligence. Why can't I get up, walk away from this house; get up, don't turn around, don't turn back, get out.

❋   ❋   ❋

The nap helped. Gene took a long, very hot bath, then changed clothes and drove up to the house, disliking the idea of having to walk down the long driveway later on in the dark.

Elton opened the door, took her coat in silence, then indicated she should proceed into the living room. She moved into the doorway to see Adele standing in front of the fireplace holding a drink and a lit cigarette. Talking to a gray-haired, long-legged man sitting in one of the armchairs. Talking to him as he turned the pages of a newspaper, obviously not listening.

Then, looking up, seeing Gene, Del set her drink down on the mantel and came across the room smiling, saying "Come in. Come meet Lawrence."

Gene was a little confused by the alteration in her voice, manner, appearance. As if, in a matter of hours, she'd been completely transformed. Into someone terribly unsure of herself, very female and vulnerable. Her mouth forming a hesitant smile as she led Gene over to Lawrence, who got up out of his chair. Up to a considerable height. To look at Gene with an amused, decidedly patronizing expression as he extended his hand to enclose hers in a too warm, too familiar greeting. As if telling her, via the handshake, that he knew things about her she didn't know about herself. Deeply personal, intimate things.

"So pleased to meet you," he said, exuding charm, displaying his teeth in a somehow predatory smile Gene found more alarming than friendly. She smiled stiffly and allowed Adele to direct her to the sofa.

"Will you have a drink?" Del asked.

Gene said, "No, thank you," and quickly lit a cigarette. There was a terrible tension in the room. Terrible. The dinner would last forever with this kind of tension. What was going on between these two?

"You're sure there's nothing we can offer you?" Del asked again, retrieving her drink from the mantel.

"No. Thank you."

Lawrence had resumed his seat, long legs extended comfortably, ankles crossed. His eyes boldly roving over her. Up and down. Staying on her breasts for quite some time.

"I'd about given up hope Adele would ever find a suitable buyer for the gatehouse," he said at last, smiling. "My wife has rather fixed ideas on certain matters."

Adele looked down into her glass, then raised it to her mouth, took a long swallow, then said, "I'll tell Sally we're ready," and carried her drink out with her. To stand for a moment in the hall praying he wouldn't successfully make a play for this woman. Not this one. Not someone so close. Surely Gene wouldn't be so foolish as to encourage him. Would she? No, no. She pushed through into the kitchen to tell Sally to serve as soon as she was able. Then again in the hallway, took another long swallow of scotch, a deep breath, and returned to the living room in time to hear Lawrence saying, "The place was on the market almost two years. It was rented for some years before that. Naturally, there were quite a number of repairs to be made before the place could be listed. But I'm sure you'll find everything in good order. Of course, any problems, you must be sure to let us know. We feel responsible."

Gene nodded, finding him unreal, too charming. As if he was set on winning her approval.

"Del liked to play around there for a time," he said. "Something to do with painting. Or was it writing?"

It was my hideout, Del corrected silently. A safe place where I did nothing and nothing was done to me. She looked at Gene. Gene's eyes on her. Questioning. Del couldn't respond to the questions in her eyes.

The pressure didn't let up at all. All the way through dinner. Which Gene might have enjoyed—Sally's cooking being superb—had this strange couple not continued their performances. Lawrence trying very hard to engage Gene in conversation, to keep her attention focused on him. As if he considered himself utterly irresistible. And she found him completely resistible, even repellent. For no particular reason. Just a series of gathering impressions. And Adele, at the opposite end of the table, ate little if anything and sat steadily drinking, looking often at Lawrence with a pleading expression in her eyes, as if begging him to stop.

Gene worked her way slowly through the fine lobster bisque, the filleted breast of chicken in a delicious wine sauce. Eating as much as she could. Which wasn't very much. Concentrating on her food, wishing she still had her conversational ability so that she might actively contribute—never mind how reluctantly—simply in order to break the many lengthy silences that occurred during the course of the meal.

Over dessert, Lawrence made an even more direct effort to capture

Gene's interest. Saying, "You must be sure to tell us if there's anything we can make available. We're glad to send Elton down if you need someone to move things about. Of course, you probably haven't much moving to do. Del tells me you're waiting for your things to arrive from New York."

Gene said, "Yes." Meaningless conversation. Except for the undercurrents running back and forth between these two mismated people. Superficially appearing to be what magazines liked to call "a handsome couple." But mismated, seeming in no way related. That terrible look in Adele's eyes. Something somehow out of character in someone so obviously possessed of insight and intelligence. She was finding herself increasingly more curious about Adele. And about how a woman like her found herself outside her own capacities—to control either the immediate situation or her susceptibility to it. Why? A woman who, in every other circumstance so far, had been very much in control. But who in the presence of this man was rendered unsteady, so patently rattled by her husband's attentions to Gene that she could do no more than smile every so often and keep on drinking.

Adele kept thinking it had been a mistake. She ought to have known better than to believe Lawrence capable of leaving any woman alone. But she'd thought that Gene's pregnancy—she'd made a point of telling him about that—and her inability to engage in conversational badinage might be sufficient to deter him from his usual efforts. But no. There wasn't a woman alive he was capable of ignoring. Or of treating with any measure of spontaneity. All a subtly conscious effort to seduce. With smiles and displays of interest and approving examinations of faces and bodies. But this woman was not responding and plainly failed to enjoy being the recipient of his dubious attentions. I like you for that, she thought. I'm so grateful to you for being able to effortlessly to resist him. I wish I could have. Years ago. Long before any of these games began. The way I'm behaving. Drinking too much. Can't stop. Why do I allow him to have this effect on me? Making me hate myself and him more than ever.

Sally brought coffee into the living room. Gene sat once again on the sofa. And, as before, Del stood in front of the fireplace. Gene wanted to leave, go home and be peacefully alone. In the future, she'd know not to accept invitations to dine with these two people.

She sat slowly drinking her coffee, realizing that for the first time in many weeks she'd actually managed to get through most of an evening without thinking of Bill. And thinking of him now, just the thought of him, the grief came rushing into her.

"Your husband?" Lawrence was asking, intrigued by her silences. As if he was unaware there was a reason for them.

"Dead," she said, lighting a cigarette.

"Mmm, sorry," he said. "Long?"

"Almost three months."

"That *is* too bad," he said, his face without the charming smile rather too long and somehow lacking in depth. Gene was very bothered by him. He simply didn't seem real. Elegantly dressed in expensive clothes. Meticulously tailored gray slacks, navy blazer, custom-made shirt, silk tie, Italian loafers. Hair freshly cut but a bit too perfect. Manicured nails. A sapphire set in silver on the last finger of his right hand. A very good-looking man. But behind his eyes something that made it almost impossible for her to relax in his presence.

"I hadn't realized it was so recent," Del said, her voice even huskier than usual. "I'm sorry." God! I've had much too much to drink. Not making sense. She's only five months pregnant. It had to have been recent. Shut up, Del! Shut up! You'll make him angry, alienate her. Oh God, I wish there was someone who loved me. I wouldn't be here, I'd leave here, if someone loved me. I don't want to be here, hating myself, the way I behave, the things I say because of you, hating myself for the things I know, knowing you'll want me tonight because your appetite is aroused by this woman and defied by her lack of response to you. You're sick. So sick. And I am equally sick, must be, for remaining here, knowing; continuing on. Knowing.

Gene finished her coffee. "I must go," she said.

"Oh, it's early," Lawrence said, not wanting her to leave just yet. Enjoying speculating on her body under the rather shapeless dress. An indication of quite full breasts. Tiny wrists and ankles. Sweet knees. He smiled, looking at those sweet, shapely knees. He was aware of Del watching and prolonged his visual inspection, knowing how much it bothered Del. Then glanced over at her, smiling. Thinking about later on. An image of her face, the way she looked when he started.

"I'll have Elton see you down the driveway," Del offered.

"I have my car."

"Oh!" I'm drunk, so drunk. "I'll walk out with you to your car." She shakily set down her glass as Gene got up and said goodnight to Lawrence, who, once more, took hold of Gene's hand. Holding it a shade too long. The warmth and pressure too obvious. Gene withdrew her hand and walked to the door, then turned to wait for Del, who seemed to be moving through glue. Her expression alarmingly close to one of despair. It was all that drinking, Gene thought, nevertheless feeling all at once tremendously sympathetic. So many New York women she'd known with similarly divided personalities. Chic, competent during the day. Working at their careers, their externals. And at night, soft to the point of breakability. Softer still with every additional glass of whatever it was they preferred to drink.

Outside, Del leaned against the fender as Gene opened the door.

"He bothered you," she said. "I'm sorry. But I'm glad. Someday," she said, turning to look at the open front door of the house, "I'm going to close that door."

"Thank you for dinner," Gene said, wishing she knew what to say that might make Del feel better.

Looking on the verge of tears, Del touched her fingertips to Gene's cheek. "I'm drunk," she said apologetically. "Disgusting. Hate people who can't drink. I like you. Do you like me?"

"Yes."

"Nnnm." Del shook her head sorrowfully, withdrew her hand, stood away from the car. "G'night."

She turned and walked slowly, stiffly—with the overcautiousness of someone who's had too much to drink and knows someone else is watching—back up the path and into the house. The door closed. Gene got into the car and drove back to the gatehouse.

Del went directly up to her room. To throw off her clothes, not without difficulty. All the dinner wine, the before and after scotches, taking their toll on her hands' effectiveness. Got everything off, pulled on a shower cap, closed herself into the stall beneath the needled blast of very hot water. Standing there feeling the heat drawing the alcohol out through her pores, sobering her somewhat. Standing with both hands flat against the wall, bracing herself. Thinking about how much she'd loved him once upon a time, how eagerly she'd thrown herself into the romance. Dinner dates, theater tickets, the ballet. A year of flight and pursuit, of Come catch me. Allowing herself to be caught. Twenty-four years old and rendered dizzy/stupid/blind by a consuming passion for the thirty-nine-year-old Lawrence Prewitt. With his studiedly casual elegance and effortless magnetism. His lazy speech and gestures. His long assertive body and well-practiced sexual persuasiveness. Her first and only lover. Lazily, effortlessly seducing her into abandoning both her body and her brain. Showing her the previously unknown other side of her nature. Showing her pleasure, pleasure.

The splashy wedding and the giddy, laughing friends. Champagne and a cruise and three weeks of lovemaking. Returning home to this house, their first and only home together, believing the future would be as intensely satisfying as their present. Deluded, stunned into submissiveness by his having shown her her capacities for response. His creating in her a grinding need for more, then more and more. All for a purpose.

She pulled off the shower cap, threw it out onto the floor, yanked the pins out of her hair, and bent back, letting the water cut through her hair, making it heavy, dragging her head back under the water's weight. Reached for the shampoo and lathered her hair automatically, mechanically, trying to remember when she'd first realized Lawrence was abusing her, the marriage, anything, everything. Using, abusing. She knew when. The precise moment. And wouldn't think about it. His afternoons and evenings spent with God knew how many other women. Coming home intentionally smelling of other women's perfume, other women's responses. Coming home. "I live here. This is my home, too. Don't tell me what to do, Del! Don't push me! You ought to be glad I come home at all!"

I'm not glad, I haven't been glad in years and years. I wish you would go away, stay away, never come back; wish I could tell you to go, not come back. I could survive it; I would. It's this I won't survive, this every day every night, until it's no longer safe to have female friends or to invite them here for fear of having to witness the death of the friendship while you cultivate their curiosity, their lust; the friends going away, all gone.

How long does this last? Another fifteen years? God! No. Not even an especially intelligent man. All appearance, all superficial. All unreal, insubstantial. I know this. More. I'm not weak or without resources. So why? Why? Letting it go on and on, letting myself be carried down, down. A little more, more, more.

She rinsed her hair and bent her head forward once more, soberer now, letting the water drum down on her back. Driving out the alcoholic haze, clarifying her senses. Familiar despair. To go on living this way. For what reason? With a man incapable of anything but more and different games.

Thinking of Gene. So gratified to find one woman lacking interest in Lawrence's synthetic charm. Of course that might only be temporary. She was still in mourning. Three months wasn't a very long time. What if, in a few more months, she began to see him differently? Please no. She closed her eyes, praying again he'd die. Then straightened, turned off the water, and stepped out of the stall, reaching for the bath sheet. Lawrence standing in the doorway, smiling, watching her.

"Nice little lame sparrow you found there," he said, tapping the ash from his cigarette into the sink.

She ignored him. His other talent, aside from the acquisition of women, was the verbal assassination of those few who found him unappealing.

"Why can't she talk properly?" he asked, watching her towel dry her hair.

She continued to ignore him. Her silences never starting out as part of any game but somehow always ending up as provocation. She draped the towel over the rack and picked up her hairbrush. Acutely aware of her body. Her damnable body. And that inverse determination to best him that somehow kept her body slim and young-looking. Her body a power Lawrence exercised over himself. She couldn't understand his needs. He'd moved into areas so far beyond her understanding that anything and everything might be fodder for his strange inner machinations. She no longer knew. There were times— how perverse!—when she became terribly afraid, fearful her body would lose its appeal for him. Because there was an odd kind of safety in being here with him. At least she knew what it was. Outside, out there, it might be worse. It might be. A lie she told herself when she found herself afraid, and angry. Angry for thinking that way. Because she didn't want him. Hadn't literally actually wanted him in years and years. He didn't care about her. Not her the person. And she knew it. So why did she stay on, keep on with him?

He came up behind her, his hands on her hips bringing her back against him. She hated it but didn't dare resist; kept on brushing out her hair but unable to concentrate because his hands were smoothing her hips, stroking. And every single time she wanted to believe, was tricked by the motions into believing. And then it was always too late to save herself. Over and over, his hands sliding up and down, around over her hips, then across; gliding over her belly, up over her ribs, closing finally on her breasts. Making her eyelids flutter and the brush hover in the air. Wishing she felt nothing, praying not to feel and then find herself captive again. But feeling too much. The hunger terrible. Just once to have it all turn right, turn good, turn to something small for her.

"Stop it," she said, barely audibly.

He smiled into the mirror, watching himself, watching his hand on her breast, his thumb pressing lightly into her nipple. The other hand sliding down her belly, slipping down. She dropped the hairbrush, trembling; caught. Telling herself to turn away from the mirror, get away. If she didn't stop watching him watching himself touch her she'd go mad, be eaten alive by the self-hate chewing away in the pit of her stomach. She moved. But of course he had her, knew he did, and bore down insistently. And then it was too late. Because there was the smallest chance he might this time make it all come good.

Mindless, brainless, she told herself; being led by the breasts back back into his bedroom. What am I, to hope, to keep hoping? What … ?

Gene lay on the cot in the dark. She pressed her hand against her side, trying to feel something—an arm, a leg? She smiled. Perhaps it would be a boy. He'd look like Bill. Dead. The smile fading. Telling herself, I must be glad of this. He might have gone leaving me nothing at all. I do have this child.

She closed her eyes. Thinking about what she'd do after the house was filled with furniture and completely livable, what she'd do after this baby was born. It seemed too far away in the future to think about. She was unable for the moment to imagine the baby out of her and in the air, visible, real. So close to her inside. It might be nice to have this presence stirring, shifting inside her forever. But it had to be born. And next week she'd have her first visit with this doctor, this Doctor Ingram, begin preparing for this birth. Alone. When she'd had a mind filled with images all having to do with Bill's being beside her, his holding her hand and helping while it happened. Bill. What's going to happen to me without you?

✳   ✳   ✳

Adele staggered back through the dressing room. Closed and locked the bathroom door from inside her bedroom. Trying to control the sounds she was making. Standing shivering in front of the window looking out at the night. Lighting a cigarette. Standing in the dark with her arms wrapped around herself, smoking the cigarette and staring out at the moonlit grounds. Reflexively wiping her eyes with the back of her hand. Her belly trembling. And her thighs. The second shower no help at all. Thinking, Perhaps I should die. Wondering why it seemed such a difficult decision to make.

Three

It was almost impossible for Gene to use the telephone. Any static or interference on the line and she couldn't make herself heard. When she tried the first time to call Leonard in New York, the operator was so rude Gene finally hung up. To get another, more sympathetic and patient operator and try again. And Leonard—very apologetic—said, "I can hardly hear you. So let me just tell you what arrangements I've made." And did. Then asked, "Is everything all right, Gene? Would you like me to come up there?"

"Not unless you have business here," she told him, forcing all the volume she could muster. Her hand wet around the receiver as she stared down into the mouthpiece, all the holes, thinking, A microphone. To amplify my voice.

"I'll be up in a few weeks and I'll come to see you. The furniture should be getting to you any day now. I'll stay on top of it from this end, make sure everything's under control. You're sure you're all right? You're getting your checks?"

"Fine. I'm fine."

She was fixed on the idea of some sort of microphone, something she could fit on or near the mouthpiece that would amplify her voice, give her some volume. Otherwise, the telephone was all but useless to her. There had to be something she could use or make up. And went through the Yellow Pages, selecting a musical supply outlet that carried all sorts of amplification equipment. There had to be something.

She drove into the city and returned home with several boxes, positive she could rig up something. Sat on the cot with everything spread out on the blanket and began fiddling with the parts.

Lawrence was going off on one of his "business trips." At the start of their marriage, she'd asked for specifics; wanting to know where he'd be and what he'd be doing, the people he'd see. She'd learned soon enough not to ask. Because it was easy to fit this with that and realize that whatever business he had to do he did it within the space of one afternoon. And the remainder of his time away was spent with new women friends or women he'd encountered on previous trips. And he always somehow managed to make a call or two where she could hear laughter and/or female voices in the background, just to remind her of his powers. Knowing it was a small killing blow he delivered every time. Leaving her wishing, longing for alternatives. But so securely roped into the situation—by fear, by habit—she could do nothing more than drink herself into a state of semi-forgetfulness.

He left. Elton drove him to the airport. And Adele stood in the living room in front of the window feeling the anxiety making its way through her bloodstream. Speculating on who and where and what. Lawrence's conquests. She couldn't stand it. Looking down the driveway, able to see the roof of the gatehouse. She went upstairs for a cardigan, pulled it on, and went out to stroll casually along the driveway—casually, as if her insides weren't in knots, as if she didn't know she probably wouldn't be able to eat for several days—to knock at the front door and wait. Wondering what she hoped to accomplish by intruding on this woman's privacy.

Gene opened the door and stepped aside, wordlessly inviting Del to enter. Del followed her inside to the living room to sit on the one chair, watching as Gene sat down on the side of the cot and picked up some small silver thing, holding it in her hand.

"What are you doing? Have you an ashtray?"

Gene got up, went to the kitchen for an ashtray, returned, and set it on the table. "Microphone," she explained, holding it out for Del to see.

"For what?"

"The telephone," Gene said, so far defeated in her attempts to create some workable system of amplification. She'd bought a small amplifier, a stand for the microphone. But she couldn't figure out any way to focus the amplification into the mouthpiece. All she'd so far managed to do was send her whispered efforts into the far corners of the room.

"The telephone," Del repeated, realizing the problem at once. Of

course, she couldn't really use the telephone. It would be very difficult at best to make herself heard. "Elton's very mechanical," she
said, staring at the equipment spread out on the cot. "Perhaps he'd be
able to help you. He'll be back in an hour or so. He's taking Lawrence
to the airport. Or even Alexander…" Her voice trailed off.

Gene put down the microphone and stood up asking, "Tea?"

"Aren't you frightened?" Del asked unexpectedly, looking at the
rounding swell of Gene's belly. "I think I'd be frightened. Surely your
things should have arrived by now?"

"They're coming," Gene said, indicating Del should come with her
to the kitchen.

"*Are* you frightened?" she persisted. Knowing she shouldn't, but
unable to stop herself. Watching as Gene filled the kettle at the sink,
then set it on the burner. Waiting, hoping for an answer. Gene
turned, her hand resting on the counter top, her eyes settling on
Del's.

"You want me to say I'm frightened?"

"No, no. Just what I think *I* would be."

"I can only die. I won't die."

"What happened?" Del asked quietly, feeling a sudden unprece-
dented ability to communicate with this woman. This petite, pretty
woman.

"Heart attack. In the sound booth. He fell on the mike. The boom."
She made a slicing motion with her hand, aiming at her throat.

Del shuddered, moved closer. To stand beside Gene at the counter,
looking at her face, her eyes.

"Were you married very long?" she asked as Gene turned away to
get two cups and a teapot from the cupboard.

"No."

"I'm sorry. Really." Del was grinding her hands together, wanting to
say something, do something; feeling desperate again. "He's gone,"
she said, eyes now on the kettle. "To California. For ten days. There'll
be some woman. He works it that way. Perhaps she'll telephone the
house in a few week's time, asking to speak to him. He'll be angry
with her, tell her never to do it again. I often wonder how they feel.
I think it has to hurt. Because they don't understand. They think
they've found someone they've always dreamed of. But it isn't a
dream. It's a nightmare that happens to you. Disguised as a good
dream."

She stopped, returning her eyes to Gene's.

"Go on," Gene said, preparing the tea.

"You think I'm crazy. Do you think that?"

"No."

"What am I doing, telling you all this?"

"You have to," Gene said, getting milk and sugar.

"Just milk," Del watched Gene's hands as she poured the tea into the cups. Small hands, delicate. "How old are you?"

"Thirty-three."

"I'm thirty-nine. I look much older, I know."

Gene handed her a cup.

"Oh, I know I do," she went on, her hand trembling so that the spoon clattered in the saucer. "You're not frightened. I wish ..." She stopped, steadying the cup with her free hand. "Have you family somewhere?"

"Father, sister. In Illinois."

"Why didn't you go there? Why did you come here?"

"Bill was from here."

"Oh!" Del nodded, lifting the cup to her mouth.

Gene picked up her own cup, trying to understand her reaction to this woman. An odd reaction. Of painful affection and a sudden longing to comfort, be comforted. Adele had such proud bearing, such aristocratic features. Yet she was so manifestly unhappy, distraught. And what am I? she wondered. Do I seem equally unhappy, distraught to you?

"Is your family here?" she asked as Del set down her cup and lit a cigarette.

"Two brothers," Del answered. "One here. One in Boston. A few cousins scattered here and there. We're not a close family. Lawrence's family is a close one. They *adore* him."

"You don't."

Del's eyes widened. "He's some sort of drug. I despise myself for keeping on and on with him. I can't get out."

Gene shook her head, reaching out to touch Del's arm. The contact made Del jittery. "I haven't any friends," Del said without inflection. "He's fucked them all. And the ones he didn't, he drove away with insults. All our friends are his. *His* friends, not mine. I wish the plane would crash." She saw the reaction on Gene's face and put her hand over the one Gene had placed on her arm. "Don't be bothered by the things I say. I have so little opportunity to say anything. And when I do, it all comes out skewed. Shouldn't we sit down? It's unfair of me to intrude on your privacy, then keep you standing out here."

"Doesn't matter," Gene said, trying to transmit reassurance through her hand. "It's all right."

"I've never been very brave. With words, sometimes. But that isn't courage. It's a deathly sort of cleverness."

What are we saying to each other? Gene wondered, finding it alarming to hear this woman's thoughts, share her confidences. But wanting it. Realizing she was in need of a friend. Just as Del admitted in her fashion to needing one. *Does* it matter? she asked herself. Does anything really matter? I need someone to break the silences.

"Come sit down," she said, carrying her cup back to the living room. Del followed, returning to the chair as Gene sat once more on the side of the cot and her hand trailed over the disassembled pieces of equipment strewn across the blanket.

"Elton really is very good with that sort of thing," Del said. "I'm sure he or Alexander will be able to help you."

"Thank you." Gene looked again at this tall, tense woman sitting in the stiff-backed chair. Willing me into communicating with you. I don't mind. Something in your intensity is so compelling. And how awful it must be being married to that man. She smiled, then drank some of the tea.

"It's my property, you know," Del said. "My parents. It was a wedding gift. The deed is in my name. All of it. Mine. Not his. But he makes references, allusions. Talking about this place. The way he did when you came to dinner. Offering to send Elton. Elton, I think, despises him. Lawrence has no way with real people. He's offensive, officious. It offends *me*, the way he deals with them."

Gene nodded, agreeing.

"Do you think your things will be here soon?" she asked, looking nervously around the empty room. Wondering if she wasn't display-ing some new, terrible weakness in confiding in this silent woman. Had she gone so far outside herself as to have lost all her perspec-tives?

"Leonard says so."

"Leonard?"

"Bill's best friend. A producer."

"Oh! And he says your things are on the way?"

"Yes."

"Good. I'm glad." Del stood up abruptly, setting the cup and saucer down on the table. "I'll ask Elton to come to see you when he gets back from the airport. Thank you for the tea. I'm sorry I barged in on you." She moved quickly toward the door, suddenly convinced she'd committed a dreadful error in allowing her thoughts to surface so freely, without censoring them.

"Come again," Gene said, walking with her to the door. "Stay longer."

Del felt so strange, so unreasonably moved. If she stayed a moment longer she might find herself saying all sorts of irresponsible things. She opened the door and stepped outside, then turned back.

"Please," she said hesitantly, "don't think … badly of him, of me. For what I said. It's just nerves. Nerves."

She pulled her cardigan tight around her as if feeling the chill of a nonexistent wind, standing looking at Gene for several long moments before turning and hurrying off up the driveway. Gene watched her out of sight, then returned inside to finish her tea, fingering the microphone parts; feeling deeply sorry. For both of them. For Del because it was all too obvious she was caught up in something that was slowly strangling her. And for herself because it didn't seem there was anything she might do to help anyone, let alone Adele.

Yet she did feel a strong desire to help. She'd begun—without any awareness—to care about Adele. And now, returning to the cot, thought, I think were becoming friends. And sat toying with the microphone, thinking about that.

Elton said, "Miz Prewitt tells me you're trying to hook up some sorta amplification gizmo to work with the telephone. Don't know there's much I can do, but I'll have a look, give it a try."

He sat, at her invitation, in the chair by the table with the various components spread out before him and she watched as he studied the housing, the contacts.

"Seems to me all you'd need is this business inside," he said, after a time. "Housing's just for protection and the way I see it, the speaking part of the receiver'd do the same job. But that still doesn't solve the amplifying problem. We get the microphone part all nicely fitted up, that's one thing. But the big thing is making what's heard on the other end nice and loud. I'm going to have to think about it, play with it."

"Will you have coffee, Elton?"

He looked up. "Thank you. That'd be fine."

She made the coffee, brought back a cup, and placed it beside him on the table before returning to the side of the cot to sit watching him examining the rear of the small amplifier.

"You got anybody to come help out when you have the baby?" he asked, eyes on the amplifier.

"No."

"I got somebody who could help," he said, picking up the cup, meeting her eyes.

His eyes were black liquid, beautiful. She felt very safe, even protected, being with him.

"My wife, Rebecca. She'd come help with the baby. Whatever else you'd be needing. She's a good woman, good worker."

"I couldn't pay much."

"Don't matter," he said, his eyes still on her. "Some's better than none at all. It'd be a help to us."

"You have children, Elton?"

"One boy. Going to the city college, learning engineering." He smiled for the first time. "If I can't figure this thing out, it's for sure Alexander will. Good coffee," he said, finishing it, then getting to his feet. "Okay if I take all this with me?"

"Yes.

"We'll study on it," he said.

She brought over the cartons the microphone and amplifier had come in and he carefully packed everything into the boxes.

"Thank you," she said, holding her hand out to him.

He wiped his hand on the back of his work pants and then shook hands with her.

"I'll have Rebecca come see you. She's a good woman."

Gene nodded and opened the door for him.

He carried the boxes off up the driveway. A large, muscular man exuding a strength more than merely physical.

She started for the kitchen thinking to make something to eat, then stopped and stood looking at the telephone. Thinking about Adele. Knowing somehow Adele was sitting up there in that huge house without appetite, lonely. The image was surprisingly painful. She picked up the telephone, dialed the number, and listened to the ringing; gathering her breath in order to try to make herself heard.

Adele answered. It pleased Gene to recognize her voice.

"Come have dinner with me," she whispered into the telephone.

Adele said, "I was just going to call, ask you to eat with me. Come here. It's more comfortable. When your furniture arrives, I'll come down there. Please don't think me rude. Come here?"

Gene said, "Yes," and put down the telephone.

We're becoming friends.

❅ ❅ ❅

"Who is Leonard again?" Adele asked over coffee in the living room. The windows open and a faint scent of lilac drifting in.

"A producer. Bill's best friend."

"I see." Del lit a cigarette. "Was Elton able to help you?"

"He'll try."

"Elton's remarkable. He can fix anything. Cars, radios, appliances. The furnace. Anything. His son's brilliant. Lawrence made a very grand, very embarrassing gesture of saying he'd pay Alexander's tuition." Her expression tightened. "Naturally, I've been paying it. I don't mind. I'm glad to do it. What I mind is the outrageous talent Lawrence has for making promises without any intention of fulfilling them. No! I won't talk about him! I promised myself I wouldn't." She was suddenly sick to death of thinking about him and hearing herself talk about him. "I won't!" she repeated, wishing she could have that part of her that contained all thoughts of, reactions to, memories of Lawrence surgically removed. Leaving her intact and once more capable of deriving pleasure from being alive. Remembering herself at twenty-four. How very fortunate she'd felt in finding him. Now, all these years later, he'd eaten away at her until little remained but a distant, fairly obsessive compulsion to best him somehow, some way. Wanting to do something, anything, that would bring her out on top with some degree of self-respect remaining. Spending hours and hours backtracking the past, wishing she'd said this at that time instead of that, thinking, If only I'd done that, things would have been different. Always thinking, If someone loved me, I'd get away from all this. If someone would just come along and ignore what they see as the obstacles strewn all about the periphery of my existence. Ignore Lawrence. Ignore everything but me. Drive right over all the rubbish, past the blockades, and help me get out.

"Rebecca is going to come see me, about helping with the baby," Gene said.

Del brought herself back into the present and smiled. "You'll like her." Thinking of how Rebecca had nursed her. Recalling the tenderness, the caring in her hands. "Rebecca is ... They're a fine family." They should be living here, in this house. A fine family. And I should be ...

"Have you started buying things for the baby?" she asked.

Gene shook her head. The motion lifting her hair. Del watched it settle about her face, fascinated.

"We'll go shopping," Del suggested brightly. "Would you like to? Go into town, have lunch, shop for your baby?"

Gene smiled slowly, answering, "Yes." Thinking, I like you. I don't know why, really. But I like you very much.

✳   ✳   ✳

During the time Lawrence was away, the two women saw or spoke to each other every day. Del walking down the driveway to chat for a few minutes. Unable to resist the temptation of simply seeing this new friend. And Gene going up to the house. For a cup of tea. Or lunch. Or dinner. To talk. Gradually realizing it no longer hurt to speak. And Del listened so carefully, Gene found it very easy to talk to her.

It did occur to her that it might appear odd, from the outside looking in. Two women actively seeking each other's company, spending increasingly more and more time together. Talking, talking, drinking endless cups of tea and coffee, smoking cigarettes—sharing each other's cigarettes; talking. Gene didn't care how it might or might not appear from the outside. She cared about the contact, about Del; wanting Del to remain available. To reciprocate the slow caring. To air some of her thoughts and memories. Each day, each conversation peeling away a little more of the reservations each possessed about the other until they were starting to talk of real things, true things; feelings, remembered pleasures and pain. Approaching larger truths, deeper truths. Talking.

Del felt rarely bold, possessed of the conviction that Gene was completely trustworthy; that it was possible to be totally truthful with her. And in admitting to the truth, she might receive in return, something—some message—that might help her to somehow alter the course of her life. She wanted more than anything else to make changes. And felt she might perhaps actually be approaching a time when change-making would be a viable possibility. So, she plunged in, without giving herself time for second thoughts. And said, "I thought I knew what I was doing." Said it feeling the anguish, the hopeless helplessness. "Age hasn't anything to do with being a fool. I don't know how to get out of it. He'll come home the day after tomorrow and I'll hate myself, but he'll find some way to make me ... be with him. The way it always happens. Coming back from the others with his appetite for me restored. It's so sick. I know it is. From this distance, I can see it so clearly. But I haven't any power face to face."

"You love him?" Gene asked.

"Love!" She turned the word into something pathetic and diseased. "I don't *love* him. Oh, once. Once I loved him. More than my life. I gave him my life."

"But can't you ... ?"

"Sitting here talking to you, I know all sorts of things. Sitting alone, talking to myself, I know. But when he's there, I'm intimidated ... It's so pointless to go on and on about it. It's disgusting, self-indulgent. I wish to God I could stop!"

Again Gene had no idea what to say. Was there anything words could accomplish here? She didn't think so. And she couldn't see why, if Del had so accurate a picture of the marriage, she couldn't just end it. No love. Advantages being taken. "Why not stop?" she asked finally, unable to understand.

"If I knew how, I'd be able to end it. Certain things *seem* so simple. There's such a lot ... things I can't talk about. Not yet. How?" she asked plaintively. "If I just knew how."

"Someone else?" Gene offered. "Someone who'd treat you well."

"I dream about that," she said distractedly, looking off into space, then returning her eyes to Gene's. "But it's a fantasy. And who'd *want* to? If you were a man, would you?"

Gene nodded slowly, answering, "Yes."

"Oh, *don't!*" Del begged, sounding agonized. "It's too late ... just a lot of fantasizing."

"No," Gene disagreed.

"It's too late," she argued dispiritedly. "Sitting here with you, talking about it, talking about all the conclusions I've come to. Talking. But he'll come back the day after tomorrow and I know me, know how I am. Know him, too. And nothing will change. Except that I've finally talked about it. And I'm glad to have you to talk to. I must go." *I've said too much too much, dangerous; putting you in a dangerous position by saying so much I must be careful, more careful.*

She hurried off.

Gene sat there stunned. Unable to relate this woman to the brittle, somewhat caustic Mrs. Prewitt of their first meeting. This woman being someone Gene could care for, care about. Was she now telling her that once her husband returned home the other Mrs. Prewitt would again return into being? And if the prospect of that was alarming to her, how much more alarming was it to Adele? An impossible situation. But the discussions had, for days on end, succeeded in keeping Gene's mind off Bill, holding her suspended above her grief. And after Del had gone rushing back to the main house, Gene got up and went to sit for a time on the front step, enjoying the daily softening, warming air; examining her waning grief. Starting to feel a very positive anticipation and longing for the baby. Three more months. Anxious to see and hold the baby. Glad of and grateful for the baby. And this new friend.

✳   ✳   ✳

Rebecca was a slender, attractive woman with an engaging smile and a soft melodious voice. She came to sit with Gene on the front step and talked quietly about the baby, working out the arrangements, the salary, the hours. Agreeing to the small weekly sum Gene was able to offer. Expressing delight at the prospect of taking care of the baby.

"You're going to be nursing?" she asked. And Gene had to stop and think about that. Something she'd promised Dr. Ingram she'd think about, but hadn't.

"Did you?" she asked Rebecca.

"Yuh. It was good."

"I think I will."

"Good."

Rebecca was very peaceful, pleasant to be with. And when she was preparing to leave, said, "When your things come, you send Elton to tell me. I'll come down and help you."

❋   ❋   ❋

Gene lay on the rented cot in the dark, looking at the moonlight shadows on the ceiling, one hand idly moving over the growing mound of her abdomen. Trying to see some destination in her future. Failing. For the first time in her life resigned to allowing the future to come as it would. Allowing Adele and Elton and Rebecca—Leonard, too—to help her move forward into the future. Because it seemed she'd lost her ability to form plans or even think very far beyond the next moment.

She lay in the dark under the light blanket and thought about Bill, how thrilled he'd been about the baby. Just a few months ago. Happy. His first child. Only child. Bill. Where do you go when you die? I'm letting life and these people carry me, letting their voices and thoughts take me here and there. I don't know what I think or feel, just about this baby our making this baby. Bill I want you back when I'm here alone in this house I had to have for no real reason except feeling I had to have it, I don't know why I'm here, can't see any point to living especially in the night when it's too quiet too empty; and dreaming I turn thinking to come up against your warmth, coming up against air only air and a friend I've found a friend we see and know in each other things we haven't yet spoken of and that's good it's just that I want you back, want to close my eyes and be back in the apartment on Seventy-second Street, with that half bathroom the toilet always going wrong and that burnt-out element on the stove, the freezer compartment always in need of defrosting; our bed our room nights are bad Bill bad, at night my eyes ache from searching all the corners of the darkness looking for you.

❋   ❋   ❋

Adele paced back and forth in her bedroom. Chain-smoking. Dreading his return. Angry and nervous because she'd said too much, talked too much. Telling too much of herself, of their private life. Disloyal. Wrong. Weak, untrustworthy, skulking off to the first recep-

tive ear to spew out her secrets, rattle off the lengthy list of sins committed against her. Wrong. God! I must stop going down there, leave
the woman alone. Intruding on her privacy. Destroying my own.
Hurrying down there like a schoolgirl currying favor with the
teacher; dredging up old tales, new secrets. For approval of some sort.
What's wrong with me?

She hadn't made good on her invitation to take Gene to lunch,
shopping. All the rain. Distractions.

She paused to stub out her cigarette, light another. Wishing she
could die. So many times she'd thought of it. An image in her mind
of a wretched and repentant Lawrence realizing, at the moment of
her death, what he'd failed to perceive throughout fifteen years of
quiet torture: that he loved her. He does love me, she insisted. He
does! If he could only stop all these games, the need for them, and
look here, see me. It can't all have died.

Oh, stop! It will never happen. And all your wishing and iffing and
what-ifs mean nothing, mean as little as your death would. He'd
make a darkly elegant showing at your funeral, then escort some one
of your old-school-days female friends home. So that she might comfort and console him. He doesn't love me. I don't love him. I'm afraid
of him. Am I that afraid? To allow this to go on and on. Life alone
would be better. Freedom. A chance to meet someone else, someone
kind who might love me. Without pain, without the need to inflict
upon me his baser judgments of my more reluctant friends. Urging
me to see other men. Those few times. Innocent dinner-party flirta-
tions when I was younger, still not convinced. He'd watched, enjoyed
it. Hurrying me home and up to his bedroom. Oh, God! There is no
love here.

Mother saying, "He's quite the charmer, Del. I'd keep a close eye on
him. There's something not quite right about the man. I can't put my
finger on it. But he puts me on edge."

Father saying, "You could do better, darling. The man hasn't any
depth. None at all. Scratch his surface and I think all you'll find is
more surface."

She laughed out loud. The sound ugly in the emptiness. She
stopped to tap off the ash from her cigarette, then continued pacing.
Her arms wrapped around herself—always doing that lately—her
hand with the cigarette moving mechanically back and forth to her
mouth. Walking away the hours until Lawrence would come home.

Remembering making love in his bedroom. His apartment. The seventh or eighth time, perhaps. When he'd succeeded in stripping away the last of her lingering inhibitions, boiling her down to a pure state of bubbling lust. Straddled over him, her teeth bared; feeling demented, at his urging hissing, "Fuck, fuck." Wanting to weep over it all. Doing what he'd wanted. And he'd gone quietly power-crazy. His hands fastened hard around her upper arms, his face indescribable. Forcing himself as high and as hard inside her as he could, hurting, his hands bruising her arms. Snarling, "Cunt!" Dragging her down by her hair, his mouth ravaging hers. Rolling her around on the bed, down onto the floor. Crazed. Animals. The memory sitting in her mind like a thorn. Immovable. The first hint of what was to come and she should have heeded, taken warning. But how was she to know this wasn't the way it was supposed to be? Only her instincts. And they might have been mistaken. The recollection leaving her brain tender, perennially bruised with the effort of attempted rationalization. But knowing now, guessing then, that what had happened was degrading. He'd taken her down past her education, her intelligence, her "breeding"—he loathed her Swiss finishing school and Sorbonne-bred qualities—bent on taking all that away from her. Cunt. Saying, "See what you are! And don't ever forget or I'll show you again and again until it's impossible for you ever to forget!"

Now that incident and so many others refused to leave her consciousness for more than an hour or two at a time—even finding their way into her random dreams. All of it embodying the essence of their relationship. And her loss of caring for herself. The fear. The cold-shakes, sweaty-handed fear.

She lit another cigarette, stoking herself with resolution, determination. Gearing herself up for the hundredth time to end it, extricate herself before there was nothing of her self left to save. I will. Some sort of confrontation. When he gets back. I will. She began placing words side by side, framing her approach. Pausing at the window—all the feverish words in abeyance—to look through the darkness in the direction of the gatehouse. Somehow infused with renewed conviction and courage by the knowledge that Gene was down there. Probably asleep. A small, dark woman. With a baby. And something, some knowledge Del longed for. An insight, perhaps. Courage, certainly. Something. Wishing they could be together talking at that very moment. So I could hear myself say what I think, how I feel.

That can't be wrong.

Tomorrow, I'll make good that invitation. Yes.

She stood for a very long time, holding Gene's image in her mind. Studying it from every possible angle. Immeasurably warmed by the exercise.

※　　　　※　　　　※　　　　※　　　　※

Four

THE INTERIOR OF THE OLD ROLLS WAS POLISHED AND PERFECT.
"My parents bought this car in 1957," Adele said, smartly tapping
her ash off into the ashtray. "It gives me an indescribable feeling driving around town in it. Like a relic. A relic inside a relic."

Gene looked at the back of Elton's head. His cap, his uniform.
Thinking about Del. Thinking, You've changed again. Back to being
Mrs. Prewitt of the first afternoon. Be Del. Not this.

"I'm making you nervous," Del said apologetically. "Why do I *do*
this? I don't mean to do it. Tell me something," she said, relaxing
somewhat, "have you ever stopped to think about how many really
marvelous women there are floating around? Splendid women.
Intelligent, sensitive, bright. Alone. Have you thought about it?
Impersonally, I mean."

Gene nodded.

"I think about it," Del went on. "I think about it quite often. And
I wonder if they don't perhaps know something I don't. If they don't
have some design for living I've failed utterly to recognize. Then, on
the other hand"—she paused to puff on her cigarette—"I wonder if
they're not all quietly dying of loneliness, believing their perfect
man, the one of their lifetime dreams, is dead after all. I wish I was
attracted to women. Have you ever wished it?"

"I've thought about it."

"It might be good. Women are far nicer to look at. And certainly, it
seems to me a woman would have far more insight into how to make
love to another woman than any man would. Women listen better,
respond more truthfully, display greater sensitivity, have keener intu-
ition."

"Some women."

"*Some* women," Del agreed. "I've thought about it. Unfortunately,
the idea of actually making love to another woman has never had any

great appeal for me. Have you ever made love with a woman?"

"No."

"Have you ever thought about that?"

"I have," Gene admitted, wondering if Del was maneuvering her way around to a suggestion that the two of them make love.

"How did you feel when you thought about it?" Del persisted.

"Funny."

"Funny how?"

Gene looked again at the back of Elton's head. Separated from them by a thick glass partition.

"Funny strange."

"Oh!" Del put out her cigarette and turned to look out the window, thinking it over. "I've had dreams," she said, eyes on the passing scenes, "about making love to a woman. Very explicit. It's amazing the things you can do in dreams." She turned. "You can do *anything* in dreams. Reality puts boulders on my brain, gravel in my mouth. Turns me into everything I'm not in my dreams. He'll be back tomorrow and I'm dreading it. I dread his going away, dread his coming back. When we were first married, I used to fantasize about his dying. And told myself I was trying to prepare for the possibility of losing him. Because I loved him. So much. And I was terrified he'd die. I thought about it constantly. Now," she said, "I go to bed at night and pray he won't wake up. I have this picture of myself walking through the bathroom, the dressing room, opening the door to his room, finding him dead. I hope his plane will crash. I wish to God he'd die. Or that I would." She felt Gene's reaction rather than saw it. An eerie affirmation of her feelings.

"I know," Gene said in her barely audible whisper. "I know how that feels."

"Do you? Yes, you do. Do you think I'm inhuman, a monster, saying the things I do?"

"No."

"How kind you are," Del said softly. "I'll buy you a gorgeous lunch," she said, laying her hand on Gene's arm. "A great big expensive lunch at Ginetta's."

Gene smiled.

"We'll have lunch first, I think. And then shop. Hamilton's is the best place. A good long lunch. That'll give Elton a chance to go over to the college and have a bite to eat with Alexander. Do you feel well?"

"Very well."

Her face, at that moment, looked so young, so innocent. Gene automatically took hold of Del's hand and placed it on the side of her belly.

Del closed her eyes, remembering again.

It hurt. The sounds. Hurting. Elton waiting downstairs in the car. The nurse—was she really a nurse?—calling him up to the office. Elton knew without having to be told. Carried her down to the car, drove her home, then sent for Rebecca. Forever after, his eyes hard when he looked at Lawrence. And Rebecca saying, "It's not right, all this bleeding. You've got to go to the hospital." The ambulance and Rebecca riding along, holding her hand, saying, "You'll be fine, just fine." And Martin Ingram asking her, "Who did this, Del? Whoever did this was a butcher, a madman. I'm going to try to make some repairs." Damage. God, the damage never ends. Two weeks later, Lawrence returned home. Casually asking, "Did you get rid of it?" Outraged at discovering he wouldn't be able to satisfy his appetites for weeks. Disgusted by the sickroom smell and bloodied dressings in the basket waiting to be taken down to the trash. Like my child was trashed. My body.

"What is it?" Gene asked.

Del opened her eyes, removing her hand. "I'm sorry. Nothing." She fumbled for a cigarette, lit one. Then sat silent for the rest of the ride into town, gazing sightlessly out the window.

Gene sat studying Del's profile. Trying to imagine how it might be to make love—not to some hypothetical woman, but to this one. Imagining Del without her clothes. Finding the image aesthetic. A well-made woman. Beautifully made. But she failed to find anything within her that responded to the idea of touching Adele intimately. It would be good, she thought, holding. I would like very much to hold you. And that surprises me. See your breasts perhaps. Hold you in my arms and try to ease you, comfort you. But how could you or anyone respond to someone misshapen, swollen? Every vein plainly defined. Patterns of blue drawn across my breasts and belly, inner thighs. No. Besides it wasn't a personal issue, but simply an objective discussion. Wasn't it?

❉   ❉   ❉

Ginetta's was wonderful. Stained-glass panels above the windows.

Authentic Tiffany lamps and antique wallpaper. Thick carpeting and silently murmuring waiters, busboys. An aura of impeccable elegance. They were given a table by the front window. Del ordered drinks and they sat looking out at the street, drinking them—a cocktail for Del, fresh-squeezed orange juice for Gene. Del saying, "This really is my favorite place. I've always loved coming here. When I ..." She stopped in mid-sentence, her throat closing at the sight of Lawrence—unmistakably him—walking down the opposite side of the street. A young, very pretty brunette on his arm. The two of them laughing.

"What?" Gene asked, frightened by the expression that overtook Del's face.

"My God!" Del whispered, then jumped up from the table and ran through the restaurant to the door. Out, down the steps to stand on the sidewalk, seeing them disappearing around the corner. She stood. Devastated. Gasping for air, for something. The feeling she'd just been slapped very hard across the face, kicked in the stomach. Her stomach hurting. She turned, feeling suddenly terribly old, stiff. Returning inside to the table. Attempting to smile. It wouldn't come. She turned away, hid her face in her hands, sobbing soundlessly. Again, again. Lies and women, more lies, more women. He'll come home bearing armloads of pain he'll wish to inflict. Why did I have to see?

"What is it?" Gene asked again, taking a tissue from her bag, pressing it into Del's hand.

If she could just die. Simply close her eyes and slide right out of her life. Why did it have to hurt? Why do I have to *feel* this? She wiped her eyes—mortified, deeply ashamed of her behavior—took several deep breaths, then picked up her drink, dropped the stir stick on the table, and drained the glass.

"You didn't see?" she asked hoarsely.

"No. What?"

"Lawrence. With a woman."

"Oooh!" Gene instinctively reached for Del's hand, holding it tight. Del had her other hand jammed into her mouth, biting down hard. Her eyes averted.

"Why do I *care*?" she whispered, agonized. "God! Why do I have to care?"

"Let's go home."

"Yes, yes," she said, suddenly overwhelmed by urgency.

"I'll leave a note with the maître d' for Elton, have him get us a taxi. I'm sorry. I'm so sorry. About the lunch. Everything."

"It doesn't matter."

❊   ❊   ❊

She dropped Gene at the gatehouse, apologizing yet again; then continued on to the house. Depressed by the house. Wishing she'd had the good sense to stay out. Have lunch, go shopping. Instead of coming back here to brood, pacing back and forth. Hating herself. Wishing she could dismiss him from her mind, her feelings, write him off. Loathing him for his deceit, his duplicity, his terrifying sickness. Pacing out her hatreds, back and forth.

❊   ❊   ❊

Gene stood by the front door, looking out; trying to think how it must feel. Seeing your husband casually strolling past with another woman, laughing. Seeing Lawrence as Bill and feeling a twisting pain. Just the thought of Bill alive and walking along some street bringing the grief down over her. Making her hands grip the door, her eyes staring hard into the distance. As if, could she only force the focus, she might return him into being. She felt so unreal. Like the microphone housing Elton had dispensed with. The insides required, the outside disposable. She was a housing for this child. And what would she be once the child was free of her body, no longer required the housing? Disposable, finally? She couldn't seem to find herself, the self she'd thought she'd known. Everything all tangled up with Del's misery and her own, losses of one sort and another. She'd evolved into some sort of machine; something drifting here and there, without real substance. Her only conscious act of will being her decision to have this house. And in making that decision, she'd volunteered herself onto the property and into the interior of this woman. This deeply unhappy woman whose reasons were all too legitimate, whose pain was too tangible; impossible to avoid or ignore.

She turned away from the door to look at the large empty living room, the fireplace, the bare wood floor. Longing to see familiar

things. The paintings, books. Chairs, sofa. Everything that was needed to take away the barren, transient look of the place, the barren
transient feeling this lack of furnishings created inside her. She
turned once again to the door to see a truck pulling into the driveway. Experiencing an excited leap inside. The furniture. Two men
jumping down from the cab. She stepped through the door, watching
as the men went to the rear of the van. Then, a car pulled in around
it, parked in front of the truck. The door opened and Leonard
climbed out. His head appearing over the top of the car, smiling at
her. She smiled back. So glad to see him. He walked toward her, looking at the two men busily removing padding from the furniture,
approaching her, saying, "I decided to come see for myself how you
are. Looks like my timing's getting better."

He stood in front of her, smiling. Someone who'd cared, who had
kept on caring; concerning himself with her welfare. A friend. She
put her arms around him, gratified that he would come considerable
distances to satisfy himself as to her well-being.

"So this is the house, huh?" He walked inside with her, admiring the
place. "I like it, Gene. This is far better for you than New York. You
were right. You made the right decision."

"I like this house," she said unnecessarily.

"I'm going to be staying in town for a few days. Plan to buy you
some dinners, feed you up. Get some business done. There's a script
I'm going to option. And a kid who's going to be doing some background music for me. Junior's getting bigger." He smiled. "And you're
getting smaller. You should eat more."

Elton knocked at the open door.

"Thought you'd want to know I called Rebecca," he said. "Told her
to come down give you a hand with the unpacking."

"Thank you."

"She'll be along in about half an hour."

"Elton. Leonard Mansfield."

The two men shook hands, then Elton stepped away saying, "She'll
be right on down. Good meeting you, sir."

"You too, Elton."

"The Prewitt's driver," she explained, watching the men set her sofa
on the grass. Its shape and fabric so comfortingly familiar. She looked
at Leonard. Kind, caring Leonard. Tall and creased about the eyes;
hair turning white. "Where are you staying?" she asked him.

"Downtown." He took hold of her hand. "At the Imperial."

"Rooms are small."

He laughed. "I've got a *big* room. How are you? Are you all right?"

"Better."

"And the baby?"

"Soon," she answered. And laughed her odd hollow laugh, her volumeless laugh.

He studied her face, for a moment hearing the rich, remembered roundness of her voice. And felt sad. Rotten sad. Her beautiful voice, her enticing laughter. Peripherally, he saw movement and turned his head to see a tall woman standing in the doorway, the sun at her back. A woman poised as if undecided whether to come in or go away.

Gene, following his eyes, turned to see Adele and beckoned her in. "Adele Prewitt. Leonard Mansfield."

She watched their two hands reach through space to meet. Interested in witnessing yet another change in Del. Whose eyes, for an instant, went wide and then settled.

Del said, "Hello," around what felt like a mouthful of cotton. In that instant deciding to avenge herself on Lawrence with this man. She would ... what? Madness, she told herself. Thinking of people in those terms. Revenge, retaliation. What have I become?

"I thought I'd come down, offer a hand," she said, forcing her eyes away from Leonard and back to Gene. "Quite a lot of boxes, cartons needing unpacking." Thinking, I should go back to the house right now. Get out of here before I make a fool of myself. Or start playing at eccentric images.

"We'll all pitch in and get everything unpacked," Leonard said. "And go out for dinner after. Come with us," he impulsively invited Del.

"I couldn't intrude," she said, looking at Gene for some sign. Was he here out of friendship or love, or both? He seemed very protective of Gene, fatherly.

"Come," Gene encouraged.

"No, no. Some other time. Thank you." She moved out of the way to allow the two men to carry in the sofa. Gene went over to point out where she wanted it placed.

"You're not intruding," Leonard said. "If you haven't already got plans, come with us." He looked at her eyes, her mouth. Mouth and eyes that betrayed her. If he took this woman into one of the empty rooms, if he touched her, she'd dissolve. He'd met two or three other women like her. And had found each of them irresistible. Naked, needing women. Misunderstood. Fiercely intelligent, uncompromising in their principles. And starving to death inside.

"I haven't any plans," she admitted, responding to the way he looked at her. Telling herself she was mad to have come here, mad to be agreeing to go out in the company of this man. Because she knew what would happen. There was no way on earth she had the will or the strength to prevent its happening. A pathetic attempt at secret retaliation. Or was it that ever-present hope of finding something solely for herself? He might conceivably be someone who would love her. God! You *are* insane! Thinking of love from strangers.

"Then you'll come with us," he said with finality. "Good!"

The furniture was unloaded fairly quickly. Rebecca arrived and set to work unpacking the boxes. Gene and Del emptied the barrels. Leonard went outside to tip the two men, then threw off his jacket, rolled up his sleeves, and began stacking the emptied cartons, barrels, and boxes outside. A couple of hours and the place looked like a home instead of some deserted waiting room.

"I'll wash up these dishes, glasses," Rebecca said. "Give them a go through the machine, get things settled in the kitchen. You all go on now, have your dinner. I'll lock up when I go."

Del looked down at herself, at her grimy hands, and said, "Come up to the house for a drink while I change, clean up."

"You go," Gene said. "We'll come for you."

Del hurried back to the house in a state akin to panic. Why should this seem such a momentous occasion? Nothing's going to happen. Yes. Something is going to happen. You're going to make it happen.

Thinking of the way Lawrence had looked at her across the restaurant that night the family had been out celebrating her parents' thirtieth anniversary. Mother, Father, Clark Jr., Emery, and herself. And Lawrence presuming upon a onetime introduction to Emery to reintroduce himself. Neglecting the girl with him. I saw that, she thought now. It should have meant something. So many warnings I failed to take notice of. But I was too engrossed in the flattery, the charm, the predatory flash of teeth, and the sexual innuendo. Why didn't I see it all then and turn away?

She pushed at the clothes in her closet unable to make a decision.

As if deciding what to wear would determine the course of the rest of her life. Stupid! Contemplating stepping outside the marriage for the first time. Mildly terrorized at the prospect. Yet determined to take as many steps as necessary in order to attain something that might be beneficial to her. She stood in front of the closet letting her eyes move slowly over the clothes hanging there, then reached for the black crêpe with the long sleeves, the low-cut neckline.

In the gatehouse, Gene stood looking at the living room. The pictures leaning against the wall waiting to be hung. The stereo, the records. Books. Ashtrays. The rugs down. Curtains sitting in a pile on the seat of the armchair. Curtain rods balanced across the arms. Home.

"Why don't you get changed?" Leonard said. "I'll give Rebecca a hand in the kitchen while you do."

"She has a hateful husband, Leonard. She's very unhappy." Why did it suddenly hurt again, trying to speak?

"Are you telling me to leave her alone?"

"No. I don't know. I care about her."

He laughed, putting his hands on her face. "We're all grown-up boys and girls. Don't worry. How are you really, Gene?"

"Don't know. But I'm happy to see you. Why did you come?"

"Does it still hurt to talk?"

Did he know things, sense things she didn't realize she was transmitting?

"No."

"I came because I care," he said. "Now go put on something pretty. Do you have anything that'll fit over this?" He patted her belly, making her smile. At the same time mildly irritating her. Had her body, with this pregnancy, become common domain? Everyone free to pat and touch her, as if her belly wasn't part of her but simply something she toted around?

"I have something," she said.

"Then go put it on! I'm hungry and thirsty."

She went off to the bedroom to have a quick wash and get changed and Leonard wandered down to the kitchen to stand in the doorway watching Rebecca removing newspaper from a large amount of glassware. He moved over and began to help.

They worked in silence for several minutes until Rebecca said, "I'm going to be helping. After the baby comes."

"Good."

"You're going to visit regularly?"

"Yes. But not that way."

She turned her head and smiled at him.

"How much is Gene going to be paying you?"

She told him.

"It's not enough. I'll see to it you get another twenty every week."

"You don't have to do that" she said, setting aside some newspapers.

"I think I do."

"All right."

"What about that husband?" he asked.

"Ain't worth spit," she said, lowering her voice. "I shouldn't talk out of turn, but he's driving that poor woman crazy. Hear her sometimes cry out in the night, times when he's home. He's the killing kind. You know?"

"Literally?"

"Oh yes! Very literally. You want to watch how you step."

"I see." He rinsed the newsprint from his hands at the sink, then dried them on a tea towel and draped the wet towel across the counter. "Take care of Gene," he said. "It's important to me."

She nodded. He went back to the living room to have a cigarette while he waited for Gene.

✳   ✳   ✳

The composer was young. Perhaps twenty-five. But he sounded age-less. Talking of musical concepts, discussing composers neither women had ever heard of. But Leonard—surprisingly—had. Gene missed his name and didn't bother to ask to hear it again. Somewhat distantly, she noted he had a very nice face and a pleasant voice, and tuned out on his and Leonard's conversation. Hers and Del's eyes kept meeting until Gene at last leaned over to say, "Come with me."

Gene stood up, touching Leonard on the shoulder to get his attention. He turned and looked up at her, at once understanding. "We'll be here," he said, smiling.

In the muzzy light of the ladies' room, Gene looked deep into Del's eyes. Not sure why but needing all at once to tell her the truth. As if the truth might affect not only this evening but the entire future. Somehow feeling obligated to be truthful in the face of what had happened at the restaurant earlier in the day.

"We weren't married," she said bluntly.

"I'd guessed that," Del said. "That came out sounding smart. I don't mean it that way. It's just that I guessed."

"I wanted you to know."

"Thank you. I shouldn't have come tonight."

"You want to go with Leonard."

"Yes. No. I can't."

"Have you ever?"

"Never. Only Lawrence. I don't know how I can even think …"

"Do it!"

Del stared at her. This was strange. Being given permission, told to go with her instincts, her whims of the moment. Was she so transparent, so utterly outside the main stream of things that her every thought showed through?

"You deserve … something good," Gene said. "You look so pretty tonight. Beautiful." Looking at Del's throat, her breasts. Very white, framed by the black crêpe. The dress the most flattering garment Gene had so far seen her wear. It lacked the usual severity and despite the simplicity of the cut, had a softening effect.

Del looked at the chiffon scarf artfully wound around Gene's throat. Pink and cerise. The beachball look of her belly. Frail-looking wrists emerging from the sleeves of the pink dress. Thick dark hair caught back with a ribbon. Sleepy-looking smudges under her eyes. Looking at Gene feeling a sudden catch in her stomach. Thinking, I love you.

Gene touched Del's shoulder and went on inside to use the toilet.

Del opened her bag for a cigarette and sat down in front of the mirror staring at herself. Deciding she needed lipstick, some color. Deciding once and for all, as she fished the lipstick out of her bag, to go with Leonard wherever he chose to take her. Knowing he would choose. Surprised to find her instincts still functional, not totally impaired after all. Telling herself, I've known one man. Just one. Thirty-nine years old and more than a third of my life with that one man. Discounting the boys I kissed when I thought I was worldly and in control of my life, my senses, my body. Boys I disdainfully allowed to touch me, puzzled by the pleasure they seemed to derive in being allowed access to my breasts and the receipt of my disinterested kisses. Bemused by it all. Until Lawrence came and put me on the other side of the wall of me and instilled in me a compulsion to offer any part of myself—no matter how degrading or humiliating—in order to experience that same, once-puzzling pleasure. Until Lawrence came and put me so far beyond the me I once knew I may never be able to find that me ever again, not ever, never. God! How frightening! Am I still inside me here somewhere?

Living all these years, never allowing myself to become interested in any other man. Knowing it wasn't safe. Yet going along wishing, hoping, for someone to love me. Thinking of love as some sort of magic elixir. Love the remedy. Love the cure. Leonard Mansfield. With round, deep eyes. And the expression in those eyes when he looked at me. I know that expression, its meaning. I know, and wish I could pinpoint precisely where and when I surrendered control of my life. So that I could go back there and resume the control. Is it too late? Have I become irretrievably victimized?

Patting powder on her nose, guiding the lipstick over her mouth. Looking up to see Gene's reflection behind her in the mirror. "You don't mind if I ... " She stopped. How did this sort of thing get said?

"It's all right," Gene said.

"I don't want to upset you."

"No."

"I have no idea what I'm doing." She turned to look at Gene. "None at all."

"It's *all right*," Gene said again. Thinking about how she could forget Bill for an hour, two, or three, then remember at the most unexpected moments. And at night. With the feeling she couldn't possibly keep going without him. Then, morning coming. And another and another. Time putting larger spaces between the periods of remembering. Injecting punctuation into the grief. Will it ever end? And why shouldn't you or anyone take what they can while they can? Why not? Go ahead!

"I care what you think of me," Del said, returning her lipstick and compact to her handbag, closing the bag. "It's important what you think of me."

Gene shook her head. I don't want to be judge and jury of your actions. It's not up to me to judge you. I accept you as you are, whatever way you are. I can't approve or disapprove. How can I, when I have no more idea what I'm doing than you claim to have?

"I think well of you," she said, then moved to the door. Afraid of new affiliations, demands being made on her nonexistent feelings.

Cold inside. All the nerve-endings deadened. All the senses blunted, burned. I am only able to care with my mind now. My feelings seem to have died several months ago. But my mind cares.

✳   ✳   ✳

The musician was leaving as they returned to the table. He smiled, shook hands all around. Smiled widely at Gene as if they'd spent the time before in deep conversation, closed both his hands warmly around hers, and then went away. A very nice young man.

Del quickly finished her drink in the ensuing silence while both Gene and Leonard watched. Then she self-consciously lit a cigarette, keeping her eyes away from their faces, wishing they'd stop looking at her.

"How about dessert?" Leonard said, summoning the waiter.

Del declined. Gene indicated she'd like the chocolate mousse which, for some reason, made Leonard laugh and pat her hand.

"Two chocolate mousses, three coffees. And brandy?" he asked the two women.

"Please," Del said, daring to look at him.

Gene refused, watching Leonard looking at Del. With the odd feeling she could read his thoughts. Able somehow to see Del as she thought Leonard must. Seeing the beauty and vulnerability beneath the anxious look to her features and despite the scraped-back hairstyle. The oddly erotic quality of the black dress. The gentle slide of small breasts, well-defined by the fabric. The absence of cleavage somehow more appealing than large breasts would have been inside that dress. She appeared finely formed, of exquisite materials. Surely Leonard was seeing it. If I am able to see it, can't he?

The desserts came. The mousse was lumpy, chalky-tasting. Gene ate a little, then sipped her coffee, listening to Leonard outlining his plans.

"I've got meetings most of the day tomorrow," he said. "Then we'll have dinner again. Meetings the following morning. Then fly back to New York in the late afternoon. Can you make dinner with us again tomorrow evening?" he asked Del.

She said, "No." And risked looking fully into Leonard's eyes. Feeling as she did as if she was voluntarily impaling herself upon something that should have been cold, sharp, hard, but instead was dizzyingly soft, warm, flexible. Feeling as if he'd put his warm hand on her naked belly and pressed gently. So that she couldn't quite catch her breath and wanted to run away but knew she wouldn't, couldn't.

"I'm tired," Gene said, breaking their silent dialogue. "You'll drop me home? Sorry," she said to them both. "I must ask the doctor for some sleeping pills. Hard to sleep now."

Del was all at once unreasonably alarmed. Never mind all her outrageous projections. Wanting to say to Gene, "Don't go off and leave me alone with this man. Please don't leave us alone together. I know what's going to happen and I'm frightened. I'm not really enough in control to be responsible for my actions. This is too real and I can't ..."

Leonard said, "I'll get the check," and again, summoned the waiter. Then smiled at Gene saying, "I'm glad as hell you've got someone who's going to be giving you a hand once the baby comes. Nice woman, that Rebecca. Husband seems nice, too."

"They're a fine family," Del put in, thinking she sounded patronizing, foolish. Lamenting every word, every thought, every deed.

"Certainly seem to be," Leonard agreed, giving her a smile that made her nipples shrivel, made the back of her neck prickle.

Leonard got out of the car to see Gene safely inside the gatehouse, then stopped her as she started to speak, saying, "Go on in, have a good sleep, and I'll talk to you in the morning. Pick you up around seven for dinner. Okay?"

Doubtfully, she said, "Yes."

He kissed her on the forehead and moved her gently into the house saying, "Goodnight. Sleep well."

She watched him walk back to the car. Peering through the darkness at the back of Adele's head inside the car. Watching Del's head turn as Leonard opened the door and slid inside. The interior light going on for a moment, catching Del suspended, an uncertain expression on her face. Then the light went out.

Gene closed the front door, locked it, and, after turning off the lights, went through to the bedroom. Smiling to see that Rebecca had made up the bed. And had placed a vase of lilac blossoms on the chest of drawers.

Five

"ARE YOU ANXIOUS TO GET RIGHT HOME?" LEONARD ASKED, HIS HAND moving the shift from Park to Drive.

Del looked up the driveway at the house. The outside lights. Sally had put them all on. She looked at the darkened windows above, then wet her lips and turned again to look at Leonard. His eyes seemed to glow in the dark. Or was it just that she was hoping so much for magic?

"What would you like to do?" she asked, her voice shrinking. Her boldness all but gone.

"A drive? A nightcap? What are you in the mood for?"

"A drive?"

"Fine." He put the car into Reverse, backed out of the driveway. Turned the car around, then sat a moment looking at her in the greenish glow of the dashboard lights. "Where to?"

"I forgot," she said, her voice sounding more like her voice. "You don't know the city. Let's make it a nightcap. We'll take a drive some other time." She was so shaky inside. Crazy shaky. Scared.

"No, let's. You navigate."

"I can't!" she said, feeling the panic again. She didn't think she'd be able to summon sufficient powers of concentration to direct him.

He reached out and took hold of her hand. Cold.

"You're cold. I'll put some heat on."

"No, no. It's all right."

"Heat on," he said quietly, his voice rumbling in the interior of the car like water booming in some subterranean cave. His hand left hers and moved to her face. His thumb on her lips. "Tell me what you want and that's what we'll do."

What I want. How can I say what I want when it's been years since I knew what I wanted or what was good for me, right for me? I don't know. His thumb grazing her lips. She blindly put out her hand, covering his mouth. Her heart pounding. Thirty-nine, without control, and feeling like a very small child in a huge, dark room.

He didn't do anything. They sat that way for several moments, then he kissed the palm of her hand, changed gears, and began driving, his hand wrapped around hers. Heading back downtown to the Imperial. As he pulled into the downstairs parking garage, he became aware of her shivering, glanced at her, pulled into a slot, turned off the engine, and swiveled around. Still holding her hand.

"A nightcap?" he asked.

"Yes. All right."

"In the bar? Or upstairs?"

She swallowed hard. Be a grownup. Be all grown up. "Upstairs."

"You're sure?"

She nodded.

In the elevator she thought she might faint. Watched the floor indicator swing slowly from left to right as they ascended. Leonard's hand closed firmly around hers. She was going to his room. He'd make love to her. And this elevator cage was transparent and everyone in the entire world knew where they were going and what they were going to do. And Lawrence—somewhere out there—would know. Thinking of Lawrence, at once in the grip of complete and arbitrary fear. Terrified, of anything, everything. The doors opened and she walked down the carpeted corridor at this man's side, her legs stiff, each step jolting her. What am I doing? Is this actually happening? Here. With this man. This producer of films who speaks about music, cares about my friend; travels considerable distances out of caring. Surely a man like this couldn't create pain?

He fitted the key into the lock, opened the door, reached inside to switch on the lights, then stepped back to allow her to enter. She walked into the center of the room, turned, realizing it was a suite. With a bar. Sofas, chairs. A bedroom down there.

Leonard stood by the door watching her. Thinking about some of the women he'd met who'd have walked in, made some flip comment, and then have proceeded to make themselves at home. But Adele simply stood there, looking at the room. Her body long and lean and poised as if for flight, the angle of her neck rigid-looking. He thought about Rebecca, what she'd said. The killing kind of husband.

"Drink?" he asked, causing her head to turn. She looked at him with anxious eyes.

"Whatever you're having," she said, opening her bag for a cigarette. Lighting one with trembling fingers as he poured scotch over ice into two glasses, added some water, then came across the room and set them down on the coffee table. Looking back to see her watching his every move. He straightened, took hold of her hand, and led her over to the sofa.

"Come sit with me." He smiled. "Midnight's quite a ways off yet."

"What does that mean?" she asked, sinking into the softness of the sofa. Surprised. She'd expected it to be hard, unyielding.

"It means"—his smile widened—"the hair doesn't sprout on the palms of my hands and the fangs don't pop until midnight. So we've got at least an hour or so before you're in any real danger."

She tried to smile. Couldn't.

"Adele," he said, as if the sound of her name was pleasurable to him and he was saying it solely for the pleasure. "Adele." His hand touched her cheek, then went away, closed, around his glass. "Ah, Adele." He sighed, relaxing against the back of the sofa, examining her eyes. "Come here. You know you want to."

He drew her over against him, his hand again on her cheek, his arm around her shoulders. She closed her eyes and allowed herself to lean against him. Listening to the deep, ongoing flow of his voice.

"You're so goddamned beautiful," he said. "But all uptight and triggered. And you don't want to be that way, do you? You want it all unlocked, smoothed out, made easy." He leaned forward to put down his drink and she sat away from him, opening her eyes.

"Let's put out the cigarette, Adele." He took it from her, stubbed it out. Her blood seemed to have stopped circulating. "Now, let me look at you," he said, turning so that he was leaning across her. "Talk to me. What's going on inside that head?"

"I'm married."

"I know that."

"You know that," she repeated stupidly. What epic stupidity! Delivering lines about being married when obviously being married hadn't anything to do with her being here. Except that it did. Everything to do with the reasons why she was here.

"No good, is it?" he said.

She shook her head, watching him.

"You want to be here, but you feel guilty."

He was being too clever, reading her too easily. But I'm not that simple, she thought. And I'm not that stupid, either.

"It's okay," he said, putting his arm back around her, bringing her against his chest as before. "I'm not trying to come across as a know-it-all, or smart. I just know how you feel. Where's the husband?"

"Here, there. I don't want to talk about him."

"How long've you been married?"

"Almost fifteen years."

"And he likes to get a little rough every now and then. Right?"

"Please." She shook her head, about to start crying. "Don't interrogate me. Nothing's ever so simple." This wasn't the way it was supposed to happen. She hadn't given any thought to words, conversations; only to the intended action.

"No, talk about it," he urged. "He gets rough and you got yourself roped in to that."

"I think I'll go." She pulled away from him. Her life was none of his business. His assumptions made her angry. Because they were at best only fractionally correct.

"Okay," he said, keeping hold of her. "I'll drop it. But let me lay it on the line. I'm too old to have any critical illusions left. You're here on some kind of personal dare with yourself. Fine. Okay. But you're here. And I'm glad. So stop thinking about all the rest of it and let's get this on."

She held herself stiff, waiting. Keeping her eyes open—feeling a terribly clinical, detached element to this encounter—as his mouth came down on hers. She closed her eyes. Shocked by the difference. The shape, feel, texture of his mouth so unlike Lawrence's. A soft insistence. But no force really. No mashing collision of teeth and tongues. His mouth moved away.

"I'm a nice old man." He laughed softly, lifting her chin. "I'm not going to hurt you. I like your mouth," he said, running his forefinger across her upper and then lower lip. "I like you."

He stood up and led her into the bedroom where he turned on one dim light, then returned to stand in front of her. She thought she might just possibly shake herself to death. Clenching her teeth to keep them from audibly chattering as he slipped his hand inside the neckline of her dress, down inside her brassiere, covering her breast. She couldn't rid herself of the panic, the sensation of being removed.

The idea Lawrence could somehow see what was happening, would know. Finally wanting him to know. Wanting to cry out and tell him, "Look! This is what it's all come to." But so sad. Being here with an attractive, persuasive man; wanting to respond but finding it close to impossible to connect herself to what was happening. Able only to think of Lawrence. One comparison after another.

He kissed her again. She didn't know what to do, thought perhaps she might succeed in forcing herself to respond. But she couldn't seem to. Leonard was setting the pace, the mood; establishing whatever control existed in the situation. And despairingly, she thought, I'm one of the sheep. I simply follow. What should I do? All this so counter to her experience she couldn't think, let alone feel.

He withdrew his hand from her breast and reached in back of her saying, "Take out the pins, Adele. Let's dispense with some of the hardware." Smiling as he took the black dress off her, then walked over to the closet and hung it up. An act that astonished her. Visions of Lawrence tossing her clothes about, often tearing them. As if the destruction of anything and everything belonging to her was his lifetime occupation. True, true. But here was Leonard displaying respect for things that were hers. And it was astonishing. Watching him loosen his tie, she lifted her arms and began unpinning her hair. Intimidated by how poorly equipped she was to handle this situation. A handful of pins. She looked around for somewhere to put them. He saw, took hold of her hand, lifted her fingers open one by one, took the hairpins, and put them down on the desk. Then, reaching in back of her with one hand—casually, as if it was something he'd done many, many times—he unhooked her brassiere, removed it; drew off her slip, placed both on the chair.

Smiling at her, saying, "Gorgeous creature." Removing his shirt, revealing a broad chest, gray-white hair. "You look as if you're going to fly away," he said, watching her hand rise and fall. Wanting to cover her breasts. "Don't fly away," he told her, arms encircling her, pressing her to his chest. Bigger, broader than Lawrence. The texture of his skin different, the entire feel of him different. All the differences registering like a series of small shocks to her brain. Why couldn't she stop thinking of Lawrence? This is Leonard. Leonard is not going to hurt me. Are you? No, you wouldn't. Would you? Please don't hurt me.

He put her down on the bed, peeled off her pantyhose, and there

she was naked on a hotel bed in the pale yellow light of a desk lamp.
While Leonard, in several easy motions, disposed of the remainder of
his clothes, then lay down alongside her, smiling; leaning on his
elbow while he took his hand over her breasts and shoulders, down
her arms, across her belly, over her hip, then back to her breasts.

"How do you feel?" he asked.

And she said, "I don't know." Her awareness refusing to shut down
and stop interfering with her reactions to his caresses. His caresses so
somehow innocent. Unlike Lawrence's manual attacks meant to
inflict pleasure like a series of injuries. Lawrence's infliction of pleasure a prelude to hurling her directly into the center of strenuous performance. She was led forward always—it seemed—by her pressure
points and a screaming, desperate need to have completed what
Lawrence so cleverly, temptingly started but always left unfinished.
So that she went about always wanting to tear the skin right off her
body in long strips or pull her hair out. Anything to take away the
monstrous need.

"Soft," Leonard murmured, his hand flat on her belly, his eyes moving over her appreciatively; taking note of scar tissue, tactfully
refraining from comment.

Her first involved gesture was generated as a direct response to the
kindness he transmitted through his hand. She lifted her hand to his
face, letting it slide over his hair, around the back of his head, bringing his mouth down to hers. Deeply frightened of offending him in
some oblique fashion with the techniques programmed into her
through the years. Those gestures so ingrained. Despicable, lacking
spontaneity; not arising from any true depth of caring, but stemming
from an intimate acquaintance with pain and her reluctance to experience any more of it.

She opened her mouth, offering access. A little more reassured by
the way Leonard was holding her, his mouth mixing with hers; grad-
ual blending. Only very subtle pressures being applied by his hands,
his body slowly coming into line with hers. But oh God! the strange-
ness. Everything about this man, this encounter, so foreign. A con-
trolled strength. His exercise of control. No angry, immediate
demands. His kisses praise on her mouth. All of him praising everything about her that Lawrence had taken and, through too many
years, turned grotesque and offensive; forcing her to despise herself.
Yet here was Leonard saying, "Lovely." Saying it again, "Lovely, love-

ly." Sighing, his hand stroking between her breasts. "You're all right?"

"Yes."

"Good, good." Kissing her again. She kept on waiting for him to suddenly leap upon her, come thrusting hard inside her, intent on wearing her down until she was compelled to respond. But no. His hands remained respectful, awaiting signals. He was making no assumption of privilege.

Surprisingly, just at the point where she was feeling her limbs starting to loosen, easing up, he got up saying, "Be right back." And she thought for several awful moments something unpleasant would surely happen now. But he returned with two lit cigarettes and an ashtray. Lay down again, placing the cigarette between her fingers, saying, "Let's talk. I can't make love to someone who's as uptight as you are. It feels too much like something I'm doing *to* you. And that's no good for either of us. So, let's talk for a while."

Talk? She couldn't *talk.* What sort of game was this?

"I can't," she said, deploring her inability to differentiate between this man and Lawrence. One man's motives and another's.

"You want to see what I'll do," he guessed, "before you'll talk. All right. Fair enough." He held the ashtray steady while she extinguished her cigarette, then put out his own, stretched past her, and set the ashtray down on the bedside table. Coming down over her so that their faces were very close together. His hands taking hold of hers, lifting them, holding them either side of her head. Entrapment? "If it's not right the first time"—he smiled—"I want an option right now. For a remake."

She was able to smile, saying, "All right," still all too frightened that this was a license she was giving him to assault her. Very aware of him hard against her thighs. Bigger than Lawrence in every way and therefore even better equipped to harm her. Would he? No. He placed his mouth on her throat, the side of her neck; keeping hold of her hands, kissing her shoulder, his tongue painting a little circle right there on her shoulder. Then bringing his mouth back to hers, his tongue painting more little circles over her lips, then around her tongue. Making her hungry now, blinding her for a moment. Her eyes locking shut at the weight of his head on her breast, his cheek smooth, soft; his mouth painting more and more circles around and around her nipples. Her knees relaxing, thighs parting slightly, lifting a little closer to his mouth painting those circles on her belly, her hips. He released her hands finally and she closed her arms around him as his mouth again came back to hers and his fingers stroked her inner thigh, higher. She opened more. Higher. Holding her breath. His fingers slipping into her, then away, caressing. Her heartbeat going faster; he was so gentle, so easy, tenderly taking her into the vicinity of pleasure. No pain, no force.

He seemed quite content kissing her, caressing; continuing until she was making small involuntary sounds he heard, interpreted, and encouraged; small signals she couldn't control. His fingers playing her. She was holding him, played out by his hands, his mouth. Her hands gripping his flesh, her eyes glazed. He wasn't using her, this was giving, allowing her to receive, giving; her fingers pressing into him. God! Are you going to suddenly stop and leave me here? Please don't do that, I'll die if you do. The sound choking in her throat, he played her all the way out, then reeled her in, holding her as he kept her shuddering on the fine edge of pleasure; then let her down, let her rest against his chest.

She received the small kisses he placed on her cheek, her temple, her ear; slowly reviving, becoming aware of the place, this man, herself. Someone who seemed to care—no matter how minimally—for her. Enough to give her this. But perhaps this was only the way he made the introductions to his particular pleasures. Was it safe? Was anything safe? It did feel safe, but how could she be certain? She opened her eyes to take hold of his hand, studying it, turning it this way and that, touching his fingers, his palm, tasting each finger, the back of his hand, placing her lips against each knuckle. Paying homage to his hand. While he watched her with the feeling that she was someone who might all too easily be shattered, smashed by any sudden movement or jarring gesture. Her hair fine, soft. He could spin it through his fingers, study it, gathering it into his hand. Something innocent, childlike about the way she examined his hand, held and stroked it; conveying a gratitude he felt no one should ever feel obligated to convey. A gratitude that brought him down, made him feel an odd anger.

"You let that happen," he said quietly, wanting to break this spell. "I don't do any special tricks."

"Perhaps you do." She raised her eyes from his hand. "Would you want to see me again?"

"I think so. What're you going to do, Adele?"

"Something," she said vaguely. Shivering at the thought of Lawrence. So that Leonard automatically held her closer. "You're being very kind. Are you this way with everyone?" Tell me I'm special, Leonard. I need to be something more than I've been made to feel, to believe.

"It isn't hard to be kind to someone like you," he said.

"I don't know. Anything." Give me something to go with. Anything. It doesn't have to be very big. "Will I see you, again?"

"Probably. I like you. You come on so brittle. And under all those external contrivances, you're a goddamned kitten. Soft and lovely. I want to make you come again. Can you?"

Color flooding into her face. Being asked about her capacities, her desires, instead of having everything pushed upon her; having what she was shoved under her nose like something on the verge of putrefaction. "I don't know," she answered.

He laughed. Not, derisively. Just delighted laughter.

"I'd like a solid week—no, make that two—in bed with you," he said, handling her with effortless tenderness.

What surprised her most was that he seemed relatively unconcerned with his own satisfaction, preferring to concentrate on hers. And despite her continuing thoughts having to do with treacherous disloyalty to Lawrence, his attention was registering; evoking further responses now. Not in the hopeless fashion in which she responded to Lawrence. Not that way at all. Simply responding because she found herself in the presence and arms of someone who cared to have her respond.

Easing her down, bending open her legs, his mouth closing in on her. Her muted cries and stroking hands offering him tremendous incentive. A woman of such passionate intensity. Incapable of withholding. Hadn't he known? Just the simplest contact had her melting. What the hell was she married to? he wondered, reveling in her undulating response to his mouth and fingers. Some fool incapable of enjoying a gorgeous, eminently lovable woman. So easy to turn on, keep on. One of the most effortless and satisfying experiences he'd had in a lot of years. Easiest thing in the world to send her off and then hold her while her body began to cool and her eyes came back into focus on his face. Questions filling her eyes and the hand she placed on his cheek; whispering. "All the things I've been taught to say, do; I start to say them and stop, thinking how wrong it would be to say or do any of that with you."

"What things?" he asked, lifting her hair back behind her ear.

She shook her head, unable to tell him; her hand traveling down his back. Feeling suddenly safe here. He wouldn't hurt her. He might even love her. She closed her eyes for a moment, frightened of love's potential. Hadn't she seen where it could go, how it could change?

"What do you want, sweetheart?" he asked, his hand rubbing her breast gently.

"Don't you want to?" she asked. Had she put him off somehow without realizing?

"What?"

"To be inside of me. Don't you?"

"Do you?"

She nodded. She wasn't sure of that at all. But it was expected. Wasn't it? Part of the performance.

"How do you want it?" he asked. And for a few seconds, she was cold; hating him. I don't want to be asked or made to tell, I want you to know, just know.

He didn't press the point, but began once more rubbing her breast, moving down between her thighs, entering her; meeting resistance.

"You're not ready," he said, lying down with her again.

"I'm sorry," she said, starting to cry. Ashamed of failing. If he hadn't asked, if he'd just gone ahead without forcing her awareness.

"Don't do that!" he said in a tone of voice that seemed to cut right through her skull. "This isn't some goddamned contest. What're you sorry for? Spend the night," he said more softly. "Forget being sorry."

She thought of all those lights burning. Closing her mind to spotlights focused on the face of that house, whispering, "Yes, all right."

She might never have another night with him. And while it wasn't safe to think about love, surely it was safe to accept what was being offered. And deal with the fear in the morning.

❉   ❉   ❉

He offered to drive her back to the house. But she said, "No. I'll take a taxi." She felt defiant. He'd assured her—successfully—that it didn't matter. She accepted that and now felt defiant. Thinking about the shopping she and Gene hadn't done, deciding she'd go first to Hamilton's, and then home. "You have appointments," she said. "It would make you late."

"Come out for dinner with us tonight," he said. "You can find a way."

"There isn't any way." You think you know, she thought. But it's all guesswork. And you couldn't possibly know. The only one who has any real inkling is Martin Ingram. And he wouldn't ever even attempt to guess.

"I'm going to take a great big step out of line here," he said seriously. "Get out of that! You're afraid of him, aren't you?"

She had to think about that. Finished pulling on her tights and stepped into her shoes. Nine-fifteen. Lawrence would make a pretense of arriving back from the airport by eleven or so.

"Answer me," he insisted. "You are, aren't you?"

"I'm afraid of *me*," she said at last. "Everything. Perhaps things will be different now."

"I'll give you a number. They always know where to reach me. If you need something, call me. Nobody has to live that way, Adele. It isn't living. And next time we get together, we're going to talk about it."

"Next time?"

"Sure, next time. A few weeks. But I'll be talking to you before then. At least have a drink with us tonight, before dinner."

"I'll try."

"Try hard. I just this minute decided I'm going to see that you get yourself untangled from that mess."

"Oh? Why?" What a proprietary stance to take about someone who's not even been able to make love to you. Do I represent some sort of new challenge?

"Because I want to spend some time with you. You need a divorce. You're not sorry you stayed, are you?"

"No."

"Good. That's a start."

You're pressuring me, she thought, pulling on her dress. You don't have the right to apply this kind of pressure to me. I don't even know you. You're telling me to crawl out from under one vise and put myself under another—yours.

❄   ❄   ❄

Determined to be calm and enjoy this interlude—before having to deal with her reactions to the night before—Adele went through the infants' department, picking things up. Feeling a one-step-removed pleasure in the act of selecting garments, tiny outfits a child would soon wear. Battling not to fall into the pit of never-filled grief for the child that would never arrive. She wrote out a check, arranged to have everything sent to Gene, then went downstairs to the street and flagged down a taxi.

Her calm deserting her the moment the taxi turned into the driveway. She paid the driver, hurried into the house, and went straight up to her bathroom to remove what remained of last night's makeup and then quickly shower. Gathering the tatters of Mrs. Prewitt together, trying to reconstruct herself in some recognizable fashion as she pulled on clean underclothes and the first dress that came to hand. Twisting up her hair. Hurrying. Then stopping, letting her hair fall, asking herself, Why am I racing this way? Behaving as if I've done something wrong. Acting guilty. But I don't feel guilty. Something, but not guilty. Strange. Different. All these years being made to feel there was an ugly, contaminated underside to myself. In one night, having it skillfully illustrated that the ugliness is contained solely within Lawrence's concept of me. He must despise me.

And the contamination had taken a strange hold on her instincts. So no matter how hard she tried, how willing she thought she was, she'd been unable to make contact with Leonard in the one way she considered most significant. Her body simply refused to contain him. Yet that didn't matter. It wasn't critical. Because he'd been happy to bestow pleasure upon her, unbothered by her body's denial of access.

Her heart beating fast, far too fast. Looking at her life, her marriage, from this new vantage point, with freshly altered perspectives. Realizing that what she'd thought of in terms of love had always been something having to do with hate. Not love. And regardless of its future or lack of future, what she'd been allowed to experience with Leonard had had to do with loving. A stranger who could care more for me than this man I've so obediently tolerated, cultivated. I *do* want a divorce. Not because it's Leonard's opinion that I have to have one. But because I want it. She lifted her head, looked at her reflection in the mirror. "I want a divorce," she told her reflection. Then felt the panic go darting like a silverfish through her bloodstream.

The telephone. She walked through to her bedroom to pick it up, saying, "I've got it, Sally," listening as Lawrence spun out a fabulous lie about being delayed, having to spend another night in California. She wanted to laugh. To scream at him. To say, "Don't *ever* come back!" But the habits were too deeply ingrained. And all she said was, "All right. I'll expect you tomorrow," and put down the receiver, wearied. All that preparedness seeping out of her, leaving her drained.

And free, if she chose, to see Leonard again.

She went down to the kitchen thinking she'd have some coffee. Wondering if Sally would say anything about her having been out all night. But of course Sally wouldn't say anything. Sally and Elton, Rebecca and Alexander. They were friends, allies. They had no fondness for or loyalty to Lawrence. And why should they? When he'd promised them the sun, moon, and stars, then forgotten all his blithe promises and she'd been left to learn, through carefully posed questions, what had been promised and not delivered. Then made good the promises. Acutely aware of the embarrassment of these people who lived on the inside of her life, their quiet anger with the man who—she knew they knew, had to know—performed nighttime plays that shook the air and sent her cries circulating like the ghosts of wingless birds.

Sally smiled, said, "Good morning," put her hand out for a cup. And Del said, "I'll have coffee with Mrs. Elliott, I think. Thank you," and left the house. Anxious to see Gene, to talk.

Walking down the driveway, thinking about Leonard; his determination to have her talk. She did want to talk. But it was easier for her to reveal her naked body to Leonard than to reveal her thoughts to him, to put words to all the feelings, experiences. Giving her body, too, was less disloyal than discussing Lawrence with someone who'd never even seen him.

And what sort of demented sense of obligation was this? To worry about her disloyalty to a man like Lawrence, who had utterly no comprehension of matters like loyalty, fidelity, responsibility, kindness. I owe him nothing, nothing. I want a divorce. I want my life. Divorce.

The word repeating in her brain. Divorce divorce divorce.

❋   ❋   ❋

Gene couldn't seem to get started. A morbid lethargy turning her body even heavier than usual, making movement difficult, making thought even more difficult. She sat in the kitchen staring at the remains of her half-eaten breakfast, nursing a cup of coffee. Worried about Del, hoping everything was all right.

Feeling on the verge of disintegration. As if anything at all might send her over the edge. Wanting to strike out, tear down the walls of an anguish that held her by the throat and wouldn't let go. Despair. Too aware of her aloneness, her losses. Longing to get up, get bathed and dressed, get moving into the day. Telling herself, Leonard will be here later, take me out to dinner. The curtains to hang, the pictures. Things to sort and put away.

Thinking about Leonard and Del going off together. Thinking about that. Without any reaction except concern for Del's well-being. Simply thinking about it. Willing to be glad if they managed to find something in being together. Wondering if they had. Imagining the two of them making love, feeling even lonelier as a result. Thinking of Bill and Sundays in bed with the *Times* in sections all over the place; getting in and out of bed. For breakfast, for a shower together. Getting back into bed to make love lazily, lovingly for hours. Dozing, waking, laughing at nothing in particular except that it seemed such a marvelous trick to have pulled off, their being together. Enchanted at finding themselves together. The sight of his in-coming beard entrancing. Bill saying, "I never thought it would happen. Being a father. It's fantastic!" Lying there with his arms folded under his head, gazing at the ceiling, talking about his feelings on fatherhood. Saying, "Jesus, I'm glad! I'm really glad. Happy. I used to think I was happy. Moments, you know. But I wasn't. Not compared to the way I feel now. What I was then was—suspended. On hold. People say, How are you? And you say, Fine, fine. Because people don't want to hear about how you really are. So you go along saying, Fine, fine. But I really *am* fine. I'm fine. You make it all that way, Gene."

Too much. She put her head down on her arms and cried. All of it fresh again, too painful. Unable to visualize any route forward. For the moment held immobilized by the grief. Thinking of Bill never seeing this child he'd wanted so much.

She heard knocking at the door and thought, Go away. Leave me alone. I don't want to see anyone. If she stayed very quiet, whoever was out there would go away. But no. More knocking. She got up, her limbs leaden, the baby pushing painfully against her, and went through to the front door.

Del said, "What's wrong?" instantly apprehensive. The look of her. The abject, broken-hearted look of her.

Gene shook her head, leaned against the wall, and covered her eyes with her hand. No words to put to the totality of her despair.

"Did something happen?"

Gene kept on shaking her head.

"Are you ill? Is it the baby? *Please!*"

Gene pushed herself away from the wall, turned, and went to her bedroom. She wanted to lie down, feeling suddenly nauseated. And disturbed at Del's having arrived to witness this self-pitying display. Yet glad, too, of her arrival. In need of sympathy. She was suddenly exhausted by the effort of carrying her burden of grief and wanted, in some way, to share the load; lessen it.

Del went after her. Wondering why there were always barriers of one sort or another standing between people. Why it always seemed so nearly impossible to go more deeply into other people. Why there was always a point at which separate selves were too distinctly defined. Without any known way to penetrate the definitions.

Well, yes, there is a way, she thought, looking at Gene curled on her side on the bed. There is one way. To proceed on instinct, without stopping first to think about appearances or hidden motives. To simply go forward. Offer one's self, one's arms.

Sitting down on the bed, bending as if she was approaching gelid water. Putting her arms around Gene, whispering, "Tell me what's wrong. I want to help."

This was what I wanted, Gene realized, soothed at once by the contact; the feel of another living body outside of her own. Eased by Del's softness, her perfume, her substance. Infinitely more substantial at this range than she appeared to be from a distance. Gene held on, gratefully accepting the comfort; rescued—at least temporarily—from the abyss of her own uncharted depths. Her feelings reviving, coming back to life. An intensely painful process.

"I *am* afraid," she admitted. Del's hair softly cool against her cheek. "Going through it alone. It frightens me."

"You're not alone," Del said, sitting up, stroking Gene's cheek. How easily they'd penetrated the barriers after all. "I'll be with you. I want to be with you."

Gene lay listening with a touching roundness to her eyes, a certain childlike hopefulness. Del found her suddenly very beautiful, fragile. Her skin so pale. Hair rich, thick, and dark. Eyes gleaming with the residue of tears. She couldn't help thinking that one incautious gesture on her part might do untold damage to this woman. Not because she was weak or too malleable. But because the present circumstances of her life rendered her too vulnerable.

"Lawrence," she said, wiping Gene's cheeks with her fingertips, "called from 'California.' He won't be back until tomorrow. I spent the night with Leonard. It's the first time I've ever done anything like that."

Gene nodded hypnotically. Wanting to listen, to hear, to know.

"He asked me to come out to dinner with you both again this evening."

"Will you?"

"I think so. He cares very much about you. But you know that."

"Yes."

"He's a kind man. For the first time in fifteen years I spent time with someone who actually seemed to *like* me." She stopped, thinking. Lawrence and I hate each other. Feeding off that. "I want a divorce," she said. "Not because of last night. Because of all the nights. Last night just helped the decision get made."

"What will you do?"

"I don't know. I'm frightened, too. There are so many things ... I can't talk about." She looked down at the rise of Gene's belly, the robe having fallen open to reveal a very pretty aquamarine nightgown. She placed her hand lightly on Gene's belly, her eyes slowly moving up over Gene's breasts to her throat. Her eyes hurting at the sight of the scars.

She wasn't bothered. Wasn't that funny? Gene thought. For Leonard to make the gesture was an offense. For Del to make that same gesture was a communication.

"I'm going to be with you," Del said, smiling; gently smoothing the hair back from Gene's face. "Why don't we have our big lunch out today? I stopped at Hamilton's this morning before I came home and arranged to have some things sent to you. I wanted to buy so many things. But I didn't. It wouldn't have left anything for you. And I hoped I could be with you when you shop for the baby. Would you like to give it another try this morning?"

Gene nodded, wanting this moment to continue; wanting to go on indefinitely contained within the capsule of well-being Del's presence and her words and gestures had created.

"All right." Del smiled more widely. "You get yourself together and I'll go change into something better-looking. Don't be afraid, Gene. I know it's all still very recent. And you loved him. But I think if you love that way once, you can love that way again. Don't you think?"

"I don't know. I can't think about it. Not now, not yet."

"You will. I'm sure you will. I'll pick you up in an hour. All right?"

"Yes."

"Good." Del bent closer, her hand cool on Gene's forehead. "I wish I had your dignity," she said, her smile gone. "My self-pity runs to hateful scenes. And terrible ... I envy you. This baby. Thank you," she said enigmatically, confusingly.

Gene continued to lie there after she'd gone. Thinking. All the boundaries and codes of her life as they'd once existed were no longer valid. She couldn't seem to make distinctions in her affiliations. And for several moments wondered if it might not be a very peaceful, very safe thing to fall in love with Adele. But no, she decided, finally getting up. I'm interpreting kindness, friendship, caring, as something romantic. I don't want to be in love with another woman. But I do want her to love me. Someone to love. All that love with Bill. Gone. Leaving such an empty space inside.

❋ ❋ ❋ ❋ ❋

Six

GENE WAS CAPTIVATED BY THE TRANSFORMATION. IN LEONARD'S PRES-
ence, Adele changed yet again. Something transpiring between one
night and the next responsible for the evolution of still another previously unseen aspect of the woman. Twenty-four hours and Adele
had gone from fearing she was behaving badly to apparently feeling
completely at ease. And as a result, laughed and chatted, smiling
almost nonstop. It would have been an altogether impressive picture
had not Gene been aware that her eyes retained a definitely anxious
light. And had Del not, every so often, taken her eyes on a brief tour
of the restaurant. As if she was the subject of intense scrutiny from
unknown quarters and in imminent danger of being publicly pointed
out and accused. But the superficial ease and rather languid gestures
seemed to Gene like some sort of underwater performance.

Leonard was Leonard. Which was perhaps why, Gene thought, it
was always so relaxing to be in his company. No surprises, no startling
changes of character. Leonard was constant. Was that why Del was so
obviously drawn to him? Thinking about Del's husband, Gene felt
suddenly chilled and lit a cigarette quickly, as if the brief flame from
the lighter or the lit end of the cigarette might offer some real
warmth.

She smoked her cigarette, listening to the two of them talking. At
a decent distance now from the morning's black depression, thanks
to Adele. Trying now to deal with this new interior view of Adele
that had presented itself to her. Examining one thought. Turning it
this way and that. Asking herself if all her thinking, her ideas were
still colored by her grief, distorted by it. But she couldn't stay away
from the idea that Del might be planning to make Leonard her new
Lawrence. Why do I think that? she asked herself. There's no reason
why I should think that. Del certainly wasn't behaving with Leonard
the way Gene had seen her behave in Lawrence's presence.

And Gene was having so much difficulty separating her responses from each other—like so many plastic-coated playing cards stuck together from overusage and sticky-fingered hands—she was afraid to accord her thoughts any large measure of validity for fear she was creating moods, impressions, irresponsibly as a result of her heightened awareness of her losses, and her inability to separate what was going on around her from her awareness of those losses. Watching Leonard and Adele laughing together over something Leonard had said, Gene feverishly wished her mind were perfectly clear, totally untouched by sorrow, so that she might more realistically appraise what she seemed to be seeing and hearing. But it wasn't possible. She hadn't any discretionary thought processes left, she decided. And gave up the attempt, turning her attention elsewhere as she smoked her cigarette and drank her coffee.

Thinking, surprisingly, of her mother. The two of them sitting out on the sagging, paint-peeling porch on a summer night. Her mother gazing into the sunset, saying, "I never thought it'd end this way, you know. I thought I'd go right the way up there"—her hand lifting into the air. "I'd have fine music and fine paintings and fine people all around me. I can see it still, clear as that one cloud there. See that cloud, Eugenie? The fat one shaped kind of like a piano? I wanted a piano," she'd said, looking down at her hands. "I used to take such care of my hands. Look at them now." Holding out her hands for Gene to see the several cuts, the jagged cuticles and rough knuckles. "I guess you've got to want things a whole lot harder than I did. I always think that. If I'd just wanted them *harder*, I'd've got it all somehow. Still'n'all, I've got you girls. And that's a fine sunset." She'd looked at the horizon for several moments. Then clutched Gene's hand fiercely, her face strangely lit from the last bursting fire of the sun. Saying, "Have a *big* life and don't let anything stand in your way. You don't have to settle. Want it all *hard!*"

My mother. I believed you. Here I am with my big life and nothing standing in my way, no compromises left to make. A house and a car and a baby I'm having. Because you pointed me in the direction of all the finer things and told me to go out and have myself a big life. You should've left me alone, let me grow with my own ideas.

But no. I can't blame you. I can't blame anyone. I chose. Nobody held a gun to my head and said I had to fall in love with Bill. He didn't force me to love him. It just happened.

Telling me, "I'm married, Gene. I'm probably going to be stuck in this marriage the rest of my life. It's not fair to involve you. At least not without telling you the truth. But I love you, Gene. And I'll take care of you."

Stop thinking about it!

I can't!

Remembering their first time. How nervous she'd been. Because her previous sexual encounters—more of them than she cared to recall—had left her sensationless. Her curiosity satisfied. But disenchanted. She hadn't felt anything much at all. Something dim and distant that might have grown but hadn't had any opportunity to because she'd been held down, held still, made captive for a few minutes that lasted days. And then had been looked upon with bleary, satiated eyes and sent home in taxis with a five- or ten-dollar bill in her hand for cab fare.

Finding herself with Bill, and unlimited sensations, and fear. Because she was bound to disappoint him. And herself, as well. But Bill. All he'd had to do was kiss her and that something dimly distant had been suddenly bright and easily accessible, and he'd nurtured it through a first meeting and then a second and a third until he brought it into flower. And afterward, held her as if she was priceless porcelain beyond currency value.

"Gene?" Adele touched her hand, her eyes bringing Gene back into focus. Del smiling coaxingly, a little afraid Gene might be returning to the morning's depressed state.

"Sorry. Daydreaming." Gene put out her cigarette and smiled at both of them. Thinking she really would have to ask Dr. Ingram for some sleeping pills. She wasn't so much down, now, as tired. Deeply tired. And covered a yawn with her hand, smiling with embarrassment as Del and Leonard laughed.

"You're just great for the ego!" Leonard laughed. "So good to be with someone you know you put to sleep. Come on, well take you home, tuck you in."

Silence.

The three of them in the front seat of Leonard's rental car. Characterless music seeping from the radio into the air. Gene thinking only of sleep, craving it.

Del planning how she'd tell Lawrence she intended to divorce him. And thinking about the fact that Leonard might succeed in putting

himself inside of her tonight. As if this act would seal some unde-
clared agreement between them. It felt odd, that she'd spent an
entire night with a man and he'd made love to her half a dozen times
so that she'd awakened in the morning feeling for the first time in
years as if she'd finally, miraculously, been purged of every last ounce
of her considerable desire. Yet Leonard hadn't taken anything for
himself. Simply saying, "Next time."

Now it was getting to be next time and she felt dizzy thinking of
having him touch her, of touching him; of having him put his hands,
his mouth, on her. A series of naked images. The two of them going
here, going there. She wanted suddenly to impale herself upon him,
fill herself with him. And could scarcely breathe, viewing the images
her brain flung before her. Greedy, hotly sexual images. Remarkably
freed from painful connotations. She turned slightly to look at Gene,
again feeling that overwhelming sense of protectiveness that had,
that morning, prompted her to promise to be there. So that Gene
wouldn't have to be afraid. Here she was. With Leonard on one side
of her. So aware of him, of his thigh pressing against hers and the cor-
responding twinge inside. Feeling as if she'd drown in the steadily
mounting lust. And Gene on the other side. Arousing in her instincts
she hadn't known she possessed. Motherly, protective, gently caring
instincts. For a moment cultivating the image of all three of them
together in bed. She and Leonard cradling Gene between them. She
turned her head sharply away from the image. An abrupt movement
that caused Leonard to turn and smile and, surreptitiously, briefly,
stroke the top of her outer thigh. Then he returned his hand to the
steering wheel. Del began thinking again of Lawrence. Seeing herself
facing him, saying, "I'm going to divorce you." An image of boldness
and self-possession; tremendously gratifying.

Gene said, "You'll make me feel guilty, spoiling your evening. Come
have a drink with me first."

The three of them got out of the car and went inside to have
brandy; sitting in the living room in thoughtful, pleasant silence.
Smiling from moment to moment at one another. Gene's radio emit-
ting Vivaldi. Until Leonard laughed aloud, saying, "Goddamnedest
seance I've ever been to! Gene, you're out on your feet, lover. Let's
get you squared away and I'll talk to you tomorrow before I leave." He
got up and drank the last of his brandy. Adele followed suit, then carried the glasses out to the kitchen and set them in the sink, return-

ing to put her arms around a fatigued-looking Gene, saying, "I'll stop by in the morning. I hope you'll sleep. You do look so tired."

Gene managed a smile and walked them to the door, thanking Leonard for the dinner. The lavish meal she'd picked at, without appetite. Just as she'd nibbled at the splendid lunch Adele had insisted on buying her at Ginetta's. Thinking for a moment of the deferential way the staff at that restaurant had treated Adele. Knowing her by name. Showing her at once to the same table by the window. Del had eaten as little of the lunch and dinner as she had. What did it mean? Did it mean anything? Or was it simply more of her incoherent intuiting?

She said goodnight and watched Leonard walk to the passenger's side of the car and hold the door open as Adele slid in. A flash of long, slender legs disappearing into the car. The door slammed. Leonard walking around to the other side, getting in. The car starting, heading up the driveway.

Gene closed the door, turned off the lights; moving like a swimming dreamer down the hall to the bedroom to take off her clothes, climb naked into bed; dropping at once into a heavy, dream-active sleep.

❋   ❋   ❋

Reckless defiance was leading Adele forward. Inviting Leonard into the house and up to her bedroom. Taking the precaution of locking the far bathroom door and the outer door to her bedroom. So that even in the unlikely event of Lawrence's returning home, there wasn't any possible way he or anyone else could gain access either to her bedroom or the bathroom. All this secured, she then turned to face Leonard. A little out of breath.

"Slow down," he said, admiring the room. The decor, to his mind, indicative of the woman he'd initially sensed present beneath the misleading externals. "Did you do the decorating?" he asked.

"Yes. Do you like it?"

"A lot."

"Thank you." She was unsure how to proceed, nervous again. "I thought I'd take a shower," she said, thinking of presenting herself to him softly warm, freshly cleansed. The idea of cleanliness and strategically placed drops of perfume oddly, appropriately wholesome when juxtaposed with the desire grinding away inside her. Contrasts. She felt as if her head might simply split from the swelling pressures on her brain.

"How about we take a shower together?" he proposed, coming forward, his head angling slightly so that she knew he was going to kiss her, could see the intent in his eyes and the slight parting of his lips. And experienced a moment of pure, tortured anticipation between the comprehension of his intent and the accomplishment of the act. His mouth descending, tongue meeting hers, sending a shaft of pleasure straight through the center of her body so that she sighed shudderingly and closed her arms around him, ready to abandon all thoughts, all cohesive action; ready to bend open right there and go plunging directly into the heart of writhing, convulsive pleasure.

He broke off the kiss and shook his head, laughing softly, saying, "You don't want to take a goddamned shower!"

"No." She could feel it happening but couldn't control or stop it. And told herself, It isn't the same because this isn't Lawrence. It's simply the way I feel. And I can't control it.

She launched herself at him like a missile. Grappling with his trousers while he let her—an unreadable smile gracing his face. Then she tugged off her tights, frantically assuming the assertive role. The control completely gone, thrown aside by the need. On the floor. She lifted her dress up over naked hips, straddling his lap while he kept on smiling that inscrutable smile—pausing only for a moment, his eyes looking actually startled—as she aimed her body and thrust herself down, her eyes rolling back. She remained motionless for a minute or two, her head hanging, hands on his shoulders as he proceeded to divest her of her clothes.

She didn't want to look, see what she'd done. Risking spoiling everything with her ungovernable needs, her commitment to the years of carefully selected input. Keeping her eyes carefully away from his face, she undid the knot in his tie, then opened his shirt, baring his chest. Feeling she was somehow bringing him down from his natural level, reducing his dignity and stature. She shouldn't be doing this to him. But she'd started, and couldn't reverse any of it now ... And his hands on her breasts set her into motion, working desperately to get closer to the feeling; to break down the once-more rigidly constructed cocoon of her accumulated hungers. Thinking how sad and defeating it was not to be able to rid herself of these appetites once and for all. But the accumulation was too great, had too many years behind it. She kept on until her body was damp, her thighs aching; failing.

"It feels great," he said at last, no longer smiling. "But I'll be damned if I know what you're trying to prove."

She looked at him, opened her mouth, closed it, stopped moving, and remained motionless. Then collapsed on his chest, grimacing in frustration as his hands stroked up and down her back and he said, "You can't do it by yourself, and I can't hold off very much longer. So"—his voice soft in her ear—"let's have a little compromise here." His hands slipping down around over her buttocks. Holding handfuls of her. "I'll just do this"—his voice dropping even lower as he held her steady and began moving—"and then we'll take care of you."

Without consciously intending to do it, she succeeded for those minutes while he thrust into her, in seeing him as Lawrence. She remained perfectly acquiescent, accepting; riding along on his chest like some parasitic animal until his hands had turned hard, he was hard everywhere, his breathing hard too as he came, sighing with the final thrusts; hurting. Then slowly relaxed. His hands once more stroking her back.

She cried silently all the way through it. Feeling the profoundest self-hatred for having set the tone, the climate; for having destroyed any opportunity for her own pleasure. For having done something, created something so nebulous it defied definition. Just something she'd done. Having taken a potentially rewarding encounter and turned it back on itself so that the underpinnings showed, the cracks and seams and patches. And now Leonard knew absolutely that she couldn't do it. When she'd so hoped this would be different. But it wasn't different. Perhaps it wouldn't ever be different. She simply couldn't respond unless a particular stimulation preceded. Had she been destroyed after all?

He tried very hard, very inventively. But she'd been right. She couldn't lose her self-awareness sufficiently to even get close to that interior door behind which everything raged and battered, demanding to get out. And finally indicated she'd like him to stop. Telling herself the fault lay partially in her having brought him here instead of going with him to his hotel. Trying to prove too many things. Failing at all of it.

Leonard stretched out on his side watching her face. Deciding tonight she wasn't so much kitten as cat. Feral, rapacious. So tense right then that she seemed thinner, older, even brittler. Reaching out for a cigarette from the box on the bedside table, she lit one, then exhaled; both of them aware of her every move.

"Is this the way it usually is for you?" he asked incisively, finding her motions and facial expression jaded, aging.

"I shouldn't have brought you here," she said, her eyes on the far wall. "It was stupid of me. Stupid."

"Maybe you're right," he said.

She glanced at him, drawing hard on the cigarette. So hard the heat burned her fingers through the paper. Thinking, It's all the same. It hasn't anything to do with this man. It has to do with me.

"No," she said at last, knowing. "It doesn't have anything to do with the place. Not really. It's right here. Inside me. Things I do, say. Thinking my doing them, saying them, will force things right. It never works. How could it possibly?"

"You're pretty tough on yourself," he said, wondering if she might not respond given a little breathing time. He was a little puzzled by her inconsistent responses. Last night one thing, tonight something else. Yet the inconsistencies interested him. She interested him altogether. He had quite a desire to study her, probe her thoughts in an attempt to find the essential core of the woman. The basic, axial essence of her. She seemed very angry now. "Give yourself a break," he said. A reasonable man seeing reason in every situation, even the unreasonable ones. "Come down from up there and relax. Or are you angry with me, too?"

This time she turned fully to look at him.

"Why should I be angry with you?" she asked.

"Who knows? Anything's possible. I've known enough women to know there are all kinds of things that get said or done in all innocence that can be the worst kinds of turn-offs. Who knows? Maybe I said something, touched you the wrong way. Those things happen."

"You haven't done anything," she said, feeling guilty. But at the same time wondering if she was being truthful. "It's me. *I'm* the one." I should have just let it happen, she thought; distressed. But I couldn't, wouldn't. God damn me! I couldn't. I don't know how to let things happen any more. Or how to direct events. I've been on the receiving end for so long I don't know how to perform except in stress situations.

"Well, I'm glad to hear you say it," he said.

"Will you still want to see me again?" she asked. At once furious with herself. Begging. Blurting out whatever came to mind. No thought, no timing. No pride.

"I told you I'd call you. And I'll probably be back in town in a few weeks. Don't you believe the things people tell you?"

"No." How could I possibly?

"Well, that's sad," he said. "That's pretty goddamned sad."

"It is, isn't it?" she agreed, putting out the cigarette. *I'm* sad. I'm very sad.

"Now don't get carried away." He smiled, drawing her down beside him. "If I was as hard on myself as you're being on yourself," he continued, planting a kiss on her shoulder, "I wouldn't get one goddamned thing done. Stop being such a critic! You're all right. Want to try again?"

She didn't answer, but simply lay looking at him. Wanting more than anything else to try again. But feeling too raw in every way, feeling worn down, used up, strung out. Needing so badly to have it all eased. Because if it was left this way, she wouldn't sleep. And might possibly be hating him by morning. The idea of having to finish for herself—an image too redolent of every encounter with Lawrence— so demoralizing to contemplate it might turn her suicidal. Seeing herself making that monumental journey back through the dressing room and bathroom, back to this bed. To huddle in the dark, furtively completing everything Lawrence so intentionally generated and rarely ever satisfied. Years of wondering, asking herself if he knew he was destroying her. Destroying her nervous system, her sanity, her life. He knew. Of course he knew.

Leonard watched her eyes. "Pride might kill you, lady," he said, not unkindly. "There's nothing wrong with asking for what you want. People can only say yes or no. And if you don't ask, sometimes you don't get. Anything."

"I know. *Please*." She placed her hand on his arm, shifting over closer to him.

"That's not asking," he said. "That's begging. Don't you know the difference?"

Why was he doing this to her? A new brand of punishment.

"No!" she said sharply. "I told you. I don't. Know. Anything. Oh, for God's sake!" she cried miserably. "I'm no good at fucking and you know it, you've seen it."

"Nice," he said wryly. "Consider me a puritanical old son of a bitch, but I hate thinking of something I'm doing with a lot of input and pleasure as 'fucking.' Spare my sensitivities." He smiled, feeling tired with all the input. "Call it 'loving.' Call it 'knitting' or 'weaving' or any goddamned thing you like. But it's too much like no contact, 'fucking.' Come on over here and let me love you a little. Don't get so worked up." Coaxing, urging her to straddle his mouth, covering her breasts with his hands.

If I think about this, I'll become hysterical, she thought. I won't think about it. She held on to the headboard and closed her eyes. Feeling humiliated at the start. Injured in some nonspecific fashion by the unpretty aspects of this, the indignity of sitting astride an aging man's face in an effort to get to something inside herself. Something that might, for all she knew, have died. But too much in need to continue questioning the posturings, the sounds. Surrendering to the need, his mouth, the concerted effort required to get over to that far side of herself.

✳   ✳   ✳

He didn't seem overly pleased with himself. As Lawrence would have. They lay quietly for some time, then Leonard roused himself, saying, "I've got some people to see in the morning, so I'd better get going."

He dressed. She tied on her robe and walked with him through the house to the door. Daunted by the darkened, empty rooms at her back. And by that damnable substance inside her that moved her so willingly into his arms to be kissed a final time. Hopeful it might all, in parting, come right. To have her breasts, her belly and thighs, stroked through the robe. To have Leonard whisper, "A solid week in bed, next time. We'll get a lot of things worked out. I took an option, remember?"

Then he was walking down the front steps, crunching his way over the gravel to the car. Opening the door, climbing in. Starting the car. Driving away. And she was left quivering inside the robe. All the fire regenerated by his final affectionate gestures. She closed and locked the door, then returned upstairs to at last take that shower she'd wanted hours before.

✳   ✳   ✳

The next morning she was standing in the kitchen drinking a cup of coffee when the front door opened and Lawrence came elegantly slouching in. Elton carrying his bags on upstairs. Lawrence making his way to the kitchen wearing his typically deceitful smile, saying, "I could do with one of your omelets, Sally. Some toast. Good morning, Del."

She said, "Good morning," through lips that felt numb. Caught every time by his cruelties. Greeting the housekeeper before greeting his wife. "How was your trip?" You liar. You sick, hateful liar. I hope Sally puts ground glass in the damned omelet. God, the childishness! The silly spitefulness!

"Oh fine," he said. "Rotten drive back from the airport. Traffic backed up for miles. Paper come yet?"

"On the dining table," Sally said without looking up, "in its regular place."

He looked at Del, his eyes narrowing fractionally, his nostrils tightening. As if he could see and smell something out of the ordinary about her, something decidedly different. She watched him over the top of her coffee cup. The words all prepared in her mind. I've decided. Had enough. It would be best if you left. You can certainly stay with your mother until you find a place of your own.

He was reading her eyes, her mouth. The swollen look to her mouth, her reddened chin. The evasiveness in her eyes. Knowing all the signs. She'd been making love. It amused him, infuriated him. Powerful reactions all detonating simultaneously. Was she intending to bluff it out? He turned and went into the dining room, humming as he slid into his chair, picked up the morning paper. Casually calling, "Come keep me company, Del. You know I hate to eat alone. And there are several things I want to talk to you about."

Del looked over at Sally, who was breaking eggs into a bowl. Thinking, I'm afraid, afraid, afraid. Why? I know why. Suddenly, she wanted people around her. A lot of people. Protection. People who cared. Gene. I'll go see her. She thought of Leonard. Leonard being so kind, trying so hard to understand. Treating her as if she mattered. As if the body that contained her was worthy of much more than abuse. She'd slept so easily, so peacefully beside Leonard that first night. And then waking in the morning to have him make love to

her again, wanting her to feel good. Unconcerned about his own sat-
isfactions. Showering together. Then sitting, smoking a cigarette
while Leonard had shaved. With the bathroom door open so they
could talk. They hadn't said all that much, really. But the effort to
communicate had been made. I'll see him again, be with him again.
I don't have to be alone here.

She refilled her cup and went through to the dining room, taking
her seat at the far end of the table. Nothing we do is real, she
thought, sitting down. None of it's been real. Way way back at the
beginning, yes. I had real feelings. Overpowering feelings. Love. So
much love. Ammunition I gave you to use against me. Love I could-
n't stop manufacturing. Love you kept handily converting to muni-
tions.

"What've you been up to?" he asked, not looking up from the paper.
The question couched so lightly, devoid of innuendo. If you didn't
know the man, you mightn't think anything at all of the question.

"Helping Gene get settled," she answered. "Her things arrived. We
all went down to help her."

"How neighborly," he said, a little acid in his tone, his hand going
to his cup as Sally came in to pour his coffee. "Thank you, Sally."

"Yessir." Sally looked quickly over at Del, then went back to the
kitchen. Where Elton was standing, having helped himself to a glass
of orange juice. Something going on here that felt bad. Elton feeling
it, too. The air all stretched, hard to move through. Elton murmuring, "Man never did come off no plane. I was there to see him coming out from a taxi."

Sally shook her head. "He knows something," she said, dishing up
the omelet, buttering the toast. "Gives me the creeps the way he's
always knowing something." She carried the plate through to the
dining room.

"Thank you, Sally."

"Yessir." Back again to the kitchen. Elton still standing there, as if
prepared for any and all eventualities. Something.

"You seem to have developed quite an attachment for your voiceless little mama," he observed. "What else have you been doing?" He
put down the newspaper, looked briefly at her, then started on the
omelet.

"Very little," she said thickly, watching him eat; loathing the sight.
Feeling sickened by the sight of the food entering his mouth. The

shape of his mouth revolting. Get the words out! Tell him right now! Tell him it's all over. That he can't ever again insult people you care about. That he can't ever again … "Will you be going in to the office?" she asked, despising her cowardice.

"Shortly," he answered, possessed suddenly of an overwhelming desire to march her upstairs, tear off her clothes, and see if the marks weren't all over her body too. A vision of her cowering, naked. Except that Adele didn't cower. He couldn't break her reserve. He could do any number of things to her, but her eyes always contained something he could never reach, something beyond his range. Her eyes forever telling him, You can do these things but you can't defeat me. You won't defeat me. Well, I damned well *will*, he thought. Riding down that desire to drag her upstairs.

"I've been intending to talk to you," he said, quickly finishing the food. He always ate so fast. She'd be a quarter of the way through her meal and he'd be ordering coffee. "I did a lot of thinking while I was in California," he said. "And I've decided the best thing for both of us would be a divorce."

The words exploded inside her head. Instant outrage. She was supposed to be telling *him*. And what did he mean? Who had he found? She didn't care. I'm supposed to be glad to get out of this, it's not supposed to matter who's doing the telling, so why do I feel this way? It doesn't matter. My God! She was possessed of so many thoughts all going in so many different directions she was suddenly trembling, unable to think at all. She put down her cup, wiped her mouth on the napkin. Replaced the silver monogrammed napkin ring.

"Don't ignore me, Del. I want a divorce," he repeated.

"You want a divorce." She got up, set the napkin in its ring down on the table, and walked through to the living room. In no way prepared for this. More infuriated by the second. She wanted to kill him. He'd taken everything she'd ever had. Now he planned to leave, but not before taking a final extra something. It wasn't supposed to be this way. She was the one. To tell him. I want a divorce. *Why are you concerned?* It doesn't matter who's doing the telling. What matters is getting out.

He got up and followed her into the living room. A laughably regretful look on his face. As if he cared at all what he did to her.

"I suppose you'll tell me you've found someone else," she said, facing him; shaking. Wishing she could be cold, killing. She should've been able. All these years of observing him at close range. She should have learned.

"What difference does it make?" he said, sounding bored.

"*What difference does it make?* Fourteen years! It's not … it isn't …" She couldn't get the words out. Her anger robbing her of her powers of speech.

"Oh, *please!*" he said impatiently. "Don't give me that! It isn't as if you haven't been out fucking around." The corners of his mouth turning down, mouth thinned to a pale line.

Oh God! she thought. He'd take absolutely everything, eviscerate her as well if he could. She wanted to throw back her head, open her mouth, and howl; scream until her lungs burst. She had no weapons at all. Nothing.

"Aren't you going to deny it?" he said. "Tell me you weren't out with some stud, humping your way to kingdom come."

"GET OUT OF HERE!" she screamed, her fists clenched. Blood flooding up into her face. Would she die of the rage? She thought she might. But it was courage, too. "GET OUT!"

"Christ, a melodrama," he said disgustedly. "Of course, I'm going to get out. Isn't that what I've just been telling you?" The dialogue was wrong. He couldn't understand it. There was supposed to be begging, pleading, demands for explanations.

"NOW! RIGHT NOW! GET OUT OR I'LL *KILL* YOU!"

Sally clutched Elton's arm, both of them staring down the hallway toward the living room. Each restraining the other from moving.

Lazily, as if it bored him to have to do it but he'd perhaps seen it in a movie once or had heard it was an effective gesture, Lawrence threw out his hand and slapped her across the face. She went absolutely rigid. Scenes of carnage, bloodshed, flashing off and on in her brain. He slapped her again. And the air rushed out of her lungs, bending her double.

Quietly, as if the voice came from someone who'd taken possession of her body and was using her voice, she said, "You'd better be going now."

"Oh, shut the fuck up!" he snapped. Annoyed with this whole silly play. What the hell did she think she was doing? Standing staring straight ahead as if she was paralyzed.

"I'd go if I were you," she said again. "Because in about five seconds, if you don't, you're going to be a dead man."

He looked blankly at her. And suddenly it registered. She actually would kill him if he stayed around any longer to belabor points. He'd finally managed to push her just a bit too hard. He'd just have to get her back on the track later. But for now, he'd play out her little scene. Went out to the kitchen, told Elton to bring his car around, then up the back stairs to get his still-unpacked bags.

Sally walked over to the bar, poured a lot of brandy into a glass, then forced it into Del's hand, saying, "Go on, drink that! You just drink that on down!"

Her eyes clicked back into focus and she looked at Sally, then at the glass Sally had placed in her hand.

"Don't matter how," Sally said. "So long as he's going. And he's going. Now you drink that up." She stood a moment, then returned to the kitchen.

Adele lifted the glass and drank. Then coughed, shuddered, and looked around the room. Unable to think. Hearing Lawrence descending the stairs. Turning away to look at the fireplace, unable to bear the thought of seeing him. Wishing him dead. Wishing herself dead. Exercising every last bit of her self-control in order not to go running outside after him to create another scene. No, let him go. Her hand closed so hard around the glass that it shattered. Glass and brandy and blood. She continued to stand staring into the fireplace, the blood dripping from her hand onto the carpet.

※   ※   ※   ※   ※

Seven

Alexander introduced himself. A tall, round-faced young man. With serious eyes and a potential about the mouth for great, wide smiles.

"I've been working on this," he told Gene. "And I thought I'd come on over, tell you some of my ideas, show you what I've done so far."

"Come in." She smiled and led him inside to the living room, feeling excited at the prospect of being able to make herself heard over the telephone.

She sat down beside him on the sofa, watching as he opened a wrinkled brown paper bag and brought out what looked like the bottom end of a Styrofoam cup with holes punched in it.

"This is kind of a working model," he explained. "See, what I thought, I thought if we could make a portable unit we could snap it on over the telephone mouthpiece. Work it on hearing-aid batteries and let the equipment in the mouthpiece do the amplifying. That's pretty much what it does anyway. This will focus the sound, direct it into the equipment at an increased volume. Good idea you had." He smiled at her. "Me and Dad have been working nights, trying to get it nice and flat, lightweight; working with a few old transistor radios and some old hearing aids we found down to the Salvation Army thrift shop. I've still got a few more things I want to work out. The housing especially. And some kind of cupping action so the whole thing'll just slide on over the mouthpiece and off again and you could take it around with you anywhere you go."

"That's wonderful," she said, much impressed. "Wonderful!"

He looked pleased.

"Another week or two and we should have a pretty good working model for you to try out. I just came by, you know, to bring you in on what we've been at." He handed her the model and she turned it over, blinking at the wiring and circuitry, the tiny, round battery.

Everything painstakingly soldered into place. She handed it back, asking, "Some coffee? Or a Coke?"

"No, thanks. I've gotta go. Promised I'd give Dad a hand with the yard work up to the house today."

"Thank you," she said, going with him to the door. "It means so much to me."

"You know," he said soberly, evidently having given the matter considerable thought, "I'll bet there's lots of people with the same kind of problem maybe could use something like this."

"Probably."

"You wouldn't mind if I did a little investigating into that?"

"No."

"Well, okay." He smiled. "It's just that it was your idea and I wouldn't want to steal it or anything."

"*Your* idea," she amended. And he smiled a great wide smile and went swinging off up the driveway.

She went back to the bedroom where she'd been before his arrival, to continue opening the packages Del had had sent to her. So many things for the baby. Vests and playsuits, sleepers. A beautiful crib quilt. Too many things really, combined with the shopping she'd done herself. A stunningly generous display. She sat on the bed looking at the array of gifts, deciding today would be as good a day as any to begin outfitting the second bedroom. She got up and walked across the hall to look at the room, mentally placing a crib over there, a chest of drawers there. A rug, curtains, a changing table. Perhaps Adele would enjoy shopping for these things. She walked back to the living room debating whether to telephone or to go up in person.

Three days of silence. She hadn't seen Del or spoken to her. Rebecca had come to help hang the curtains, mentioning that Lawrence had gone; Sally had been instructed to pack his things. But that was all Rebecca had said. And Gene wondered what was happening. Because something was definitely happening. She could feel it.

Hearing the sound of the riding mower, she looked out the window to see Alexander riding back and forth, cutting the grass. And Elton close to the house pruning the bushes. The car, waxed and polished, sitting on the drive in front of the garage. The effect was of a fully staffed house with no one living in it.

She moved outside. To stand for several minutes looking at the house, at the gleam of its many windows, the chimneys, the broad front door. A very large, commanding house, set at the apex of the circular drive. In her mind, Gene thought of Del as small inside that house. Nowhere near large enough to in any fashion populate all those rooms. And now Lawrence was gone. She was glad. She hadn't liked him at all. But still, the feeling was all wrong. Somehow, Del should have been out and about, celebrating. Her lengthening silence was slightly ominous. She'd walk up to the house, invite Del out—a return lunch. And, at the same time, satisfy her curiosity, as well as the small anxious spot that seemed to chafe when she thought of the silence. Aside from all of that, she reasoned, she needed the exercise. Her legs swelled now after a few hours of being on her feet, and the baby seemed to be growing pounds heavier every day. So that it required considerable conscious effort to keep her spine from bending forward over the weight of it.

✳   ✳   ✳

It really was a very good thing Adele didn't know where he'd gone. Although making a few telephone calls would soon enough tell her. But she was exercising her will power, not making those calls because that really would be the end of her. All too easy to give in to the positively overwhelming desire to find him, get him on the hearing end, and say all the things she'd wanted to say for so long. Hurtful, vengeful things she'd been unable to say at the time. Her mind kaleidoscopically turning with ceaseless images of confrontations where she, each time, emerged victorious. Fantasy. She knew it. There was no way she could hurt him. But he was eminently capable of returning to hurt her. And that fact was acid, eating its way through her every thought and action so that she was scarcely aware of anything but the constant interior monologue she revised, edited, revised, both asleep and awake; as if the perfect set of words delivered at the perfect moment could keep her safe from harm, protected.

There was a small, calmly logical part of her brain that kept warning her to be careful. This was not the way Lawrence did things. Lawrence did not go away and stay away, maintaining silence.

There was a larger, irrationally optimistic part of her brain that kept telling her, It's over. Forget it. It was what you wanted. You got it. So forget it. But she simply couldn't. There were too many loose ends.

Too much invitation about this house.

So on and on she went, preparing for a second play. Convinced it couldn't possibly all end this way. A bit of stage managing, some new directions, fresh dialogue, and surely the scene would play to perfection? What was she thinking? Telling herself it was petty, unworthy, not to accept that it was played out, finished, unalterable. But no. One part of her would patiently hear out the determined voice of logic, then turn aside and indulge anew in all the recriminatory and accusatory lines of scathingly appropriate dialogue. She had to be prepared. Fight with suitable ammunition, be prepared. She longed to kill him with well-turned phrases, leave him stunned and broken by the cleverly penetrating usage of true words, true facts. Truth was strength. Wasn't it? On a treadmill of hating, fearing. Hating herself for being unable to accept his departure, his never coming back. Fearing his capacity for clever deception. Not above creating a scene like that simply in order to bring her into line. Except that she hadn't cooperated. And he'd had to make good the threat. Now, it was his turn for a countermove. Oh God! she thought. I'm going mad, finally.

Guiltily, she thought of Gene alone in the gatehouse. She was probably wondering about the sudden break in contact. But Del couldn't detach herself sufficiently to get up, go down, and explain. She couldn't, in fact, even summon the strength or take the time out from her frantic musings to get dressed. Or sleep. Or eat. She paced back and forth in her robe, paying scant attention to the trays Sally brought up and took away; every so often lunging at some bit of food that caught her eye, wolfing it down—disgusted by the sloppy sounds of her own eating and her contemptible appetite—then pushing the tray away to get on with replaying that last scene, pinpointing the faults, the omissions. It was by no means finished. The only conclusion she could draw. The only one safe to draw. And she was exhausted, terrified.

Had he defeated her finally, once and for all, with this? It felt that way. She thought of all the pills in the bathroom. Certainly enough there to see her into a safe and permanent oblivion. She was holding the pills in a safe corner of her mind, distantly deciding she would indeed use them. Just as soon as she was able to get her thoughts clarified.

From time to time she looked at the bandage on her hand, remembering watching Sally rinse the deep cut with disinfectant. She'd felt nothing, but Sally had winced. Then Sally had wrapped the hand with gauze, taped the edges. And looked at Adele finally with an indecipherable expression that could have been sympathy or disguised contempt. Everything so distorted now, so completely out of focus she found it impossible to trust her senses; knowing absolutely that nothing she saw or heard or thought at this time was in perspective. Knowing only that this was not ended and she was not safe.

She walked a path into the bedroom carpet, embracing images of her dead self laid out for public viewing. Grotesquely painted images. And a picture of Lawrence playing it out abject and broken-hearted as he valiantly guarded her waxy remains and silently savored his ultimate success.

She'd never wanted anything more deeply, more passionately, than to be able to cleanse her mind of Lawrence and of her thoughts of his multifarious sins against her and her pathetic fear of him. Pacing back and forth, back and forth, feeling like a sick rat in a cage, manically testing the strength of the enclosing walls, searching for a weak spot where she might break out. Or someone else might break in.

She smelled bad. She knew it. Three days without bathing. Three nights without sleeping. Her face felt like something congealed at the bottom of a frying pan. Her fingernails were dirty. Her body felt oily, thick. As if she'd been swimming for weeks in malodorous mud and had at last climbed out, allowing the stuff to dry on her body. Her hands itched to shred her skin, tear it away from her bones and musculature in fatty, bloodied strips.

"God, God!" she whispered, moving, moving; her arms wrapped hard around herself. "Get me out of this! I've got to do something to get out of this!" If she didn't find some way to break out of the cage, she'd go into the bathroom and swallow everything in the medicine cabinet. And she didn't want to, knew she mustn't. That action would be too in accordance with his plans. I *am* mad! I've gone over, finally. Yes.

Sally knocked at the bedroom door.

Del jumped, her insides racing. Startled further by the sound of her own voice asking, "What is it?"

"Miz Elliot's downstairs asking to see you."

Gene. Gene had come to see her. She couldn't let anyone, especially Gene, see her in this condition.

"Give her some coffee, tell her I'll be down in a few minutes!"

"Yes'm." Sally went away.

Leaving Del suspended in the middle of the room. Thinking about how depressed Gene had been. And how she'd promised to be with her. Given her word. Thinking she'd be all right with Gene. Yes.

She ran into the bathroom, pushing her filthy robe into the hamper as she climbed into the shower and began scrubbing at herself, in a hurry to get rid of the thick feeling, the smell. So exhausted from all the sleepless nights that her body kept twitching and her eyes seemed to want to stare and her hands kept wanting to fall limply to her sides. But she forced herself to hurry. To see Gene.

Gene sat at the kitchen table with the cup of coffee Sally had pro-vided, watching Sally preparing bread. Something she hadn't seen done in years. Remembering her mother's fifty-fifty successes with the bread. Sometimes it was perfect. Sometimes it came from the oven gluey and inedible. So fifty percent of the time, Dad grunted and tore off hunks. And fifty percent of the time he casually back-handed Gene's mother across the head and went out to ride into town in the pickup and down some brews at the tavern, bypassing dinner altogether. She'd always understood his anger—from a certain distance. But had never been able to generate any sympathy inside herself for his need to strike out. Why couldn't he have just yelled instead of hitting?

Sally slammed the dough down on the floured board, kneading it hard with very capable-looking hands, practiced hands. Her knuck-les sinking into the dough, then slinging the dough around, slamming it down again. Gene found it relaxing to sit drinking the coffee, watching Sally; breathing in the yeasty smell as she looked around the large, spotless kitchen. Yellow. Everything gleaming, new-look-ing. All of this to provide for the appetites of one woman. Something about this reality striking Gene as decadent. One person didn't need a kitchen this size, all these appliances, all these cupboards full of china and glassware, that pantry over there with shelves laden with canned goods, dry goods.

"How many rooms?" she asked Sally in a quiet moment

"Ten," she answered, not looking up. "Looks bigger, though. Five bedrooms. Five bathrooms. Living room, dining room, kitchen, library, sunroom. Miz Prewitt used to spend all kindsa time in the sunroom years back. Past few years, I just dust around." She went silent again. Wondering if it was her place to talk about what used to be around this house. Wasn't up to her to worry whether the rooms got used or not. But still, she couldn't help thinking back to when Miz Prewitt's brothers used to come visiting. And the old folks. Friends spending weekends. Parties ... No more of that.

"I haven't had home-baked bread in years." Gene smiled.

"Make you up a loaf," Sally said, paying close attention to the loaves she was shaping. "Elton'll bring it down later on."

"Thank you."

"Just gets wasted anyway," Sally said. "She ain't been eating much. Ain't been eating at all, truth be told." She looked hard at Gene, then quickly returned her eyes to the bread she was setting in the pans, covering with wet cloths. "Guess I shouldn't tell tales, but I'm glad you come on over. I was moving myself to have Elton fetch you. She's been in a bad way. Up there." She looked at the ceiling as if she could see Adele through the floor. "Up there, just pacing away, talking to herself like a crazy woman. Crazy scared." Her eyes fixed on Gene's again. "You're her friend," she said. "That woman she don't get out this house, they'll be coming to *take* her out. She ain't got cause to be as scared as she is. We all're here." She shook her head and went to the sink to rinse her hands, then poured herself a cup of coffee and leaned against the counter. "You never in your life saw a person change from day to night the way that girl changed. She was so pretty it made your heart big just looking at her. Happy. And not six months, she was looking old, looking—surprised. Like somebody hurt her in the baddest possible way. Evil," she said, her face suddenly grim. "That man. Things I've heard in the night in this house. She's needing a friend," she said. "And she needs to get away out of this house for a time, get back inside herself." She studied Gene's face. "You could see me with my walking papers for saying all this. But you won't, 'cause you care. Just like I care. And Elton, Rebecca. Somebody's got to care about a woman locks herself up three days without eating or sleeping, just walking night and day, talking out loud; scared half crazy out of her mind."

"*You're* her friend," Gene said, both sad and frightened. She'd had no idea things were as bad as this.

"I'm not a friend like you're a friend," Sally said patiently. "It's not the same thing."

"It should be," Gene said, meaning it.

"For you. Okay. Maybe. Not for a lot of folks. For her, fine. But not at a time like this. That's why I'm telling you, stepping outa my place, telling you."

Gene nodded soberly.

"How's that baby coming along?" Sally asked with a sudden smile, liking Gene.

"Good," Gene answered distractedly. "Glad when it's over."

"Don't I know it! Last weeks're the longest. But that child'll be here before you turn around. And then you'll be wondering how one little baby could keep a person so all-fired busy."

Sally stopped talking abruptly and Gene turned to see Del standing in the doorway. And seeing her was a shock. Just days and Adele had turned thin and old and haggard. As if someone had taken away the laughing, chatty woman of a few nights before and substituted an elderly, poorly-made look-alike. She understood exactly now what Sally had been trying to tell her. And wondered what might be done to reverse some of the damage.

"I intended to call you," Del lied, trying for lightness as she opened the cupboard, took down a cup, and poured some coffee. "I've just been so busy since Lawrence left I haven't had time to think."

"Of course," Gene said, looking down into her cup. Mrs. Prewitt. Mrs. Prewitt. Where's Adele, Mrs. Prewitt?

"Getting his things out of the house," Del went on. "Getting *rid* of him, I can't tell you what a relief it is!" She stood with her back to the cabinets, both hands around her cup, lying so hard she thought surely the entire world must be shrieking with laughter at this preposterous display. Her hands shaking wildly as she held the cup to her mouth and drank some of the coffee. Watching Gene nodding earnestly, her eyes very alert. Suspicious? Didn't Gene trust her?

"I came to invite you to lunch," Gene said. Thinking she just might cry. "To shop with me."

Stop pretending! Del told herself. I'm not fooling anyone. Why do I have to try to fool these people? They know. They know everything. Sally does, I'm sure. And Gene, haven't you guessed?

"I'd like to," she said, suddenly filled with longing for someone to hold her. Hold her hard, tight; keep her safe. There was a part of herself that longed to see her dead. And she was struggling with all her might to resist. I don't want to die. I really don't want to die. I'm so afraid. Don't let me die.

"In an hour?" Gene said, getting up, placing her empty cup in the sink. "My car?"

"Fine," Del agreed. Her face appearing to be on the verge of disintegration. Putting her cup down carefully on the counter, trying to hide the uncontrollable shaking in her hands. But Gene looked, saw, and took hold of Del's hands. In her husky whisper saying, "You'll be with me. I'll be with you. That's fair. An hour."

Del nodded stiffly, the tears clotting in her throat, behind her eyes. Not daring to speak or meet Gene's eyes.

Gene held Del's cold hands a moment longer, then let go; thanked Sally for the coffee and walked through to the front of the house.

Sally, still holding her own cup, quietly said, "Go on get yourself dressed up. Get out of here."

"I'm going insane, Sally."

"You're going *shopping* with your *friend*. Ain't nobody gonna kill you. And *you* ain't gonna kill you! We're all here, looking out for you. Go on, go change!"

Dumbly, Del turned and went up the back stairs.

Thinking, No one's going to kill me. And I'm not going to kill me. I am not going to kill me, I won't die, I will not I can't won't must not die.

She could barely get her hands to function. But forced herself to light a cigarette, take a deep breath, calm down. Did up her hair. Then some makeup. Perspiration streaming down her sides. Stomach heaving, dancing. The litany going on, on. I won't die won't die will not die. I'm so scared scared so scared, but I won't die, won't.

She forced herself to pay attention to remarks Gene made, forced herself to offer opinions on the crib, the changing table, the chest of drawers, the mattress. Forced herself to eat almost half the lunch Gene generously bought her. Forced herself to talk to Gene on the drive back. Commented on the fine quality of the 450 SEL's ride. Forced herself to get out of the car when Gene pulled up beside the gatehouse. And then, suddenly beyond the need for forcing, reconnected with herself, she stared down at the gravel, trying to think of what to do next.

"Stay here." Gene said. "Don't stay there alone. Stay here."

"Yes," Del accepted. Exhaustedly, gratefully. And went into the gatehouse with Gene. Appreciating Gene's look of health, her soft-looking roundness. The thick fall of her hair. The scarf tied artfully around her throat. The swell of her breasts against the bodice of her dress. She looked young and healthy, alive.

The evening went away from Del without her awareness of its departure. It simply went. And then Gene was looking at her with dark, concerned eyes, saying, "I'll make up a bed for you here on the sofa, lend you a nightgown."

Gene had the eerie feeling Del wasn't hearing or seeing her. All afternoon and all evening, the feeling that Del's body was present but the woman had gone off somewhere, and there seemed a frighteningly distinct possibility she mightn't ever return. Yet when Gene brought her the nightgown, Del said, "Thank you," and, "May I use your bathroom?" and went off to remove her makeup, to bathe, and finally emerge clad in one of Gene's pre-pregnancy nightgowns. And, shivering despite the warmth of the evening, lay down on the sofa, pushed her head into the pillow, and wrapped herself tightly into the blankets, murmuring, "Thank you very much. Good night." And closed her eyes.

Feeling somehow defeated, Gene turned off the lights and went to prepare for bed. Thinking what an incredibly emotional week this had been. Thinking, for the first time since he'd left, of Leonard. How Del and Leonard had lifted her out of that brief, horrific depression and set her back on her feet. Now Del. That so-charming husband. It was infinitely better that he was gone. And what Del had claimed to want. Yet she was so distracted, so nervous and fearful. Surely she couldn't want to *keep* that man, could she?

She took one of her sleeping pills and smoked a cigarette, giving the pill some time to work before turning off the light and slipping down further under the bedclothes, waiting; ready for the synthetic sleep to claim her. Looking into the darkness, her hand moving over her belly, feeling the now-sleeping bulk of the baby. Picturing it coiled inside her, asleep. Tiny fingers and toes. Knees and elbows. Someone alive inside her body. The concept was sexual, taking her back to Bill. Bill moving in her, sweet friction, his words and body urging her to accept him, accept the child he wanted them to have, wanted to give her, moving her, his open hands welded to her upper thighs, watching himself moving in and out of her, watching her lift to meet him, whispering, Jesus, you're beautiful! Look at you—beautiful! Teasing her with his fingers, making her moan, the pleasure inverting her, making her come, leaping, crying, making this baby.

❋   ❋   ❋

Adele kept her eyes closed, willing herself to sleep. But it wouldn't come. She couldn't get past the thoughts, the thinking. Unable to get warm.

❋   ❋   ❋

Gene looked up. Del was a figure in the doorway, indistinct.

Whispering, "I can't ... I'm so ... please let me be near you for just a few minutes, I'm so cold, please."

I should be afraid, Gene thought, but I'm not. She's so unhappy. It can't hurt. How can it hurt? And turned, caught for an instant by the crisp sound of the sheets rustling—the sounds magnified—was it the pill? Del whispering, "Please, just for a few minutes," slipping into the bed, curling up on her side, gazing at Gene in the darkness. Whispering, "If only it could have been me who did the telling. I wanted to be the one to say it was over because then he'd have known it was real. To say, You have to go. But he took that away, too. Why did he have to do that to me? I don't want to think about him, but I can't stop. There isn't anything else, if I could just think about something else, something pleasant. I can't stop thinking about all the things he's done to me, years and years; things he's said, made me do." Her whispering voice breaking, the tears lending an odd cadence to her words. "He destroyed me, took away what I wanted most, the babies. I wanted them so much." Her cool hand reaching under the blankets to touch Gene's belly. Her touch light, skimming; strangely comforting. Gene lay still, listening, receiving Del's hand. The pill slowly taking her over. Del moving a little closer, her hand closing gently over Gene's breast, whispering, "Oh, my God! Please! I need ... so much just to be close, touching."

Frightened, Gene said, "I can't make love to you ... I ... I can't." Yet, even while saying it, she was asking herself, Why can't I? Why not? Who's making the rules?

"Just let me touch you," Del pleaded, a frantic whisper in the dark.

The movements of her hand suspended. The lush ripeness of Gene's body, the baby inside drawing at her in a way nothing and no one ever had. The promise of a communion deeper than any she'd ever known. Without thought, only a longing to hold; be held; touch this woman lovingly, without fear for either of them. Because she didn't feel at all afraid or doubtful here. An instinct stronger than any other she possessed urging her to touch, caress, give love with words and gestures. And, in return, derive a pleasure and comfort previously denied her. Unable to stop herself, her hand encircling Gene's breast. Drawing in her breath with the sudden, intense satisfaction. Abundance and awesome softness.

Gene didn't stop her. She didn't really want to. This was life returning to her, an infusion of warmth. Del would never harm her. Del might even make her feel happier simply about being alive. And perhaps, most importantly, they might help each other. So Gene consented by not consenting. Simply present, receiving; her limbs turned heavy by the drug.

"Oh," Del whispered softly, lost in the depths of new feelings, important feelings, "you're so beautiful. Your skin." Her eyes adjusted now to the dark, the tremors still shaking her, she looked down at Gene's face, her eyes, mouth. Lightly pressed her lips to Gene's, then to her breasts. Resting her cheek against Gene's breast, the panic leaving her, the madness and anger and fear all leaving her. She felt Gene's hand gently stroking her hair, and her eyelids fluttered closed. Lying loosely within each other's arms, pills and exhaustion prevailing, they slept.

✻ ✻ ✻ ✻ ✻

Eight

HI, THIS IS GRADY. REMEMBER? I WAS THERE THE OTHER NIGHT. WITH Leonard. Remember?"

Gene said she did, wondering why he was calling her.

"Okay," he said. Then, as if adding an afterthought, said, "Must be really rough getting yourself across on the blower. Okay. The thing is, I really didn't get any kind of chance to talk to you that night. Leonard and I had a lot of stuff to cover and then I had a late session. Recording. Some people can't do it except late at night They can't get their voice up during the day. Anyway, I thought we might get together, have dinner."

She didn't know what to say to him. All she could remember was a young-looking man with longish hair and an exotic knowledge of music, composers.

"I can hear you thinking." He laughed. "Trying to figure out what this turkey's doing calling you up. Maybe he's into some weird stuff or something like that. Listen, it wouldn't be good for my image, you know, going around molesting pregnant women. But Leonard told me some about … what happened. And what the hell! I thought you might just like to get out, have something to eat, talk a little."

"When?"

"Any time you like. Tonight? Got anything going for tonight?"

"No."

"Okay. Great! I'll pick you up. Seven, okay?"

"Yes."

"Boy, it's rough trying to hear you. I'll be there at seven. Don't get all fussed up or anything. We'll just relax, unwind, eat some good food."

She put down the receiver and looked at Del.

"I have a date." She started to laugh.

"Who?" Del asked, smiling.

"Grady. The composer that night with Leonard. Remember?"

"Not really. Just that he seemed very young. Nice-looking."

"That's about what I remember. Pancakes," Gene said. "Let's have pancakes."

"I'm really not hungry."

"Have to eat," Gene said firmly. Wishing she could use her voice. Inflections, emphasis. Goddamned whisper that conveyed so stinking little. Just the essential words. Relying on whatever facial contortions she could drum up for accompaniment to add the appropriate weight to those words. Wishing, too, she could remember more about him. Longish dark-blond hair and young-looking. Other than that, his features were a blank. She hadn't even retained any impression of his size or height. I must be out of my head, accepting an invitation from someone who's probably ten years younger. Me, enormous with this baby. I must be crazy. He must be even crazier, wanting to go out in public with someone looking the way I do.

She switched abruptly from that track to a fuzzy recollection of the night before. Feeling only a residual warmth. She turned to look at Del as she mixed the batter. Her memory expanding to include a further recollection of how slight, how fragile Del had seemed. The feeling that she'd held a child in her arms, to her breast. More loving than sexual. Her continuing response one of deep caring, concern.

Del was smoking a cigarette, one hand around her coffee cup; gazing down at the table. The smoke from the cigarette floating up through her hair. Her profile arrestingly lovely, pure. Without makeup. Her hair falling softly about her face. Her expression thoughtful. Her features smoothed out. She looked young. Troubled.

"Are you all right?" Gene asked.

Del looked up. Her face still holding its thoughtful composition. "Why can't I stop thinking about him?" she said, pained. "I'm so tired of it. I'm a bore on the subject and I know it. Every time my mouth opens and I hear myself talk about him, I want to cut my throat; hating myself for being so small, so damned subjective, such a rotten coward. I've got to do something. Get away. Or something. You're right. I can't stay in the house. I've got to do something." I wouldn't sound quite so demented if I could just tell you, explain the feelings. But I can't. That would be dragging you right into the middle of it all, somehow. And unfair to you.

"A holiday?" Gene suggested.

"I don't know. I just don't know." Leonard had said he'd call. Sally would know to tell him to call here if he did. Perhaps she could go see him for a few days. Anything to put some distance between her and these thoughts. An image of dressing up, packing, going off to the airport; flying away. To be with someone who cared. Never mind how much or how little.

But then she thought again of their last meeting and felt the blood seeping into her face. Was it some brand of lunacy to hope to perpetuate something that had started out with failure? But he'd said ... No. Maybe Sally's right. Maybe, just for once, it is the way it seems to be. And it's all right for me to relax, get on. Maybe. But then, why does it feel so unfinished? Obsessive. Impossible to explain.

Looking at Gene's body under the robe. Filled again with a yearning for what she couldn't ever achieve. A baby would have meant so much. So very much. I will never have what you have. And nothing, nothing, must happen to you or this baby.

Watching Gene pour circles of batter onto a Teflon griddle. Then, stand holding a spatula, watching the pancakes bubble. While butter was melting in one pot and syrup warmed in another. And sausages spit under the broiler. The smell of food causing Adele's stomach to contract painfully, hungrily.

"I am hungry," she said, causing Gene to turn and smile, saying, "Good!"

"I didn't ... upset you, did I?" she asked in a hesitant voice.

Gene stood for a moment, then crossed over and touched the top of Del's head. Feeling a pang of mixed responses as Del's eyes closed, then slowly opened.

"I'm not upset," Gene said. "Nothing to be upset about." She moved back to the stove to turn the pancakes over. "You're making me re-examine my values, perspectives. I think that's good. It doesn't feel at all bad."

"I'm always forcing people," she said, eyes on the tabletop. "Wanting everything to come out the way I want it and not letting things happen by themselves, in their own time." Forces exerted simply by my being alive. The fact of me an exertion of force.

"Stop then," Gene said reasonably, stacking the first batch of pancakes to one side of the griddle to keep warm, opening the oven door to check the sausages. The kitchen filled with good smells, homey smells. Sunday morning breakfasts with Bill. Taking turns. He cooked

one Sunday, she cooked the next. He'd liked to try exotic foods, difficult things. Crêpes, Swedish pancakes. Remembering the one
Sunday when she'd bought the expensive new griddle and for the first
time in her life prepared perfect sunny-side-up eggs. Perfect. Serving
them to him feeling ridiculously exhilarated. Those perfect eggs. "I'm
happy you're here," she told Del. Grateful for her presence. "And you
couldn't force me to do what I'm not willing to do. My sister and I
shared a bed as kids. It was warmer. Amelia's older. She used to let me
touch her, feel the ways her body was changing. Before *she* changed.
It was natural, nice. Close. I've never felt guilty about it. You don't
have sisters?"

"Two brothers."

Gene turned over the second lot of pancakes, then opened the oven
door and removed the broiler pan, using tongs to set the sausages to
drain on some paper towels. Put the broiler into the sink, squeezed
liquid detergent into it, then filled it with hot water. Del watched,
admiring her efficiency, her orderliness. Then got up saying, "Let me
at least set the table," and found place mats, dishes, cutlery. Lifted out
of her lassitude by the simple acts of movement, the minimal thought
required in setting the table. Distantly admiring the pretty
blue-and-white flowered pattern of the plates, the matching place
mats. Scandinavian flatware. Gene liked modern things. All the living room furniture was the finest teak, upholstered in rough-looking,
unusual fabric. The rugs were Berbers. Beautiful, natural things. The
lines of every piece in the living room clean and flowing. Large,
heavy art books. Rows and rows of books. Hand-potted jugs and
vases. A huge, plainly hand-woven basket beside the fireplace for
kindling. For the first time, Del thought about Gene's career. How
she must have worked. And succeeded. And how much it had to hurt
now, having lost it forever. Why haven't I thought about that? she
asked herself, annoyed at this omission. The good clothes, the car.
Even the cosmetics Gene used were the most expensive, the best.
Those scarves she wore so casually were designer scarves, beautiful.
I've assumed so much about you. And most of it's probably wrong. I
must stop thinking solely of my problems, of myself, and think about
you, others.

They ate in silence for several minutes, then, slowing down, Del
said, "I haven't told you. Your things are beautiful. The rugs, the furniture."

"Thank you."

"You chose them?"

Gene nodded. "Bill liked them, too."

"Did you know a lot of men before him?"

"Quite a lot," Gene admitted. "Enough to know Bill was special."

"Lawrence has only ever made me feel ... desperate. Like a contestant."

"Leonard?"

"He's a kind man."

"A very kind man. He took care of everything when Bill died. So strange to talk about it, think about it. Bill died. Almost four months. Sometimes it seems years ago. Other times, I can't believe he's dead. But I know he is. I wish you'd stay here with me for a while. It's good. To have someone to talk with. To be here."

"But you've got a date ..."

"So what? I'm not about to bring him back here and make love to him." She studied the idea, found it hilarious, and burst into almost silent laughter. The two of them sitting, laughing. Neither of them really sure why.

Grady sat back down at the piano feeling very pleased. With himself. With life. With the prospect of seeing Gene. His mental image of her so softly enticing, he wondered if he wouldn't be disappointed at seeing her a second time. But he'd watched her the entire time he and Leonard had been talking; watched her and the other woman and the way their eyes had communicated. A lot of very fine feeling going down between those two women. And that had given him kind of a nice high. For no particular reason. Except maybe that he liked women, liked the way they could be to each other when it was a close thing, a caring thing. It broke all the standard image patterns, two women caring about each other. Otherwise, looking at the whole picture, it could've just been one typically tight-assed society babe who, for some unknown reason, was cultivating a small, dark, very pregnant lady. Perhaps just tolerating her presence for the duration of the evening in order to be there with Leonard. No question the society babe had eyes for Leonard. But the thing of it was, neither of them was typical. Not the society babe. And not the small pregnant one.

For another thing, Leonard wasn't the type who just indiscriminately fucked around. He was the go-easy kind who didn't go chasing hard after women. At least that's the way Grady had it taped. Because this was maybe the fifth or sixth time he'd done business with Leonard, and he'd never even seen him with a woman until that night at dinner.

Funny thing about reading people. The society babe was what she was. And there weren't any other ways of reading it. *But.* She was a great-looking lady and there was a certain kind of something about her deep boozy voice and big sad eyes that blasted the stereotype. She was sharp, smart. A good head, you could tell. Lots of machinery upstairs. Nervous hands. And something missing he could feel just from watching the way she smoked those cigarettes. He'd liked her. Because she really wasn't a tight-assed society babe. She only looked like one.

And Gene. You couldn't pinpoint what she might be. Except that she definitely wasn't society. She didn't have that kind of granny-nanny training—like the other woman—that kept her snapping her spine straight every time she remembered. But what she did have was this unbelievable sort of warmth. Just incredible. The kind of cozy lady it'd be dynamite to cuddle up with. Because she'd be soft and she'd bend. And if she touched you, it'd be gentle, good.

He hadn't been able to stop thinking about her. And after the session, that next morning, he and Leonard were having breakfast in the hotel coffee shop, and Leonard laid the story about Bill on him, how it'd happened. And that kind of cinched it. Asking Leonard, "D'you think it'd throw her totally if I called her up, invited her out?"

And Leonard had thought about that and said, "Play it. I'm no goddamned good at telling people what to do. Do whatever feels right to you."

So all week he'd been thinking about it. Trying to guess what her throat had to look like under the scarf. Thinking about what a downer it had to have been. Projecting himself into the future deaf, say, like Beethoven. Or maybe with his hands wrecked in some accident. And it scared him nuts. Put him into a state of the shakes just thinking about it. Going deaf. Or breaking his hands. And if it felt that way to him just thinking about it, about all the maybe's, then she had to feel … Man! He couldn't even begin to imagine how she had to feel. And having the guy's kid on top of all that.

So, along with being so goddamned sweet-pretty looking, she had balls. And he was high as hell on the idea of seeing her, having an evening with her. He'd take her to the good Greek place. And then, maybe, if she was into that, he'd bring her back here, play some stuff for her. They'd rap. It'd be good. Great. He switched on the gooseneck and looked over the last few bars of the score. Then uncapped his pen and changed two notes.

❋   ❋   ❋

"I'll be here," Del was saying. "If you're sure you don't think it's ..." She shrugged, lost for the appropriate words. "In any case, there are a few things I want to get at the house. You're quite sure you want me to stay?"

"Very sure."

"All right then. I will. You look lovely," she said a little shyly. "Have a good time." She let herself out and walked up the driveway toward the house. Feeling strange, almost elated. She'd go to the house, do a few things, then return to the gatehouse for the night. And not be alone. Why was it, she wondered, she felt more at ease, safer, in the gatehouse—even alone—than she did in the main house? It had always been that way. Which was why she'd been so reluctant to sell the place. Needing a refuge, some place she knew could contain her safely. For some irrational reason, she'd always believed nothing bad could happen to her in the gatehouse. And some summers, she'd gone down just to putter around on the pretense of making certain things were in order there. But really just to walk from room to room wishing she lived in the gatehouse. Knowing how comfortable, how contented she'd be, being contained within those sound, stone walls. Insulated, sheltered, secure. She'd bring books and a thermos and sit on the floor of the empty living room, drinking iced tea and reading. Every so often lifting her head to breathe in the summer smell of the air and the illusion of freedom being there gave her.

Wasn't it odd how the closer she came to the main house, the less elated she felt? She'd only stay a few minutes. Long enough to get a book or two, a nightgown, a robe. Have a quick chat with Sally. No, Sally was off this evening.

Maybe, she thought, I should sell this house. Move into town. Take an apartment. Something I could handle alone. All these rooms. The grounds, the taxes. Five years of mortgage payments left. The mortgage because the accountant advises I need the interest deduction. But I love this house. It isn't the house. It's all that's gone on here.

She opened the door, switched on the lights, and went upstairs to her room. And as she entered, her eye was caught by a shaft of light at the far end of the bathroom. A light on in Lawrence's room. Was Sally here after all? She walked through the dressing room, the bathroom, stopping in the doorway, her heart clutching in on itself at the sight of Lawrence opening and closing dresser drawers, tossing things on the bed. She hadn't seen a car. What was he doing here? How had he come? I must remain calm. I can deal with this.

He went on opening and closing drawers for several moments, then seemed to sense her presence and turned, stopped, and stood looking at her.

"I thought you were out," he said, sounding guilty. As if she'd caught him at some highly illicit pastime.

"How did you get here?"

"I drove, of course," he said evenly.

"You drove. I didn't see a car."

"It's parked at the side."

"I see." She didn't know how she felt. She hadn't ever felt quite this way before. Strained, yet able to maintain her calm. He looked different. As if she'd never actually seen him. And somehow, she suddenly didn't care what he did or where he went or if she never did say all the cleverly hurtful things she'd been brooding about saying to him for close to a week. She felt sorry for him, sorry for herself. And anxious simply for him to be gone. For the game to be ended once and for all, for good, forever. Ended.

"I won't be long," he said a little nervously.

"Take all the time you need." She returned back through the bathroom to her own room, lit a cigarette, and sat down in the chair by the window, examining this new calm inside. What had happened to the rage, the fear? Could it all go, just go so easily? What was happening to her?

Sitting quietly smoking, feeling quite at ease. Hearing him moving around down there. Then silence. Looking up to see he was standing just inside the room, lighting a cigarette, saying, "Can we talk? Or are you going to leap up out of the chair and cut my throat?"

"Talk," she said, turning again to look out the window. Still light outside. So why did it seem so dark inside the house?

He sat down in the other chair, crossing his ankles, looking at her.

"What's going on?" he asked, sensing even more changes.

"Nothing. Absolutely nothing."

"I don't know why I did that," he said, his voice different, subdued. She turned to look at him.

"Did what?"

"Said I was leaving. The divorce business."

"Oh?" Her eyebrows lifted. The game had boomeranged on him and he was actually admitting it. Should she trust any of this?

"You slept with someone else," he said a little thickly.

"Yes, I did. You've slept with dozens of someone elses."

"That's different."

"It isn't different."

"It *is* different, Del. You cared, I never did."

"Explain that to me," she said, leaning forward to put out her cigarette.

"Oh, Jesus!" he said tiredly, all at once looking his age "Who the hell knows? The whole thing's gone wrong. Who knows any more what it all means? I came back, looked at you, and knew you'd finally done it. I never thought you would. I never thought any of this ..."

"Why wouldn't I?" she said softly, a little frightened of believing they might finally be communicating. Don't trust him! her interior voice warned. Don't let your guard down! "I've certainly never had much of anything from you."

"I didn't really want to leave," he said. Trying to get angry with her.

"It's a little late for that. I was getting ready to ask for a divorce."

He slouched somewhat lower in the chair and drew on his cigarette. It seemed to be getting gradually darker in the room. "Was it any good?" he asked. Aroused just by the thought of it. Picturing her naked, another man.

"That's none of your business," she said without inflection.

"I didn't go to California," he admitted.

"I know that. I saw you. With one of your someones."

"And that's why you did it," he guessed.

"That isn't why I did it," she said patiently. "I don't have a whole set of reasons all laid out for what's happened. I did have a lot of things I wanted to say to you, though."

"And?"

"All of a sudden, I can't be bothered saying them. It doesn't seem worthwhile."

"I see." He sat up to extinguish his cigarette, then leaned forward, arms folded across his knees, studying her face. Restraining himself. "Are you going to marry him?"

"I'm not marrying anyone. I'm still married to you. Remember?"

"Are you planning to?"

"I have no plans."

That was good. He felt a little better. A chance. "Do you want to have dinner?" he asked. "Or have you already eaten?"

She felt the first stirrings of alarm mixed with optimism and didn't feel she could trust her reactions.

"I don't think so," she answered carefully. Her heartbeat starting to accelerate.

"Come on! Have dinner. We'll talk some more."

"It's too late," she said. "There's nothing left. I no longer care."

"You're just going to write the whole thing off?"

"Lawrence, fifteen years! I'd be the fool of all time to believe one word you said at this point. You've paraded your women in front of me. You've done … unforgivable things to me. Marched me off to doctors to have my insides torn up. Marched me off to other doctors to have my insides put back together. You've lied and lied and lied until there's nothing left. You've done every conceivable … I'm going to write the whole thing off, yes." You want me now, she realized, because for the first time I'm actively resisting you. With my thoughts, my words. And it's tantalizing to you. My God! You think I've taken the game down another track.

"You're hard," he said, disbelievingly. "You're so hard."

"If I am, finally, it's the result of all your efforts. I don't care enough about you any more to degrade myself for your benefit. It's over. I'll get a divorce. It's what I want. Funny." She smiled sadly. "I knew you'd come back. And I was so desperate to have the words all prepared. But now I don't care. I just don't care."

"Oh, you care," he said, some of the familiar self-assurance edging its way into his tone. "You'd care if I took you over there." He waved in the direction of her bed.

She shook her head. Refusing to be afraid, to back down, be intimidated.

"No," she said. "I wouldn't. You're welcome to try. But you'll be disappointed. It's all used up, gone. I don't have the strength or the inclination to allow you to work me into a frenzy. And then ... auto-eroticism. Do you know that that's what it was? I find that very interesting: that I spent most of fifteen years turning myself on for your benefit. To make you want me. To make you want me happy. I find that sad."

"You love me."

"I *loved* you. A long, long time ago. Now, I don't know what it was about you I thought I loved. I think the truth is I was in love with my own feelings for you, not anything you ever showed or gave me. You can't do to someone all the things you've done to me and expect that person to keep on loving. Well, perhaps it happens. But I've stopped caring. Even the ghost died." She smiled, enjoying this rare opportunity to verbalize about a tremendous accumulation of feelings, fears. "How could you expect me to love you," she said quietly, no longer smiling, "when, aside from all the other things, at your insistence I lost the one thing I wanted and needed the most?"

"That wasn't my fault," he said, flustered; always hating it when she brought that up. "How could I know that would happen?"

"You made me do it. Just as you've made me do everything else. You might as well have held the scalpel yourself. The end result's the same. How could you do these things to me, Lawrence? I wish I could understand that. How could you put someone you claimed to love through such a long, long nightmare?"

"It's not my fault," he repeated, anxious to get away now. "You know I can't help it." He had to get away to think, to straighten things out in his head. She'd changed all the rules. Every one of them. He'd have to figure all this out.

"Have you found everything you came for?" she asked, reaching for her cigarettes, lighting one.

She was dismissing him. How had she suddenly taken over the control? He stood up, very confused, unsure of himself. "Come have dinner," he said. "We really should talk."

"No, thank you. I'm all talked out. Please make sure you take everything you want. Because I'm going to have the locks changed. And I think I might even go away for a while. I don't know. I'll have to think about it. In any case, take it all now, Lawrence. Because you can't come back here. Ever again."

He stood for several moments looking down at her, then cleared his throat and lifted his eyes to the window. He'd have to do something about all this. "Will you sell this place?" he asked.

"I don't know. I haven't really decided anything."

"Del." He looked back at her. "I know you probably won't believe me, but I'm sorry. I'm sorry it all turned out this way. I took a big chance. It backfired. It was in the back of my mind all the time to come back. You know I can't help all the rest of it."

She shook her head. "You can't come back. I don't want you." She wanted to add, "See a doctor. See someone. Get help." But that might be dangerous.

He didn't say anything further. Just turned and walked away back to his own room. She continued to sit looking out the window, the darkness slowly taking over the room. The palms of her hands wet. He might come flying back. No. She heard him going out and waited for the sound of the front door closing. Then she put down her cigarette, got up, collected her books, nightgown, and robe. And, in the dark, ran all the way back to the gatehouse.

❄   ❄   ❄

Perhaps it was because she was pregnant. Or maybe because she had a friend she knew would be at home, waiting for her. Gene felt no pressure. Simply relaxed. Able to listen to Grady, to smile and talk to him while she ate with better appetite than she had had in months. He was very good to look at. Although her original impression that he was very young remained with her.

"How old are you?" she asked, after the waiter brought their coffee.

"Guess!" He smiled, showing his teeth. His eyeteeth slightly overlapping.

"Twenty-five."

He laughed. "No way!"

"How old?"

"How old're you?" he countered.

"Old. Thirty-three."

"Shit! That's not old."

"No?"

"Old is my grandmother. She's eighty-eight. And even she's not that old. Guess again!"

"Younger?"

"No." He laughed, taking hold of her hand, squeezing it. "*Older.*"

"Twenty-eight?"

"You're lousy at this," he said, enjoying himself. "Thirty-one. Coming up thirty-two in August. So, you're not so old, granny."

She smiled, looking at his hand around hers.

"You thought I was a kid, the junior league, right?"

She nodded.

"Wrong!" He laughed. "I'm in your peer group, Madame. We are of the same generation. We are con-tem-po-rarees!"

"You're crazy!"

"Yup! Wasn't that a great meal? Christ! I could live here. Best pita anywhere. They make it right here, you know. The desserts, too. D'you mind if I ask you something?"

She shook her head.

"Does it hurt to talk?"

"No."

"You could use one of those gadgets, couldn't you? Those things you hold against your throat?"

Her face froze and she remembered the doctor holding the cylinder to his throat, to show her, the inhuman sound that had emerged. Had he gone on one second longer, she'd have gone completely insane.

"Hey!" he said softly, again squeezing her hand. "I'm laying a bad trip on you. I'm sorry. We won't talk about it if it's such a downer."

"Why did you ask me out?" She looked at his eyes.

"Because you're pretty. Because I thought it might be fun."

"How could it be fun, taking a pregnant woman out to dinner?"

"People'll think I'm out with my old lady and the soon-to-be kid."

"Are you *serious?*"

"Sure. Why not? What the hell?"

"You want to make love to me," she accused.

"Maybe. Aren't you allowed to?"

She put cream into her coffee, added a packet of sweetener, unable to conceive of making love to anyone in her present condition. The idea that another man's body—not Bill's—entering hers might somehow contaminate the child.

"I'm not going to push it," he said. "I'm not into pushing people, throwing my weight around. I mean, it wasn't the whole setup I had in my head to get you out tonight, then take you back to my place, score. I don't have that kind of head. I don't have kinks. I just thought maybe you'd like to come back, hear some music, maybe smoke a little. Maybe you're not allowed to smoke?"

"I don't think I should."

"You've smoked before?"

"Before," she said vaguely. Thinking of Bill sitting on the sofa with his feet on the coffee table and his eyes half-closed, holding the smoke down in his lungs. Then passing it to her. Back and forth until it was gone. And then naked together. On the floor. For hours. Fingertips touching and nothing else. Lying there looking into each other's eyes. Wells. She'd never had an experience like it. An intensifying of emotions, a fusing of responses. Moving entirely out of herself and into him. The feeling, too, that she'd finally managed to embrace the complete man, all of him. And after that first time, they'd done it once a month or so. Sometimes oftener. Rendered so peaceful, brought so completely together. I must let you go, she thought, her eyes moving over Grady's face. A fine, open face. I must begin letting you go. You're gone and you're never coming back. And I have to keep going. I must.

"I like you," she said.

"Good. I like you too."

"You're not married?"

He laughed, his face once again very youthful.

"Oh sure! I'm married. With six kids. And for kicks, I like to escort a heavily pregnant lady around town. Just to keep everybody clued as to what a high-powered, heavy-duty stud type I really am." He picked up her hand, turned it over, then put it down again. "I'm not married. Were you married?"

"No.

"Didn't think so," he said, serious again. "Must be rough. When I started thinking about it—about the parts Leonard told me—I thought it has to be really rough. That blonde lady a tight friend of yours?"

"What does that mean?"

"I mean, who's looking out for you?"

"I am."

"I know that," he said. "But what if you have to go to the hospital or something?"

"Del's with me. Why do you concern yourself?"

"I care about people. I care about you. How much longer will it be?"

"Six weeks or so."

"What I'd like to do," he lowered his voice. "Two things. I'd like to take that goddamned expensive *bandage* off your neck. You don't need that. You've got a scar. Be proud of it! Don't go around with it all covered up! Show the world! Say 'Fuck you' to everybody! That's the first thing. And the second thing. I'd like to kiss you all over your nice big belly. Maybe rap awhile with the kid. You know, exchange taps back and forth. I'm crazy about your big belly."

She smiled, finding him funny.

"You'd probably get a foot in your face," she told him.

"Hey! I'm willing to risk it."

"You're crazy."

"All the really good, really bright people are. D'you want to come back, hear some sounds?"

"Another time. Not tonight."

"Another time for sure?"

"If you like."

"It's hard as hell trying to talk to you on the phone."

"I know that. Some people are working on it for me."

"Good! 'Cause if it wasn't so damned hard, I'd be calling you every ten minutes. You know what's kind of nice about this whole thing?"

"What?"

"I have to stop and listen, really pay attention to what you say. And you say just what you have to say. No extras. That's kind of a good thing. You can get tired having to listen to all the superfluous garbage people feel they've got to say to keep your attention."

She waited to hear if he'd add anything more.

"That's all," he said. "That's the whole thing. Just that you don't say a whole lot, so I've got to pay heavy attention to what you do say. Are you scared?" he asked bluntly.

"Sometimes. Are you?"

"Sometimes. Particularly when I think maybe I've taken on more than I can really handle. I wish you'd come back, let me play some things for you."

"Next time."

"That's a promise?"

"Yes."

"Well, at least I get to have you as a captive audience for forty minutes while I take you home."

She smiled and he leaned all the way over the table to kiss her on the tip of her nose.

"You're like an ice cream sundae," he said, taking both her hands, steepling her fingers. "I'd like to eat you up. A little bit at a time." He looked up from his efforts with her fingers to see her studying him quizzically. "It's okay," he said. "It's common knowledge I'm not playing with a full deck. You all set to go?"

"Yes."

"Okay. Maybe I can drive *very* slowly and drag it out to an hour."

❋   ❋   ❋

He pulled in, put the car in neutral, and turned to look at her. "I don't scare you?"

"No."

"Do I get a goodnight kiss?"

"No."

"Okay. No harm in asking." He jumped out and ran around to open her door, extending his hand to assist her out of the car. "I'm not really nuts," he said quietly, keeping hold of her hand. "And I *don't* want to scare you. It's just that it doesn't make any difference to me, your being pregnant. That's all. I'll phone you tomorrow. Okay?"

She changed her mind. Just like that. Put her hand on his cheek to bring his head down and kissed him on the mouth, then stepped away and stood looking at him, smiling. "I do like you," she said. "Thank you for dinner."

"Thank you for the bonus. And one other thing," he said, stopping on his way back to the car. "You're the most righteous-looking pregnant lady I ever met." He waved and kept going.

❋   ❋   ❋

"You had a good time?"

"Very good."

"I'm glad."

"What did you do?" Gene asked her.

"I had an interesting encounter with Lawrence. He was at the house when I went up to get some things."

"Oh?"

"It was funny. For the first time, I felt ... brave. I just wanted him to go away and stay away. He couldn't believe it. I couldn't either. I've never defied him. But I did. It was how I felt."

"Why?"

"Because I knew I could come back here, be with you, talk about it with you."

"That's good."

Del put out her cigarette, then turned out the light.

"He wanted to make love to me," Gene said.

"What did you say?"

"I wanted to. But I wouldn't, couldn't. If he's still interested after the baby's born ..."

"I know what you're trying to tell me," Del said.

"I don't know what I'm telling you. But I love you."

"I know," Del whispered, safe again. "I love *you*."

"I thought I was dead. But I'm not."

"God! Don't say that!"

"Don't *you* think of it," Gene said surprisingly. "It's important to me having you here."

"I want to be here."

PART
TWO

Nine

I‍T WAS AT LEAST THREE WEEKS TOO EARLY. BUT IT WAS HAPPENING. SHE got up out of the wet bed and stripped off the sheet, the mattress pad; carried them out to the kitchen and pushed them into the washing machine. Then had to stand and wait until the next contraction passed. She picked up the gadget Alexander had presented to her the week before, assuring her, "It works. Dad and I've been trying it out. Just fit it on over the mouthpiece and whoever's on the other end will hear you clear as day." She removed her wet nightgown and pushed that into the machine as well, then moved slowly back to the bedroom and got dressed. All the while she was dressing looking at Alexander's invention on the dresser.

She hated to call. It was so late. And Leonard was up there at the house with her. They were most likely asleep and she'd wake them. She toyed with the thought of calling Grady. He'd said the idea of being around to see the baby born really appealed to him. But she couldn't go through this with Grady, not someone she knew so slightly.

She picked up the receiver, stood looking at it for a moment, then slid the attachment on over the mouthpiece, dialed, and listened to the ringing.

"It's me. I'm sorry, but I'm going to have to go to the hospital."

"My God! The thing actually works! I can hear you so well. Have you got your bag?"

"Yes."

"I'll be right there."

"Not Leonard," Gene said.

"I understand. Five minutes."

Adele drove with careless skill—a surprising new facet, this skill—sending the car along the highway at a speed well over the limit. Yet Gene wasn't in the least frightened by her driving. She seemed more in control than she'd ever been. Glancing across every so often to smile, asking, "How is it? My God! I'm so excited!"

"Fine. I'm still drowsy from the sleeping pill."

"You called Martin?"

"Yes."

"Does it hurt?"

"No."

"Leonard's going to England to do a film. He's asked me to meet him there."

"Will you?"

Del looked over. "I don't know." She thought how odd it was, these weeks. Lawrence hadn't called, hadn't returned to the house. Odd. What she'd asked for, received. But couldn't quite believe.

"You should go."

"You're making faces as if it hurts."

"Not any more than a bad period."

"You're sure?"

"Yes."

"Do you think they'll let me be with you?"

"I think so. Do you want to?"

"God! Yes, I want to. You really wouldn't mind?"

"All I care about is having it. That's all."

❋   ❋   ❋

Del paced up and down, smoking a cigarette, feeling a little ridiculous in the outfit they'd given her to wear but too nerved up to care much. Pacing. They'd told her she'd have to wait. But what if something happened to Gene while she was in here waiting? "Someone will come tell you when it's time for you to return to the labor room," the nurse had told her. And she'd been led to this lounge and presented with this outfit, told to put it on. The nurse, wearing an amused expression, saying, "This is a newey. But then nothing much surprises me any more."

It was taking ages. Over an hour already. Maybe they'd forgotten all about her. And Gene was alone. She put out the cigarette and at once lit another. Thinking about Leonard. Hurrying out, leaving Leonard half-awake in her bed. Telling Leonard, "I'll call you after. You sleep." And Leonard saying, "Tell her I'm with her."

She'd tried to exercise some self-control, to relax and let it happen. But it kept on happening. And surely he wouldn't go on indefinitely putting up with this? He'd arrived with gifts. Laughing, saying, "You're saving me expense money. I figured I might as well bring something for the hostess." Giving her two just-published novels and a small box from Tiffany's containing a sterling silver bee on a fine chain. Laughing, hugging her, saying, "Sting me! Go ahead and sting me!"

Lawrence hadn't given her anything in years. Years. The last gift had been something utterly meaningless. A subscription to some magazine. And a check she hadn't needed or wanted and didn't ever cash. So that he'd become furious and accused her of screwing up his bank balance. And then had graphically illustrated just how really angry she'd made him.

Now, her lawyer and his lawyer were having telephone conversations, working out the details. What details she couldn't imagine. The house was hers. He had his money. She had hers. Jointly, they owned absolutely nothing. Details. There were no details. Just under three months and it'd be all over. Perhaps, then, she'd be able to breathe more freely.

"You can come along now," a young nurse said from the doorway. And Del crushed out her cigarette, grabbed her bag, and went hurrying down the corridor after the nurse. Back to the labor room. To see Gene. Her face small and very pale, her eyes darkly circled, sunken-looking. Her hair pulled back, tied with a ribbon. Lying propped on her side, saying, "I'm so glad you're back. It's not my favorite place, here."

"How is it? What did they do?"

"It hurts," she said wearily. "What they did was make me feel like some sort of inconvenience. Despise hospitals. My back aches."

"What can I do for you? Is there something I can do?"

"Just stay. Hold my hand."

Looking at Del's blanched face, Gene thought, She looks like she's the one having the baby.

Somehow, being processed that way—shaved and purged like some impure, bloated sea creature—had robbed her of the pleasure she'd experienced until then. Now, it was all just something to get through so she could at last see and hold Bill's baby, their baby. That did it. Thinking of Bill. She started to cry. Tears simply leaking out of her eyes as she lay there, thinking of Bill. A cigarette would've helped much more than those nurses handling her as if she was an imposition, a waste of their valuable time. And where was the doctor?

"Why are you crying?" Del asked, distraught. "Is it bad?"

She couldn't answer. Thinking if she ever had another baby she wouldn't come to a hospital to do it. Hating this place. Looking at the walls of the small room and finally at Del. "That last nurse said not much longer." She smiled grimly as Del wiped her face, then gripped Del's hand hard, getting through another contraction. She closed her eyes, her face turning scarlet. Then exhaled noisily. "Don't look that way," she said. "It's all right."

Del's features relaxed a little.

The doctor arrived, smiling. The smile—to Del—seemed incongruous.

"Hello, Del," he patted her on the arm and neatly moved her away to stand at Gene's side. "How's it going?" he asked Gene.

"Fast."

"So I heard. I'm going to take a look. Del, would you mind?"

"She stays!" Gene clutched his arm, forcing him to look at her. "She's *staying*!"

"All right." He removed her hand and moved down to the foot of the bed.

"Are you really sure?" Del asked her again, once more taking hold of her hand.

Gene nodded, giving herself over to the pain. Not fighting it. Simply allowing it to take her. She didn't care about the pain. She only wanted all this ended. Unaware of her nails digging into Del's hand. Unaware even of Del. Except as a presence she tuned back in on every so often. And then was glad of.

Del concentrating on not looking at what Martin was doing, yet unable to altogether avoid seeing. Holding her breath as Gene made an odd animal sound deep in her throat. Then letting out her breath when Gene did. Silently praying, Please don't let anything happen to her, let this all be all right, nothing can happen to her, please. Frightened by how small and pale she was and how large the mound of her belly was in comparison.

"Everything's fine," Martin said, stripping off his gloves. "We'll be moving you across the hall in a few minute. This is going to be a nice, easy one."

"Is it?" Del asked without thinking, causing him to smile.

"It is," he said, again patting her on the arm. Finding the question considerably less amusing on second thought. She *would* be greatly concerned in a matter like this. "I'm going to get suited up," he said. "About ten minutes and we'll get this show on the road."

"I don't know what to *make* of him!" Gene groaned after he left. "Never wants to *tell* me anything."

"I know," Del said. Remembering how he'd treated her after the abortion. Like a fool. Like someone who shouldn't have been let unescorted into the world. Nothing he'd said. But the look on his face. And he had kept her alive. He'd done that. No. Rebecca had done that. By sensing something was wrong and phoning for the ambulance. Martin had come along—to this very hospital—to sew her back together. The first time. The second time. Taking this out, that out, leaving this in, that in. Shooting her full of hormones so that for months after she'd had all the symptoms of menopause and wished she hadn't survived after all.

But he was right. It did seem easy. Two or three minutes after they'd moved across the hall, Gene's face contorted, her hands flew out to grasp whatever hands were there to be held, made a terrible sound, and began pushing. Pushing so hard perspiration poured down her face, kept pushing until she collapsed back and Martin was handing the nurse a wriggling, blood-stained baby, saying, "You've got a boy, Gene. A big, healthy boy." To the nurse, he said, "Put him down, let her see!" And she sat up on her elbow to look at the baby, touching him gingerly with her hand. Not daring to smile because it felt as if something was breaking inside of her and she couldn't seem to catch her breath.

Martin saying, "Take the baby!" to the nurse. And, "Del, *out!*"

Terrified, Del backed away, seeing Gene's eyes rolling back in her head. Seeing blood splattering on the floor. The nurse carrying the baby out, other nurses pushing into the room, forcing Del out into the corridor where she stood gaping at the door open-mouthed, convinced Gene was going to die in there. Petrified of that. She couldn't move, couldn't think. Just stood outside the door watching the surging movements inside the delivery room. People making purposeful gestures. A nurse slapping instruments into Martin's hand. Someone else rushing to the door, nearly knocking Del over, shouting, "*Get out of the way!*" as she went running down the hall to the nurses' station to pick up the telephone, talk frantically into it, then came rushing back, ignoring Del, pushing back into the room. Covering over the window.

Del backed up until she came up against the wall and stood there, gasping, praying, so frightened she was incapable of moving. Watching as an intern came charging down the corridor carrying what looked like plastic sacks of blood. And then someone else came. And someone else. And the P.A. system delivered hollow-sounding announcements that echoed up and down the corridor. For hours and hours. Days, weeks. While she stood with her back to the wall, unblinking, every part of her fixed on that door and what was happening behind it. Until at last people began emerging. And Martin came out, pulling off his head-dress, saying, "Go get yourself some coffee or something, and relax. She'll be all right."

"What happened?" she asked, dry-mouthed.

"It looked worse than it was. Go have a cup of coffee. With a lot of sugar in it. You're not going to pass out, are you, Del?"

She blinked and looked at him. "No. The baby's all right?"

"Just fine."

"And Gene's all right?"

"She'll be in her room in about an hour. Go on."

"You're sure?"

"Yes, I'm *sure!*"

"Yes. All right." She got her bag from the labor room and went back to the lounge to get a cup of black coffee from the vending machine. Then fished a dime out of her bag and called Leonard.

"You sound lousy," he said. "You're sure everything's all right?"

"Martin says it is. It's a boy, by the way."

"And you were with her the whole time?"

She sighed, finding it tedious talking to him. "I was with her."

"You know something?" he said.

"No. What?"

"You're okay."

"Thank you very much."

"When d'you think you'll get back?"

"An hour and a bit. I want to see her first. Tell Grady, will you? I think he'd like to know."

She slumped down on the battered leatherette sofa, lit a cigarette, and drank the coffee, knowing she wouldn't completely relax until she saw for herself that Gene really was all right. She kept on seeing Gene's eyes rolling back to the whites. And the blood splattering on the floor. She shuddered.

Leonard saying, "You're okay." Approving her. It only made her tired. Because she didn't care if he approved or disapproved. In fact, she didn't care about anyone's approval. Not anyone's. The people who mattered weren't judging. And everyone else could go straight to hell. Lawrence in particular. And Leonard in general.

Grady put down the phone, jumped out of bed, then stopped and scratched his head, thinking, deciding. Went into the bathroom to shower and shave. He wouldn't waste any time, but get something to eat at the hospital. A boy. That was so great! He wished it wasn't so damned early. He really had wanted to show up with all kinds of stuff for the kid. But maybe by the time he got there and grabbed some breakfast, some coffee, the gift shop would be open. Fantastic! He just couldn't get over it.

Martin went down to get some breakfast. Lousy, wet, cold scrambled eggs. Cold toast. Pisswater coffee. Just amazing people didn't die of starvation in this hospital, eating garbage like this. Got another cup of the coffee and went back to the table. Thinking about Del. She had a way of looking at him, through him, as if he didn't exist but was simply another instrument or machine upon which she was dependent for certain services. What kind of woman was that? He yawned. Tired. Too tired to pursue any one thought.

An hour later Adele went along the corridor to the room. Stopping to look at Gene, thinking she looked somehow too small in the bed. With intravenous stands on both sides. Her face so completely without color she looked dead. Martin had lied. It had been as bad as it had looked. Why had he lied? She moved into the room and stood looking at Gene, caring so much it made her dizzy. She touched the back of her hand to Gene's cheek and Gene's eyes opened. She seemed to find it very hard to focus.

"He wouldn't tell me why," she said, moistening her lips. Feeling so groggy, dopey.

"Why what?"

"Why the surgery."

"I don't understand. What surgery?"

"Look. Under here. Look."

Del lifted back the blankets, her eyes on Gene's. Gene prompting her to lift the hospital gown and see. Del raised the hem of the gown to see blood-stained bandages covering most of Gene's abdomen.

"Has he been here? What did he tell you?" She covered Gene over carefully.

"Just patted me. 'Nothing to worry about.' And went away. Find out!" She had a deep, terrible fear that parts, vital parts of her interior had been removed without her knowledge or consent.

"When was he here?" Del asked, feeling even dizzier.

"Few minutes. Just left."

"Then he's still around somewhere. I'll find out and be back."

She hurried out into the corridor, then stopped, looking up and down, deciding the logical place would be the doctors' lounge, and went there. As she was about to go in, a nurse materialized saying, "You can't go in there."

Del turned, fixing cold eyes on her, saying, "Go play with your bed pans and don't tell me what I can and cannot do!" Then she opened the door and walked in to find Martin in his shorts and socks, getting dressed.

"Nice of you to knock," he said, pulling on his shirt.

"What did you do to her?"

"Some repair work," he answered, doing the buttons.

"Specifically," she said, "what repair work?"

"She was hemorrhaging. You could see that for yourself."

"I saw that. What did you do?"

"I had to find the damage, fix it, stop the bleeding."

"Go on."

"That's all. There was a tear. Quite a bad one. These things sometimes happen."

"Why didn't you tell her that?"

"I didn't think she was in any condition to hear the logistics." He stepped into his trousers, zipped the fly.

"You know," she said, leaning against the door watching him, "I've always thought you an excellent doctor. A fine technician. But you've got all the sensitivity of a wart hog. She's a *person*. Someone with a full set of feelings, all functioning. How could you just pat her on the head like she was some sort of mental defective and leave her there, terrified you'd taken half her insides away without her consent? What sort of doctoring do you call that?"

"You've got a pretty lofty opinion of yourself," he countered. "Not to mention your right to presume."

"Oh, yes," she agreed. "I presume a lot. Is that the truth? Is repair work all you did?"

"That is *all* I did."

"Then why the hell didn't you *tell* her that?"

"It wasn't the right time."

"I'd like to hit you," she said quietly. "'The right time.' You'd just leave her there until your afternoon, or maybe your evening, rounds and then casually—having left her to suffer through an entire day—reassure her she's intact. You're a son of a bitch!"

"She was bleeding to death."

"And you fixed that," she said, keeping a tight control on her voice. "Is the truth so difficult to deal with? You saved her. Couldn't you simply tell her instead of deciding you've got the wherewithal to determine the reactions of other people? God! You stink, Martin! I hope to hell you never get sick and have to suffer the well-intentioned, *kindly* ministrations of your associates. Or maybe I hope you do. You might develop a bit of realistic sympathy, some understanding, and start treating us like people with brains instead of plastic playthings you can pat on the head and talk to later. You're going to go back before you leave here and tell Gene exactly what you did and why, and satisfy her that she's all right."

"Am you threatening me?"

"Yes. Yes, I am."

"Don't threaten me, Del. It's a little ludicrous."

"Martin, you're going to go to her and tell her why you had to do the surgery and reassure her. You *are* going to do it. If you don't, I promise you you'll be very, very sorry and wish for the rest of your life that you had. By the time I've finished, there won't be a woman within forty miles who'd allow you to put one hand anywhere *near* her,

You may in fact find your practice reduced to prepubescent girls and geriatric cases. If you think it's ludicrous, don't go talk to Gene and see just how ludicrous I can be. You don't have the right to treat anyone that way. You may think you do, but you don't."

"And don't you think you're overreacting just a little?"

"If anything, Martin, I'm exercising a self-control that could make history. Don't you have any feelings? How would you like to wind up in a hospital bed with bandages all over your belly and no one to tell you what's been done to you? And your good, trusted doctor just pats you on the head as if you're some sort of pea brain, not bright enough or possessed of enough intelligence to be informed as to just what's been done. Pretend you're human!" she said, winding down. "Just walk down the hall and talk to her. God! If you'd been through just a quarter of what she's been through you'd be a babbling idiot. She deserves a simple explanation. And I can't for the life of me see why it's so beneath your dignity to give it."

"Why're you making such a damned case out of this?" he asked. Thinking he probably should've been getting angry. But he wasn't.

"You *can't* be that stupid," she said, exasperated. "The woman's my *friend*. Surely you have friends, Martin. People you care about. Don't you?"

He sighed and shrugged on his jacket. "You're being a pain in the ass," he said. "Seeing what you want to see but not things as they are. You don't see that we saved her, that our 'technical' expertise saved her. You see that a few social niceties have gone unobserved and that offends your sense of ethics."

"You're wrong," she said, lighting a cigarette. "You're a good doctor. And I know it. I've always trusted you. It's just that as a human being, right this minute, I find you offensive. So, I suppose that makes us equal. Just do me a favor and do it. It'll take you five minutes and you'll put her mind at peace. Surely you can do that."

"If you'll excuse me," he said, "I'd like to take a leak."

"By all means. If you'll excuse *me*, I'll just wait to make sure you have a little talk with Gene before you leave."

He stood for a moment, his eyes boring into hers.

"None of this is that critical," he said finally. "And you know it. It's a hell of a lot more personal than that, isn't it?"

"What do you want, Martin? Some sort of true confession?"

"Isn't that the case?"

"As it happens, that is *not* the case. My God," she said softly. "Don't you care about people?"

"I cared enough to put what was left of you after that botched-up abortion back together again. Not to mention sundry other little visits. Doesn't that count for anything?"

"Of course it counts. I concede your abilities, your skill."

"Then why the fuck don't you get off my case, Del?"

"Why the fuck won't you admit you made a mistake?"

Surprisingly, he smiled. "Okay," he said. "I was tired. I thought I'd talk to her later. When she was awake and I wasn't so tired."

"Why was that so hard?" she asked earnestly. "I can understand that. It's human. Why did we have to go through all this?"

"Your good husband still around, practicing his little acts of bestiality?" he asked.

"That's dirty."

"It wasn't intended to be, really. Is he?"

Feeling as if she'd had the air knocked out of her lungs, she said, "He's gone," and took a puff of her cigarette.

"You should give those up." He pointed to her cigarette. "And you should get yourself another gynecologist."

"Why?"

"Because. It's unprofessional to see a client privately. And I'd like to have equal time for rebuttal one evening soon."

"You're *serious?*"

"I'll go talk to Gene. You keep Saturday night open."

"That's not fair! It's blackmail."

"Isn't it fair? Think about it. I'll call you." He opened the door and paused. "You tell me something," he said quietly, no longer smiling. "How could you talk about sensitivity and feelings and come in month after month in the condition you did? And how did you suddenly get the balls to end it? Seriously."

"I didn't," she admitted. "He did."

"And you're sorry?"

"No."

"Well, that's good, at least."

"Are you trying to hurt me back, Martin?"

"You don't give people much of a chance, you know, Del. You just came barging in here with a bug in your ear and that was that. I was standing here telling myself I shouldn't have done that. Shouldn't have handled Gene that way. But I was tired. That was one very rough hour. And I was deciding I'd stop in and see her on my way out, talk to her, tell her."

"Then why did you argue with me this way?"

"I guess because in the—what?—thirteen years I've known you, you've never taken a stand on anything. Coming in to the office all torn up, quietly suffering like some dreary martyr. And believe me, I've got more battered wives lying through their teeth than I care to talk about. All patched up and off you'd go, home for some more. All of a sudden, here you are the lady tiger, flinging your fists out six ways at once, taking a stand. A little out of line. But to tell you the truth, I enjoyed it. I'm not insensitive and I do happen to care about peo-ple. A lot. But what you don't seem to understand is, there are an awful lot of the women I see who rely on the consistency, the pats, the cute remarks. It's a kind of quiet trap, and I have to work damned hard not to fall in and stay in. But I'm not a chauvinist pig and I hap-pen to like women. I happen to like you. I always wondered how someone like you, with all you've got going for you, could keep on with a life like that. Never mind. I'll call you and we'll get together. Maybe have a whole selection of topics to fight about. Okay?" He smiled.

"Yes, all right. I'm sorry if I offended you."

"I'm sorry for what you *think* you saw happening. So let's forget it."

"Yes."

He extended his hand and she placed hers in it. All at once seeing him, not as someone in possession of unfair and unreasonable pow-ers, but as someone human, likable. With sandy hair and tired lines around his eyes and mouth. And an appealing, quite whimsical smile.

"Jesus, but you're tough all of a sudden!" he said admiringly. "Woke me right up." He released her hand and went out.

She remained standing there, amazed. The moment Gene had entered her life, her life had started changing. *She'd* started changing. And now there were two men displaying an interest in her she'd never have believed possible. Because she'd started taking stands on certain issues. Because she'd finally broken out of Lawrence's careful-ly constructed prison.

She laughed aloud, put out her cigarette, and went back to see Gene.

❄   ❄   ❄   ❄   ❄

Ten

IT MADE HER LAUGH. AND SHE DIDN'T WANT TO LAUGH BECAUSE IT hurt. But how could she not laugh at the sight of Grady staggering through the door, laden with stuffed toys and boxes of chocolates, magazines tucked under both arms, blowing a kazoo. He deposited everything in one of the chairs and came around the far side of the bed to lean on both elbows inches away from her face, saying, "Hi there, Mom! What's with all the interplanetary receptors?"

"What?"

"Those things." He nodded at the I.V. stands. "They've got you wired like a Moog. You been misbehaving again?"

"Crazy!" She smiled at him, trying hard not to laugh. How could he look so *young*?

"I hear you got yourself a nice little boy to play with."

She sighed, nodding.

"I was never in on having a baby before," he said. "You think they'll let me into the nursery to eyeball the kid?"

Another nod.

"D'you check to make sure he's got all his equipment—fingers, toes, ears, and whatevers?" he asked.

She laughed again, then winced. "Don't make me laugh. It hurts."

"How come it hurts?"

"Surgery."

"You had one of those Caesar jobs?"

"No."

"Oh!" he said, serious. "But you're okay?"

"Fine."

"You're so pretty." He smiled. "Even up close you're pretty. Why is that?"

She lay looking at him, noticing how long and light his eyelashes were. And bits of black in the blue of his eyes. The rounded V of his upper lip and its fullness. His mouth was very pink, pleasingly shaped.

He stuck out his tongue and crossed his eyes.

"*You're* not supposed to be looking. *I'm* looking. It's not your turn."

"Oh!" Smiling. His face so close she could see every little detail. His skin soft-looking, babyish. A dimple at the right side of his mouth. And one in his chin. He was wearing a red and navy striped rugby pullover with a white collar.

"You've got a great little nose," he said, tilting his head to one side. "A nose of character." He tilted his head back the other way. "And I can look all the way up your noseholes, straight to heaven."

She laughed. Tears sprang into her eyes. "Stop!" she pleaded.

"Okay." He straightened and dragged the other chair over close to the bed and sat down. "When do they unhook the lunar probes?"

"Later this morning. They said."

He bent down and lifted the bedclothes saying, "Hey! You know what *else* you've got? A whole Baggy full of pee-pee. You naughty girl!" He leaned on his elbow on the bed and grinned at her. "You're a wonder to behold," he said, scratching his cheek. "No kidding! It's not every day I get to come into a place and see stuff like this. They keeping you in here long?"

"A week."

"A week, huh. I don't suppose you've had a shot at the kid yet, being all hooked up here?" He pointed to the Styrofoam boards to which her arms were strapped.

"No."

"And I don't suppose it's occurred to you that some deranged pervert could come in here and tickle you to death and you wouldn't be able to do one single thing about it?"

"No."

"Well, you don't need to worry. It's my day off. I only practice my perversions on alternating Thursdays and Saturdays. I practice lechery, debauchery, and archery on subalternate Wednesdays and Fridays. And Mondays and Tuesdays I keep open just in case. So, listen, cookie, what's new?"

"Oh God!" she cried. "Go away! You're killing me!"

"Are you aware of my advanced medical degree from the Juilliard school of phonetic surgery? No. I can see you're not. Well, I happen to know—I *know*—that excesses of laughter, coughing, and sundry other contractile reactions are excellent for getting everything all knitted back together again."

"How do you know that?"

"Hey!" He leered theatrically. "Wanna see my scars? I'll show you mine if you'll show me yours."

"What did you have?" she asked interestedly.

"You wouldn't like it."

"No, tell me."

"How about getting stabbed by a mugger?"

She looked horrified.

"No?" he said. "Okay. How about gored by a bull?"

She smiled.

"No good? Appendicitis? No? Very extensive root canal work? No, huh?"

"What?" she asked.

"Stabbed by a mugger."

"Truly?"

"Truly. I wasn't smart. He said, 'Your money or your life,' and I tried to play Jack Benny saying, 'Wait a minute, I'm thinking that over.' He didn't think it was one little bit funny. In the end, I didn't think it was all that funny either. Eighteen days in the other wing here. About six zillion stitches. Now, you wanna mug me, you can have everything I've got including my gold crowns. How come you're so pretty? I could just sit here all day trying to figure that one out!"

"What did he get?" she asked.

"Who, the mugger? Twelve dollars, a cheap digital watch, and my school ring. The hospital bills nearly wiped me out. I mean, d'you have any idea what they're probably charging you for this nifty little room? Anyway, I try to keep off certain streets at night. And I've got a real wallet and a mugger's wallet. I hand over the special one with a ten and a couple of singles and keep the real one tucked out of the way. Okay if I come back and see you again later tonight?"

"Yes."

"Okay." He got up off the bed. "I'm gonna go see the kid. What's his name, anyway, so I can introduce myself?"

"William."

"William. Classy. I'll stop back to say good-bye and then come again tonight with chow mein and spare ribs and some shrimp fried rice. No, don't tell me! You can only have mush. I know. I'll be back in a couple of minutes."

He got up and made a show of checking both intravenous stands, then waggled his fingers at her and went out. She lay back trying to catch her breath, hurting from having laughed so hard.

He stood out in the corridor telling himself she couldn't possibly be as sick as she looked. Exhausted from the effort of being funny to cheer her up, to keep himself from a dose of terminal fear. He took several deep breaths and went down the corridor to the nursery where a duty nurse asked him, "Which baby?" and he sang, "'Big bad Bill is sweet William now.'" She laughed and pointed out the baby, then returned inside the nursery.

He stood with his hands flat on the glass, laughing. Thinking, William. You're dynamite, William. Absolutely dynamite. The baby screwed up his face, yawned, waved one tiny fist around, then went to sleep.

"Boy, that's some jock kid," Grady told her, hanging from the door frame by one hand. "I've gotta go now. Anything you need?"

"No. Thank you."

"William said to tell you hi and that everything's cool and would you please send money and new moccasins."

She smiled sleepily.

He walked over to the bed and said, "You rest up and I'll see you later. Okay? I'm sorry you had kind of a rough time."

"Okay."

He turned to go. She said something he didn't hear and he turned back.

"What?"

"What's your other name?" she asked.

"Morrison. Grady Michael Morrison. *Junior.*" He smiled.

"That's nice," she said dopily. And closed her eyes.

❊   ❊   ❊

What came over Del in the shower was something she hadn't experienced since her earliest days of childhood. A feeling of I-don't-care. Of I'm-all-right-and-that's-what-matters. An extraordinary sense of well-being, of being dependent upon no one but herself; of being, finally, self-contained. Free of fear. It was very nice that Leonard was there but, examining it closely, she couldn't see that she'd mind all that much if he wasn't. It was a bit demoralizing having to turn around every few minutes and come face to face with her continuing failure. Still, he wasn't making an issue of it and seemed quite content to let things go as they would.

It was very nice that Martin wanted to take her to dinner on Saturday evening. But if it didn't materialize, that would be all right, too. What did matter was this tenuous-feeling containment of herself. Experimentally, she tried thinking of Lawrence. And merely felt tireder. Thinking of Gene, she automatically smiled.

Still, she warned herself, it might merely be a transitional phase. And it would be unwise of her to count on this new feeling as a constant. But wasn't it a rare, profoundly satisfying sensation: to feel at ease with her own actions and decisions? She wasn't at all ashamed of having gone after Martin the way she had. Perhaps she should have been going after any number of people—most specifically Lawrence—for years. How had she allowed all that to simply *happen* to her?

She felt the color rush into her face when she thought of seeing Martin socially. Knowing as much as he did about her. Did he possibly think she enjoyed that sort of thing? Making mention of battered wives. I was never that. Something. But not that.

If she thought about it, Martin's tight-lipped look of grim concentration during all those past office visits said all there was to say about his feelings on the matter. But why hadn't she ever noticed or thought about his reactions before? And if she'd been unaware of that, what else had she failed to see? The implications were frighteningly extensive.

I must *think*, she told herself. Debating whether or not it would be a good idea to meet Leonard in London. She was too tired to think clearly. But she did feel well. So well.

He looked like Bill. So much. Around the eyes and the shape of the mouth. Bill. Bringing him back with stinging clarity. Bringing him back so hard, so strong if she turned her head she might actually see him standing there. That déjà-vu sensation that had been with her all those weeks in the hospital in New York. Suddenly it was all raw, all mixed grief and joy, lying there holding Bill's baby while the nurse bustled about the room doing this and that, chirping about "Baby being hungry," and other annoyingly cute remarks.

They'd given her a shot to dry her out. Because she was, Martin said, far too weak, had sustained too critical a blood loss, to nurse. And that was another blow, because she'd wanted to feed William from her own body. All of William of and from her. But she couldn't. So sat holding the small bottle of glucose and water to his mouth, crying but trying to control it because she didn't want to transmit anything negative or unhappy to the baby. It wasn't that she was unhappy. Because the weight of the baby on her arm, the hungry moving reality of him, was an exultant feeling.

She looked at the soft skimpy hair on his head and the faint arches of his eyebrows, the ecstatically closed eyes and greedily sucking mouth, and was astonished at her body's accomplishment. But why couldn't Bill at least have lived long enough to see his son? It seemed so terribly unfair for him to have died without ever seeing what they'd succeeded in creating.

And all this child might ever have of his father would be his one name. There was no legacy. A few photographs. Some old movies that might still be playing, perhaps on television, when William was old enough to watch and comprehend. References in movie and the-ater books. The public persona that would live on for some time to come. But nothing of the private man. Except memories, some gifts, occasions she could examine over and over again in her mind. And that was about all.

Playing out her role as Mrs. Elliott would drape William's life in a mantle of supposed respectability. For having had a father who'd died. The only incidental problem being that his father hadn't ever been married to his mother. Not that it had mattered to her then. But it mattered to her now for their child. She couldn't bear the project-ed image of William as the recipient of taunts and childish cruelties because of his having only one parent, because of his illegitimacy. Because William was a bastard.

Words out of some gothic novel, maybe. But the pain of sitting propped up against the pillows feeding this baby, watching him and thinking, You're a bastard, a bastard, was very real, very potent. And nothing that savage was going to happen to her son. What did a lie matter if it meant a happier life for this child? It didn't matter a damn. But at some point she would tell him the truth. Yet, facing the prospect of one day having to sit down with William and say, "I lied to you," filled her with dread.

She'd thought of all these things and more during the pregnancy. But that was when the infant had been simply a cumbersome weight she'd carried around and not someone alive out here in the air, breathing and hungry; not someone real, with a name. His reality rendered the future suddenly difficult, problematical. Why had she thought life might be easy? It was never easy, wouldn't ever be easy.

But at least she did have the child.

I must be realistic, she told herself, stopping crying. Bill might have died leaving nothing at all behind. I do have a child. And I'm all right. And nursing, not nursing, doesn't make any difference. I have a son. And Bill is dead.

A nurse wheeling a trolley filled with flowers stopped outside the door and came in with an arrangement of pink roses and lilies of the valley. Smiling, saying, "I'll put this on the window sill. Isn't it pretty? Would you like to see the card, dear?" She put the card down on the bedside table. Went out and came back with more flowers. Anemones. Another card. And a pot of chrysanthemums. And a huge vase of red American Beauty roses.

The pink roses from Adele. The red ones from Leonard. The anemones from Grady. And the mums from Elton, Rebecca, Alexander, and Sally.

The sight of all the flowers gladdened her immeasurably and she sat gazing at them for several minutes until the nurse came to take William away, saying, "This one's a champion sleeper. He'll probably be sleeping through the night real early. You'll be glad of that."

She turned to look again at the flowers. Feeling better and better.

In the lobby, Del and Leonard were having a very quiet but very fierce argument.

"Dammit!" he said. "This is something I intended to do right from the start."

"Why are we arguing about it?" she asked, annoyed. "Let's just split the whole thing right down the middle."

He lost a good measure of his angry look and paused for several seconds thinking that over.

"Let's just sit down over here for a minute," he said, taking her arm and directing her to a sofa. "I think we've got a little bit of clearing up to do before we go to see Gene."

"I'm listening," she said, thinking of smoking but noticing a sign that said, "We thank you for not smoking."

"Either way she's not going to like it," he said. "Whoever's footing the bill. It's going to smack of charity, and Gene's never wanted anything she didn't work for."

"Let me pay it, Leonard. I can promise you there'll be no problem."

"We'll both pay then!" he said, angry again. "This is ridiculous! Fighting over who's going to pay. *Ridiculous!*"

"Why are you so angry?" she asked quietly. Was this where he turned into Lawrence? Did it start now?

"Because, damn it, it was always my plan!"

"Plans change."

"A gesture," he said. "For a lot of things that went before."

"You're subtly saying I'm an interloper and haven't the right to come barging in and start making gestures."

"Maybe. This whole thing is goddamned ridiculous."

"I'll have the office send the bill to me. I'll pay it. And when I meet you in England, or when you're back, you'll reimburse me for your half. Fair enough?"

"Fighting over money." He shook his head impatiently. Looking like an old, angry lion. "No, it's not the money. It's like some kind of goddamned contest. Trying to prove who cares about her more."

"That's not why," she said.

"Are you all that *sure?*" he challenged.

She looked past him. *Am I sure about that? I'm not sure about anything. Maybe that is what I'm trying to prove. And maybe this isn't the way to do it. But are you any righter than I am? You're trying just as hard to prove yourself as you say I am. And maybe I do think I love her more, and differently, than you do. Or ever could. Do I have to prove that? There are other ways, perhaps more important ways, to show my feelings. And it's demeaning to do battle with you over money.*

"All right, Leonard," she conceded. "You pay it. I don't see it doing either of us any good sitting here quibbling over who has more of a right to pay Gene's hospital bill."

"Now you're upset with me."

"No, I'm not," she lied. "Could we drop the whole thing now? I'd really like to go up and see Gene, the baby."

On their way through the hospital she thought about the almost endless telephoning that had gone on since Leonard's arrival. Within minutes of his walking through the front door, he'd started placing a series of calls on his telephone card. Leaving her number with people all over the country. Forty minutes nonstop on the phone. Then he'd sat down with her for a cup of coffee and the return calls had started coming in. And it had continued on that way until they'd finally left the house to go out for dinner. When they'd returned late that first evening, Sally had been waiting up with a list of messages. Leonard took them and went directly to the telephone. Del had seated herself on the living room sofa with the latest copy of *Newsweek* and become so engrossed that she'd failed to realize he'd not only finished on the telephone but had been sitting beside her for several moments rather peevishly waiting to get her attention.

He was, he told her, producing *and* directing this picture. And was therefore more deeply embroiled in this project than in any other he'd ever done.

Fine.

But something about the ceaseless telephone calls—coming in, going out—and his preoccupation with the budget and the actors and the locations and the crew was getting on her nerves. It might be a very bad idea going over to be with him on location. There was an element of overblown self-importance and ego to all these goings-on that disturbed her. As if it was some sort of game—of a new and different variety—that required an amount of attentive input she was extremely reluctant to give.

And. Aside from all that, she was curious about Martin. Who was younger than Leonard, for one thing. And so totally different in every possible way she could see that she was quite anxious to test her own responses. To spend an evening with someone she'd known—at best on a purely superficial level with a few social encounters thrown in for good measure—for a good thirteen years and hadn't ever really thought of as completely human. Now, suddenly, there was the distinct possibility he was very human. And the prospect of being able to talk truthfully about Lawrence to someone who'd met and known him was singularly appealing. Not to mention the fact of Martin's having had the only first-hand opportunity to witness the results of Lawrence's attentions to her. She very definitely wanted to have an evening with Martin. For all sorts of reasons.

And, a little guiltily, was anxious for Leonard to leave.

She went to the nursery to see the baby and thereby allow Leonard some time alone with Gene. Out of deference to his prior friendship with her. She pushed through into the nursery and stood outside the glass looking at Gene's baby, once more swallowed by yearning for the infants. Any one of them. To simply walk around behind the glass, lift one out of its crib, and hold it. Her arms aching to hold one of those babies. She looked at William, watching him sleep; again thinking of Gene.

To have given me this. Look at the babies. Beautiful and clean with their small funny faces and waving fists. Sleeping their small sleep, dreaming warm, floating dreams. I'll never have one. Never. I'll never know any of the pain or the pleasure, none of it. But at least I'll know William. And I'm so glad of that.

She left the nursery and went to the ladies' room to blow her nose, repair her running mascara. Looking, with curiosity, at her reflection. Thinking it couldn't be possible. But she actually looked different, younger. And the sight of her own image no longer filled her with despair. I need a haircut, she thought. And some new clothes that don't look quite so thoughtlessly selected. New things.

Then for a moment found herself once more in the grip of fear. Wondering if she wasn't just sidling blindly into new, different kinds of delusions. Fooling herself. Believing changes of clothes and a new haircut could make permanent these new feelings.

Am I just grasping at air? she wondered. Or is all this real? Please, let it be real, let me finally, at last, be safe.

✳   ✳   ✳

When Leonard presented himself to the cashier, he was told, "I've already got billing instructions for Mrs. Elliott. It's all taken care of."

"What d'you mean?" he wanted to know.

"Are you a member of the family, sir?"

"No, I'm not a member of the family, but ..."

"I'm sorry."

Del looked very indignant. And said, "If it's been taken care of, I know nothing of it. And I have no intention of going another round with you on the subject." But she wondered who'd done the "taking care."

Gene, suspecting Adele or Leonard might attempt to make some sort of gesture, had taken the precaution of prepaying her hospital expenses, with the proviso that she would be billed at home for any additional charges accrued during her stay.

Eleven

GOING FROM ONE MAN DIRECTLY TO ANOTHER. THE IMPRESSIONS OF Leonard were still so strong on her mind it was almost impossible, yet again, not to make comparisons. Martin was younger, taller, leaner-looking, more directly attentive. And somehow kinder. It was kindness that made the deepest, most immediate impression. And she simply couldn't understand now why she'd ever accused him of lacking sensitivity, caring, when it was so patently obvious he was very caring, very sensitive.

"If *you* think this is strange," he said, "it's twenty times stranger for me. Until the other morning I'd thought of you as some kind of willing victim. It's not up to me to volunteer my opinions when someone comes to me for medical attention and makes not a single reference to how she came to be in the condition she's in. As I told you, I've got carloads of women. Most of them lie. But the other morning"— he shook his head. "That was a whole new you. And I've just been diddling around since Barbara left with the kids. So I decided, why not. And here we are. And I'm a bit stunned to find myself sitting here having dinner with about the last woman on earth I ever dreamed I'd be out with, having dinner."

"Some kind of willing victim," she said, turning that concept over in her mind. I'm still afraid. Does that mean I'm still a willing victim? "Maybe that's the truth. What *did* you think?" she asked, holding her drink with both hands. "Or did you think anything?"

"Oh, I thought all right. I thought, Maybe she enjoys this. It's none of my business. And I thought, Maybe he's into some kind of black-mail and this is the payment. It's none of my business. And I thought, Maybe she doesn't even care that a few more years of this and she's going to have nothing left to repair. It was none of my business, Adele. The professional ethic. You don't volunteer advice to people who have no apparent desire to hear it."

"What could you have told me, anyway?" she said, looking down into her glass. Nothing anyone could have said would have made very much difference. She'd had so many reasons. Justifications, rationalizations.

"I know that," he said, watching her light a cigarette. "What I'm curious to know is what finally happened."

"I'm not really sure," she said dishonestly. Gene had happened. But was it safe to tell people that love could save lives? She might talk about it and find that not only had she betrayed Gene but also that she'd managed to create a false image of herself. People in general seemed to talk such a lot about love, but individually seemed highly suspicious of it. As if love was fine from a philosophical distance, something to idealize and keep safely at arm's length. But up close, within touching distance, it might be lethal. And people who went around talking about love just might be crazy. Some brand of dement- ed latter-day revivalists, all hipped up, hopped up, crazy on love. "I've been saved by love," when it used to be, "I've found religion." She looked at Martin closely, wondering if he was someone who'd quiet- ly hear her out and then, just as quietly, at the end, narrow his eyes and say, "Bullshit!" Hadn't Lawrence treated the majority of her con- cepts that way? Listening as if there was some measure of compre- hension sitting behind his eyes. Then, having heard her out, pro- nouncing it all bullshit. And warning her that if she didn't watch her step, the next thing she knew she'd find herself carted off to an insti- tution. And he'd meant it. Regarding her with an expression that put her into the ranks of the fanatics, the fantasists, the cultists. But maybe that was all just part and parcel of Lawrence. Gene certainly knew and understood. Even Leonard seemed to. But Martin. What are you? she wondered. With your large medical practice and junior and senior partners, with your custom-tailored suits and scrubbed fin- gernails, with your Sulka shirt and your expensive tastes and rather sad-looking eyes. What are you? If I tell you someone I could care for came into my life and gave me some of her courage, gave me her thoughts and her words unstintingly, would you think us both worthy of being immediately institutionalized? If I told you that without even the faintest lascivious trace I held another woman and derived enormous comfort from the act, would you at once brand me with a title? Because I don't think of myself as being this one thing or that other thing exclusively. I just am. And I care. And caring, for the first time in fifteen years, has enabled me to care about my own self. Are you someone who might understand these things?

"You've gone very thoughtful," he said. "Something I said?"

"Mmm. And something I was thinking."

"Tell me about it."

"I don't know. Perhaps later. It's a bit early."

"All right. Are you ready to order?"

They ordered. The waiter left. And Martin watched her light another cigarette.

"If someone nagged you enough, would you give up cigarettes?"

She looked up at him. "Why?"

"Because they're rotten," he said equably. "You're taking years off your life."

"And if I tell you maybe my life is already too long and I have absolutely no intention of giving up something I enjoy that gives me pleasure?"

"Just the kind of silly defeatist talk I would've expected from you ten years ago. It doesn't quite jibe with the flying tiger and claws-bared protectiveness you showed a few days ago."

"Doesn't it?"

"No."

"Well, don't nag at me, Martin. I'll smoke these forever. It's my *right*. You'll notice I'm not 'presuming' to pick at some point and nag at you."

"True."

"I feel like getting drunk," she said, fingering the rim of her glass, looking at his eyes.

"Go ahead. I'm known for my reliability. I'll make it my responsibility to see you safely back to the House of Usher."

She laughed, her apprehensiveness broken. "Is that what you think of the house?"

"Manderley?"

She laughed again. "Surely you don't see me as some sort of fey heroine?"

"You've got too much money to qualify." He smiled and finally tasted his drink.

"What's money got to do with it?"

"Oh, lots," he said, setting down his glass. "For one thing, you can't be the heroine of one of those sagas unless you're at the mercy of strange, nutty people with lots of money and power over you. And for another, having money can sometimes blind you to a lot of simple values, important values. Not having money, on the other hand, can be equally as blinding. But in different directions. However, the lack can sometimes be conducive to a careful examination of the other things you do have. What do you do with yourself from one week to the next?"

"I don't 'do.'"

"Maybe you should."

"Maybe you're right. Any suggestions?"

"Are you being sarcastic?"

"Yes. You keep wanting to tell me what I should and shouldn't be doing. You seem to have a lot of very specific ideas on the subject." Interesting, she thought, how oddly circumspect they were being, how covertly they were trying to close in on each other.

"I have some pretty specific ideas about *you*," he said.

"What ideas?"

He laughed. "Not before dessert."

"Really? You want to make love to me, Martin?"

He flushed, looking terribly embarrassed. Then he laughed. "Is that part of the new emancipation?"

"It might be. Seriously. Do you want to?"

"I suppose I do," he admitted. "I sure as hell wasn't prepared for this tack."

"Why not? Obviously it was on your mind. Do you?"

"What would you do if I flatly answered, Yes?"

"I'd say, All right."

She'd managed to throw him so completely he'd lost some degree of his cool control. "Why, for heaven's sake?" he asked her.

"Why not? I'm no good at all at it, but if it's something you'd like, I don't see why we shouldn't. It's perfectly safe. You know that."

"Let's change the subject," he said, taking a good swallow of his drink. "The conversation's turned a little bloodless."

"Why did that upset you?" she asked, genuinely curious. Wondering why he, as a man, might make any number of suggestions along lines sexual and nonsexual and feel perfectly at home and in the right doing it; but she, as a woman, was being bloodless by being willing to openly discuss the prospect of their becoming sexually involved.

"I'm just not used to it," he said truthfully. "Especially not with you."

"You don't know me."

"That's true. I don't."

"Martin, what are you? Who? Tell me about you."

"I think you know about all there is to tell."

"I know you're a doctor. But you're not the sort of person I always thought you were. And, obviously, I'm not the sort of person you assumed I was. Tell me."

"What do you want to know?"

"Why did you ask me out tonight?"

He smiled, watching her exhale smoke from her nostrils.

"Because the other morning I really started liking you. And I wanted to see if we could take it farther, find out if there was any mutuality."

"Ah!" She took her time putting out the cigarette. "And before that you *didn't* like me?"

"I didn't *dislike* you. I found you ... frightening."

"How?"

"Frightening in the way it's frightening to see a child drowning and be unable to help because you can't swim and if you go in after the child you'll wind up responsible for two deaths instead of one. But being in possession of that knowledge, that logic, doesn't make it any easier to have to stand there helplessly watching that child go under."

"You perceive me as a child?"

"I saw you as someone enmeshed in something you thought you understood but obviously didn't, and couldn't control. Nobody lets all that happen to her without reasons, Del. Why, for the love of everything sacred, did you go on and on with it?"

"Partially because I felt sorry for him. And partially—out of vanity, I think—because I thought I knew the rules. But he kept changing them."

"What finally ended it?"

"All right," she said. "I'll tell you. It was Gene." She stopped and looked at him for some reaction.

"Go on."

"Just Gene. A friend. Someone I cared about who cared back. Without price tags. It gave me something I hadn't had before. The feeling that what I was, the person, was acceptable to someone I respected. I wasn't being judged and found wanting. What I was was all right. There was also another man."

"I see."

"No, you couldn't possibly. I'm not minimizing your intelligence or ability to understand. But it's just not that graphic, that black and white. The other man part of it was really very secondary and, truthfully, not very successful. I honestly think it was just something that had to happen. Inevitable. A firsthand meeting with kindness. But Gene. To know someone who's been through such a lot and still had caring to give to others. I love her." She tensed, fully prepared to be misunderstood.

"I'd say that was fairly obvious. You certainly did battle for her."

"You're not shocked?"

"Do the two of you have a sexual relationship?"

"Not really. No. I'm the one with the sexual interest. And I'm not altogether sure it is sexual. I've discovered there are areas where the emotional and the sexual start overlapping. I don't think I actually want to make love to her. When I think of that, of the clinical aspects, I know I don't. But when you're close to someone you love, you don't concern yourself with the clinical aspects. You're carried along by the feeling. The truth is, I don't know precisely *what* I am any more. If I ever did know."

"But you'd make love with me?"

"I will."

"Why?"

"Because I want to," she said simply. "Don't *you* want to?"

He nodded very slowly, as if he was agreeing to partner her in a political assassination.

"Well, then we will," she said conclusively.

"Actually," he said, giving it thought, "I think I like what you say about Gene, your feelings for her. From my own experience with her, I can quite easily see where the attraction might lie. For both of you."

"Can you?"

"Maybe it's just that you need each other. Isn't love a lot of that? Don't you think? I honestly can't see anything unnatural or shocking about what you're telling me. Even if it was sexual, I don't think I'd react very much differently. It's not up to me to evaluate other people's needs, behavior."

"I don't know. I'm still trying to analyze all this 'love' business; see how it relates, if it does at all, to me. I may be busily working it through for the next hundred years. The only thing I do know is I'm going to find out as best I can what I really am, after all. Who I am. I'm so tired of sustaining injuries for the sake of what I *think* love is. And the only thing I know for absolutely certain is that what I had with Lawrence wasn't love and didn't have one damned thing to do with it." Saying his name. Feeling a sudden clutch of fear. Being so bold, so truthful. Was it all, unknowingly, playing with dangerous explosives?

"Well, you sure are truthful." He smiled, moving his glass aside as the waiter set down their salads.

"I'm starting to learn."

❋   ❋   ❋

"Why did you say you're not any good at it?" he asked.

"Because I'm not. It's the truth."

"How do you know you're not? Did someone tell you that?"

"*I* told me that."

"Would you care to tell me on what you base this conclusion?"

"You mean clinical details?" She turned to look at him. "Could we have the air-conditioning off? I'm freezing."

"Sure. Sorry." He reached over and shut it off, then sat back, his eyes never leaving the road. "Be specific," he urged. "I'm curious. Personally and medically. Christ, I've met a lot of women who thought they were performance incarnate. A whole lot of technical bravado and somewhat maniacal flourish. I think the truth of all that is they're trying to convince themselves they do like something they actually don't like. But I have to admit you're one of the few women I've met who's expressed a willingness to proceed despite the fact that you don't think you're 'any good' at it."

"Really? They go into it telling you they're good?"

"Well, not quite. But the implication's there. 'I'm terrific, fella! Boy, I'll do things for you you never dreamed of!' There's only so much you can do, you know, Del. And what's important isn't the versatility factor or the inventiveness. What's important—to me, anyway—is the chemical reaction between the two people in question, the emotional quotient. So, immediately, I'm curious about why you'd say something like that." As soon as he said it he thought, I'm being an idiot. Of course she'd think that. Just think about it and you know that's the only logical response. What're you trying to make her say?

"I'm not quite that emancipated," she said, unable to put it into words for him. She didn't know him nearly well enough, couldn't yet be sure he wouldn't whirl around and start proclaiming her every remark bullshit.

"Okay," he said quietly. "That's a tough one. I know it."

"Why did Barbara leave?"

"Oh, we ran out of things to talk about. And the chemical composition went flat. The emotional content just kind of dribbled away. Nothing critical or unpleasant. We just agreed we'd come to a dead end. We're still good friends. She wanted to try walking on her own feet, see if she could provide for herself in a lot of ways. I admired her for wanting to try. She's a good person, an intrinsically good person. We sat down together one night and held hands and said, 'This is dwindling down to nothing. So let's end it before it turns dead and ugly.' And that was that. It really was very quiet, relatively painless. Certainly without bloodshed. She made no unreasonable demands. Either for money or support. That sort of thing. And I was willing, happy, to give her whatever she thought she needed. End of Act Two. Curtain."

"Why 'Act Two?'"

"Act One was med school, internship, residency, et cetera. Act Two was Barbara, the children, the house, the practice, et cetera."

"And what do you envision for Act Three?" she asked.

"I don't know yet. At this point in my life, I want to think pretty carefully about that."

"How old are you?"

"Forty-five."

"Lawrence is older than you," she said. Then was very annoyed with the irrelevancy of that fact and that she'd bothered to introduce him into the conversation. Why had she done that?

"How old is he?"

"Fifty-three."

"God, I don't know," he said. "How the *hell* did you ever get into all that?"

"I'll tell you later. I'll tell you a lot of things later."

"Would you like some brandy? Or coffee?"

"A little brandy." he said. "Thank you."

She poured some into two balloon glasses and went to sit beside him on the sofa, handing him one of the glasses. She tucked one leg under her, wondering what he'd do, how he was feeling, what he was thinking. He was beginning to seem quite familiar to her. She was actually ready to go upstairs with him. And wondered if she wasn't perhaps going off into some new extension of herself where she'd make love to one man after another, never succeeding, but always trying. Visualizing a long procession of middle-aged men removing their clothes in her bedroom. A prelude to attempting to immerse themselves in her body. Like some improbable contest. The image was frightening. Was this going to be the permanent aftereffect of Lawrence? Was Lawrence actually done with her? At some moments, it didn't feel as if he was. His lengthening absence and continuing silence were more alarming than reassuring. She'd never known him to simply admit defeat and go on to other things. And she had defeated him in this, hadn't she?

Martin sat sloshing the brandy around in the glass, for some inexplicable reason seeing her face as it had looked on those seemingly endless office visits. Tight and withdrawn, sealed off. As if, had he dared say anything direct or personal to her, she might simply have turned and walked away; gone elsewhere for the necessary medical attention. That aspect of her had always frustrated him. Because he'd entertained a very mild but nonetheless continuing curiosity about her. She stood apart from the ranks of his other patients. A young, beautiful woman allowing herself to be slowly, painstakingly destroyed for no visible or explainable purpose.

Certainly, she was still young enough. And perhaps even more beautiful. That hostile preparedness had left her eyes so that her face appeared more open. The woman inside seemed more accessible. For the second time in less than a week, he was aware of a definite fire in her. A heat of determination. Stating she loved another woman. It failed to bother him in any way. If anything, there was an aspect of purity and innocence to her declaration of love that aroused his respect, his deep admiration. Not to mention his interest. It seemed to him quite a brave thing to do, to admit to loving. Never mind who. The who's were secondary. But to admit it. To say, I love so and so. It did seem admirable.

She was studying him. Holding her glass against her mouth, her eyes moving over his face.

"What do you hope for, Del?"

"Hope for? I don't know. Nothing. Anything. I don't know if I have any hope left at all." I hope to be left alone, safe, unharmed. That's all. "What do you hope for?"

"Someone," he said. "Just someone."

"Why?"

"Because I know what it takes, what I need to get through."

"I envy you that," she said softly, her heart suddenly pounding. "I wish to God I knew what I need."

"This other man," he said. "What about that?"

"Oh, parts I like. Parts I'm not sure I care for very much. I don't know what the hell I'm doing. Can't you tell that?" She brought her other leg around under her and sat against the back of the sofa, facing him. Braving out the truth. Prepared for anything and everything. But he seemed very relaxed, pensive. His jacket an attractively appealing soft looking camel-colored cashmere. Silk tie, linen shirt. "I've never seen you in civilian clothes." She smiled. "You have fine taste." But then so does Lawrence. Impeccable taste.

"Not quite accurate." He smiled. "You caught me the other morning. Or didn't you notice?"

"I didn't actually."

"Lions one, Christians one." He laughed. "You've got beautiful legs."

She looked down. Then felt stupid. Her legs were tucked under. "You think so?" she asked him.

"I do think so. I like long-legged women."

We're starting, she thought. The panic leaping into her system. Curiosity and anticipation turning her vision soft at the edges. So that his eyes were suddenly different. Were they different? She hadn't really examined his eyes. Had that quality been there before? What was that quality? The other morning. Yes. For the first time looking at what her brain had recorded that her anger had failed to allow her to see. Stepping into his trousers, buttoning on his shirt. She'd known, seen; without knowing, seeing.

"I"—she smiled against the rim of the glass—"like long-legged men." I'm a fool, a sucker, a patsy for long-legged, tastefully dressed men. Did I fall into a pattern once upon a time? Am I caught in that pattern now? Could I get out if I wanted to?

"When did you start wearing your hair down?" he asked, falling into the rhythm.

"Yesterday, the day before. Recently."

He sat comfortably smiling at her, recalling an incident that had happened years before. Eight or ten years. When the Prewitts had given a large dinner party. He and Barbara had attended. Adele had been out in the kitchen with Sally, helping prepare the dinner. And he'd wandered in, thinking to chat, at the precise moment Lawrence was berating her in a deadly undertone for neglecting their guests. He'd had his hand on her upper arm, squeezing. His knuckles white with the pressure he'd been applying. And Del, just as quietly, had explained she was trying to help Sally. He'd leaned close to her then, saying something Martin hadn't heard. The effect on Del had been startling. She'd lost her color and looked at the man with an expression of such fear, Martin had wanted to strike him. For putting that look on her face, for maintaining his white-knuckled grip on her arm. Instead, having been unobserved, he'd gone to find Barbara to ask her to give Del a hand in the kitchen. And later on that night, as he and Barbara had been preparing for bed, she'd asked, "What was that all about?" and he'd replied, "There was something very ugly happening there. I wanted to get him off her back." Which hadn't properly explained the scope and intensity of that brief little scene or his reactions to it.

They'd only been at the house on one other occasion. About three or four years after that dinner party. He couldn't remember much about the evening except that Adele had been drinking when the guests arrived and kept on drinking throughout the evening. And every so often, he'd seen her looking at her husband with an expression of such contempt and fear that Martin had been forced to look away. Yet when he'd later risked looking at her again, she and Lawrence had their eyes on each other. And Lawrence had been in possession of the contempt. While she had retained only the fear.

"Mind if I say something?"

"Say anything at all," she said.

"I don't suppose you remember. But Barbara and I came to dinner one night. Eight or nine years ago. And I came out to the kitchen just to say hello or some such, and Lawrence was with you. I don't know why I remember it so clearly, but I do. Just a couple of seconds, really. But I've never forgotten it. Del, *why?* How could you stay for fifteen years with a man who treated you that way?"

"Are you sorry for me?"

"Of course not," he said quickly. "I might have been then. But I'm not now. I don't do things, make gestures out of pity."

"I don't *know* why," she said. "Oh, I suppose I do. Reasons. I could put them together for you. But it's over. What's the point?"

He finally tasted the brandy, letting it sit warmly in his mouth for a moment before swallowing. Both of them waiting for the break. Might as well be now, he thought.

"You're too far away," he said. "I can't possibly make a move. I could if I were Plastic Man. Remember Plastic Man?"

She laughed and moved slightly closer. "I loved the way he went through letter slots and under doors."

"The best was the arms that could just shoot out to there." He extended his arm. His hand closed gently around her wrist.

All her new-found courage drained right out of her leaving her nervous, suddenly uncertain. She sat staring at him, able only to see an image of herself riding Leonard in a disheartening attempt to achieve a state of satisfaction she simply couldn't get to. I don't want to go through that again. Please don't make me stand face to face with any more of my inadequacies. I don't think I can take it.

"What happened?" he asked, observing her change of expression. "I put my hand on your wrist and suddenly the whole thing changed."

"I'm scared. I talk a fine game. But I blow it in the clinches."

"There's nothing here that *has* to get done, you know."

"Oh, yes there is," she said in a low voice.

"I guess you're right. There is. But it doesn't have to be now, this minute, tonight. It can be next week or next month. Next year, if you like. Although lately I find myself very aware of time." He removed his hand and looked down into his glass. "I don't really care much for brandy," he said, setting the glass on the coffee table. "As a matter of fact, I don't care all that much any more for booze. Would you be interested in getting high in the company of a very square medical practitioner with secret vices? I've got some grass."

"Really?"

"Yes, really. We can do whatever you like. I've discovered in my advancing old age that it's better not to do the things that come with a pressure kit. And booze doesn't do for me what grass does. I could probably let everything go to hell and just sit around all day in a lawn chair, smoking—breathing and looking at the trees and watching the clouds go by. Exercising nothing more strenuous than my awareness."

"I suppose it would be a lot more appealing than having to deal with women's problems all day long."

"There's that," he agreed. "But mostly it's the idea of living. Just *being.* I have moments when I resent the hell out of being stuck in that office. When the sun's shining and everything looks bright and alive and I have the scary feeling that I'm not, that I'm living my life behind plate glass."

"But you're all for me getting up and going to work."

"Ah!" He smiled. "You've probably never smoked grass."

"Lawrence once injected me with heroin," she said, feeling that clutching inside again as she said it and saw the reaction take hold of Martin's face. "I think he thought it would be the ultimate perfect answer. He'd turn me into an addict."

"*Jesus,* Del! I honestly don't think I want to hear that."

"It was interesting," she said, looking off into space. "I was so utterly euphoric nothing he did bothered me at all." Her eyes moved back to his face. "Lawrence," she said, deadly serious, "should be committed. He's a very sick, *very* sick man."

"I'm beginning to believe it. And what were you, Del?"

"Sick and deluded and scared. A victim. You weren't wrong."

"Heroin, for God's sake! How did he get it?"

"You can, with enough money, get anything. You know that."

"You're right. I know it." He looked disgusted.

"That was the same night he decided to branch out into embellishments. Why am I telling you this?"

"Do you have to?"

"Maybe I'm trying to put you off because I suddenly got scared."

"Maybe."

"I didn't want to be an addict," she said, running her finger around the rim of her glass. "I didn't want to be any of the things I was." She took a breath audibly and set her glass down, noticing her hands had started trembling. Why? Thoughts of Lawrence's capabilities. And fear. Fear of him, of this, of anything, everything. She'd been fairly bold with Leonard. True. But this wasn't Leonard. This was Martin. Who'd stitched and scraped and cleaned and cauterized her interior. This was Martin, who'd disposed of her destroyed ovaries.

"I'm sorry," she said. "I'm being revolting."

He put his arms around her.

"It's all over. Remember?"

"I think it's a bedtime story I like to tell myself." Thinking, Contact. I come up against the substance of your reality and derive comfort from it. "But I have the feeling I'm living at the whim of someone else. My life ..." She stopped and turned her head, lifting her hand to study the contours of his mouth with her fingertips. Dismayed. I've done all this before. With Leonard. Do I keep on doing the same things over and over, forever? It doesn't feel the same, though, as it did with Leonard.

"Tell me about your life."

She shook her head.

"Still scared?" he asked, smoothing her hair. A soothing motion.

"Yes. But let's go upstairs."

❊   ❊   ❊

They lay side by side. Silent. She didn't seem to feel any perceptible difference. A very pleasant calmness. But that seemed to be all. It was pleasant to be there. Martin was pleasant to look at. He seemed in no apparent rush to commence an involvement with her body. She'd chosen to undress in the bathroom and had returned in her robe. Silently lying down beside him. Sharing the inhalations of strange-tasting, strange-smelling smoke until it was all gone.

And now here they were and it simply didn't feel any different than before. The mood was much the same. Although her robe did feel unusually confining. Martin appeared comfortable enough in his shorts. Arms folded under his head, ankles crossed. Relaxed, that's all. Nothing like the sort of enervating euphoria she'd experienced from the heroin. Drugs. Did this qualify as a drug? Martin hadn't had to hold her down, force her down, push a needle into her thigh.

"Is it a drug?" she asked lazily, turning her head to look at him. Her mind still containing an image of herself fighting, pleading. And then the pain of the needle. Plunging in, in. The wrenching despair, the sense that everything was lost, gone.

"If it is—and I personally don't consider it to be—it's certainly about the least harmful one I know. Feel it?"

"I don't feel anything. What am I supposed to feel?"

"Peaceful. That's all. Concentrated, focused."

"I don't think I feel any of that."

"I want to take that robe off you," he said. "Any objections?"

"No. Do you want me to take it off?"

"No. I want to."

He turned over and looked into her eyes, then molded his hand very lovingly—it did feel loving—to her cheek. He opened the robe and took his hands down the entire length of her body. Exquisite. She'd never been touched more perfectly, more beautifully. She moved to sit up, thinking she'd get the robe out of the way altogether, but discovered sitting up required quite a considerable effort.

He watching her, smiling, saying, "Sneaks up on you very quietly. Feel heavy?"

"Incredibly."

"You'll get used to it." He drew the robe off her and let it fall to the floor.

"Are you going to take those off?" she asked, sinking back against the pillows. The softest pillows in the entire world. And she'd never before noticed.

"You want me to?"

"I want to see you."

He dropped the shorts over the side of the bed, then was once more looking into her eyes. "Now," he said. "Tell me what you're no good at. Tell the medical practitioner."

She laughed happily. "If you're inside me—if you can *get* inside of me—I won't come."

"Ah!" He nodded sagely. "But otherwise, you will?"

"Fifty-fifty." She laughed again.

"And if I prove you wrong?"

"And if you don't?" she challenged.

"Then we'll have a very, very nice time finding out who's right. Do you know you have very pretty nipples?"

"I do? What's so pretty about them?"

"They're very full and very pink and very edible." He grinned into her face.

"Are you going to kiss me?"

"You don't know it"—he smiled—"but you're high."

"I must be. It's wonderful. Are you going to kiss me?"

"All over."

"Start here." She pointed to her mouth.

Was it him or some smoke-induced response? She couldn't tell. But his mouth on hers, his lips and tongue, were very potent, immensely stimulating. And his hair so soft under her hands. Soft, welcoming. Feeling lovely to her fingers. When his mouth left hers, she was breathlessly smiling; giddy, drunk. He kissed her throat, her shoulders, her ears, then moved down to her breasts. Deliberately licking and sucking at her for what felt like hours. Generating a tremendous response. She wanted to move but felt she couldn't for the moment. It might fracture or lessen the impact of the pleasure.

When he stopped, finally, and was once more grinning at her, face to face, she found him suddenly too compellingly lovable to resist. And engaged him in another of those potent kisses while her hands went independently traveling over him. Finding his smooth body, smooth skin, the most completely satisfying she'd ever known. And might have been content to lie forever kissing him, her hands learning his body.

"Feeling good?" he asked, letting his weight down on her. "Feeling very, very good?"

"Marvelous." She sighed. "I'm sure if I tried right now I could walk on water."

He laughed and rolled off her, looking up and down the length of her body approvingly. "Beds are so terrific," he said, walking to the foot of the bed, taking hold of her ankles and slowly pulling her toward him. "And you're beautiful. I was right about your legs." He dropped to his knees, eased her legs open, slipped his hand under her buttocks and lifted her to his mouth.

She went moaning and shuddering straight into the center of annihilating pleasure. And with a knowledge that might have been her own, he maintained just enough pressure and contact to drop her in and out of that pleasure two or three more times until he eased her down again. His hands slipping up over her back, he raised her so that she fell against his chest like a rag doll. He stood up and carried her to the armchair by the window, backed into it, and sat down.

"How did you *do* this?" She laughed, finding herself on his lap with her legs dangling over the arms of the chair. "You're turning me into a contortionist."

"Just wait," he said, smiling, smiling, his hand between her thighs, fingers wedged inside her, his thumb pressing against her so that she jerked reflexively against him. "Still think you can't?" he asked.

"God!" she whispered, afraid she'd topple over backward. "What are you *doing* to me?"

"Stop?"

"No!"

She was shaking, her teeth colliding with his as she leaned in to kiss him. His mouth drawing her out, his fingers moving. Something in her brain telling her it should be hurting but it didn't. It felt wonderful. Fantastic. Involuntarily, she moved, wanting to perpetuate the feeling. Moving with and against the feeling. On and on and on until he'd tightened his arm around her and she was dying there, impaled on his hand. Groaning as her body took off in a series of violent contractions, leaving her gasping against his chest.

"Is it because you're a doctor?" she asked.

And he roared with laughter, hugging her. Saying, "Fifty-fifty."

And then, only distantly aware of the movement, they were back on the bed, their legs oddly tangled, and he was deep inside her and, with no time to think about any of it, she was once more riding frantically into the pleasure. He was taking her all the way through. Start to finish. No games. No promises. No threats. All the way down to the end.

Still, finally, she held him in her arms thinking she'd never release him but just keep him there forever, heavy on her body, holding her safe, protected.

"Still good?" he asked, his face in her neck, nuzzling.

"I can't talk," she murmured.

"You may not be able to talk, but you sure as hell are good at this."

"Am I really?" Is that the truth?

"Very, very good."

"Are you going to gloat and say I told you so?" Are you going to hurt me now?

"That's for kids. If it's good, good. That's all."

"I'll fall in love with you," she whispered. "And want to smoke your grass and make love with you all the time."

"Okay. Fine."

"Don't make jokes, Martin. I'm serious."

"I'm not joking. One little nudge and I'll be right over there with you."

"Meaning?"

"Contact has been made. I have this nice little picture in my head of the two of us gently stoned on some hot Caribbean beach making love like lunatics."

"Is that what you want?"

"One little picture."

"Why me?"

"Why not you?"

Oh God! Right this minute, now, I feel as if I love you. If I love you, will you begin to despise me, want to destroy me? Will you begin dreaming up tortures and start buying terrifying objects with which to hurt me?

"Was it the grass," she asked, "or you and me?"

"Some of both. You're scared again. Don't be scared." Draping a necklace of kisses across her throat. "Don't be."

He eased off her, fitting her into his arms. Thinking about the fourteen-year-old girl who'd been in a few days earlier. Pregnant. With cervical cancer. And he'd had to tell her everything would have to go. Very few things any more that painful. But she took it. Sat there and heard him out, asked a few questions, then said, "Thank you very much," shook his hand, and went out to tell her mother. "I'll tell my mom. I know how to put the downers so my mom can handle them."

Thinking about thirteen years ago trying with every bit of his skill and knowledge to save this woman. Some madman's handiwork. And on a second occasion, he'd had to tell her almost everything would have to go. Further effects of that same madman's handiwork. And other damage the causes of which he couldn't begin to guess at. And she'd sat there and heard him out, asked a few questions, then said, "I see," had got up, walked out of the office. Not another word about it, then or ever. But her eyes had said it all.

Thinking about eleven years ago and nine years ago and eight and seven and six, month after month.

Thinking about the last few years of his own life. With Barbara gone. And the kids gone with her. The house gone, too, sold. An apartment he couldn't even be bothered furnishing. Stacks of books on the floor. Unopened cartons. Sleeping there, showering there. Boiling water for the occasional cup of tea. Plugging in the percolator for his morning coffee. A toaster he'd used perhaps twice. An electric frying pan that Janet what's-her-name had given him, telling him it was the absolutely perfect utensil for a bachelor. Still in its box.

Thinking about the nights he spent out. A woman here, a woman there. Demoralized by what appeared to be their terrible gratitude.

He didn't want to go around giving parts of himself away, making women grateful when he seemed to feel very little of anything except a grinding fatigue. Waking up in the morning with a taste like death in his mouth and the feeling he'd just attended his own funeral.

And now Adele. He'd never even *thought* about her, except within a clinical and diagnostic framework. She'd been just another of the patients. One of the ones he used to see more often than the others. Then, suddenly, she'd come flying at his throat and he'd *seen* her and thought, I like you. You're being a little absurd and you're jumping the gun, but all of a sudden you're alive and I like you.

Christ, I like you! And what kind of year-after-year effort did he put into destroying your belief in yourself? And your body. You're no good at it? You're wonderful. It's simply astounding you've got any responses left at all. But you do. Big, giving ones. And something, quite a lot of things, reaches into me, touches a part of me that's been sitting way down there going cold and stale and hard at the edges.

"You're better than good at it," he said, kissing the palm of her hand. "You're great, delicious!"

She could feel the euphoria leaving her. And didn't want it to go. Wanted to hang on to the wonderfully free, completely involved feeling. Looking at him, finding him infinitely more accessible than Leonard. Or was it an illusion? He did seem to be within her immediate grasp. And unlike Leonard, his body wasn't yet showing the more pronounced signs of age and stress. And unlike Leonard, he didn't affect to emulate youth by letting his hair hang down over the back of his neck. Unlike Leonard, he was young-feeling, young-looking. In fact, the youngest man she'd ever made love with. And the way he made love to her. As if it was a privilege, a gift she was giving to him. And he was anxious to illustrate to her just how much he valued the giving. And she did very much want to give him something. Now. Before the mood was entirely gone. Before there was a chance to find the feelings actually unreal, illusory, created and inspired by the smoke.

She liked the look of him. And his hands. Very strong, beautifully made, so clean. His thighs, long, muscular. Good legs. Unlike Leonard, relatively hairless. Unlike Leonard, not too thin in the hips and thighs. Leonard's age was showing badly in those areas. His legs looking vulnerable, insubstantial. His skin crêpey in repose. Martin's flesh was still very tight to the bone, elastic. She slid her hand down over his belly, down across his inner thigh. Then, liking the idea of it, shifted; letting her hair trail across his chest, down; pleased by the silent intensity of this communion and his immediate, swelling response.

He wanted to stop her near the end, but she shrugged his hand away. Telling herself, This is Martin. *Martin.* Voluntary. But for a few seconds, another image. Inescapable. Silk scarves. Bondage. And Lawrence. Choking her. Tears and slime. And how reluctantly he'd released her, doubtfully watching her stagger away into the bathroom. No. This because I want it not because I've been forced or bound. This because yes. Martin. Letting her hand play over his belly, feeling his muscles contracting here, and there, there. Yet the quality of the man unchanging. Martin yes.

He held her against his chest. And she started to cry, unable to stop herself. Wanting so badly to believe in possibilities and consistency. Yet so afraid of unfinished business and the darker corners, dark empty rooms. And a man who'd die or see her dead before he granted it was ended.

He sensed it best to leave her be, let her get it out, and stroked her gently, tenderly. Saying, "In spite of my better judgment," he lit one of her cigarettes and passed it to her. "Go on," he encouraged her. "I'm not going to nag."

She lifted her head and rested her cheek against his, her eyes moving over the room, then returning to his; whispering, "Stay, will you?"

"Are you sure, Del?"

"Stay." I'm afraid again. I need you to stay.

※　　　　※　　　　※　　　　※　　　　※

Twelve

GENE COULDN'T BELIEVE HOW WEAK SHE WAS. SHE FELT WELL ENOUGH. But getting checked out of the hospital and coming home had exhausted her.

"Why don't you go lie down?" Del said. "Rebecca's here. I'm here. And nothing would make me happier than to sit and hold William for a while."

So, with Rebecca's help—and she did need it, was grateful for it— she got into bed. And without being aware of anything further than Rebecca's hand coolly touching her forehead, was asleep.

And then awake again. Feeling dizzy, hot. Becoming aware of wetness. The bed was feeling sticky wet. She pushed away the blanket and sat up, looking at the stained sheet. She'd have to change it. Got up and made her way unsteadily to the door, into the hall. Looking down to the living room to see Rebecca standing, talking to Del. Del sitting on the chair, holding William; smiling.

She couldn't make a sound. Tried, but didn't have the strength to make herself heard. Then Rebecca's head turned and she came hurrying forward, her arms very strong as Gene felt herself slipping, sliding. Weightless, bodyless; disappearing.

Del put William in his crib and then undertook to get Gene out of the soiled nightgown and into a fresh one while Rebecca quickly, efficiently stripped the bed, changed the sheets.

"Don't get yourself worked up," Rebecca said quietly. "She's just a little thing and she's worn out. She'll be fine."

Fine. Del set the nightgown to one side and reached for the clean one. Stopped for a moment by how truly small and frail Gene seemed now without the mound of belly. The bandage—a smaller one now— gracing her abdomen. "This is no good," Del said, wondering if she really could do this. It had to be done. And she did want to do it, although she knew if she didn't, Rebecca would.

Rebecca looked over, went out, and came back carrying a small plastic bag and a napkin.

She did it. Didn't stop to think about it, but just did it. Then accepted the warm washcloth from Rebecca and cleaned the tops of Gene's thighs, bathed her tenderly, carefully. And, finally, with Rebecca's help, got Gene into the clean nightgown and back into bed. Rebecca went out and closed the door, and Del lay down on top of the blankets watching Gene sleep. Was it sleep?

Sitting in the chair, turning as Rebecca hurried down the hall. To see Gene just dropping. As if her body contained no bones, nothing of any substance. Folding, crumpling. It seemed like sleep.

Gene opened her eyes to see Del lying next to her.

"How do you feel?" Del asked, touching her forehead. "You seem cooler."

"Better. What time Is it?"

Del looked at her watch. "Just after four."

"William?"

"Sleeping. He had his two o'clock bottle and we had a lovely visit and then he went to sleep. He's so beautiful." She smiled, continuing to touch Gene's face.

"I want to be up," Gene said impatiently. "I'm sick of this. Days, weeks in bed."

"You'll be up tomorrow or the next day. There's no hurry."

"I still want to be up." She looked more closely at Del. "Something's different."

"I had my hair cut some." Del sat up to show her, then leaned back on her elbow. "Do you like it? Or do you think I'm trying for the impossible?"

"No, I like it. Something else, though. Not just the hair."

"I went out to dinner with Martin."

"You did?" Gene smiled, raising her eyebrows.

"I did." She smiled back. "And, yes, we did."

"You're getting very popular."

Del's smile faded. "I'm getting very confused."

"How?"

"I told Leonard I'd probably meet him next week. I've got a reservation, everything's arranged. But I'm not at all sure it's a good idea. I don't like the idea of leaving when you're still not altogether well. And for another, I don't really have any idea what I'm doing. It feels like too much, all of a sudden." Too many things happening. Other things left incomplete. The awful feeling that something's running behind me, just a few steps behind; waiting for me to stop for just a moment. An instant. And it'll pounce.

"Go and not see Leonard?" Gene suggested.

"I might like to do that," she said consideringly. "Just for a change of scene. Grady phoned. He wanted to know if it would be all right to come see you this evening."

"What did you say?"

"I told him to call back when you were awake, that I'd ask you."

"Grady." Gene looked up at the ceiling. Asking herself, Do I want to see Grady this evening? Yes, I want to see him this evening. She smiled and looked back at Del. "He's so funny."

"I've noticed."

"The sheet," Gene said, remembering.

"Rebecca and I took care of it."

"All of it?"

"Everything."

"Oh!" Gene closed her eyes, needing to think about that.

"Are you bothered about it?" Del asked, concerned.

Gene opened her eyes. "Yes. No. I don't know. How could you?"

"One summer, I think I was seventeen, Mother and I went up north to stay for a week with my Aunt Kate at her summer place. Aunt Kate was my mother's older sister. But very different. Not at all like mother. They really didn't even look very much alike. Kate had been married and was widowed quite young. Late twenties, early thirties. Young. Anyway, I used to love to visit her. She was so ... vibrant, alive. Not reserved, dignified like Mother. Not that she wasn't dignified. But she was *younger* somehow than Mother seemed to be. And everyone in the family talked in whispers about Kate's scandalous behavior. Because she had *lovers*." Del smiled. "Awful. Shocking. Actually she was fun.

"In any case, my period started when we were in the car on our way there and, naturally, the first thing I did when we got there was to go to my room, get some clean underwear out of my bag. Whatever. And very carefully, stain side in, folded my pants and left them on my bed to rinse out later.

"After dinner, I went up intending to unpack and do that. And discovered the pants were gone. I went into a kind of quiet panic, try-

ing to imagine what could have happened to them. Had I inadver-
tently dropped them on the stairs? Had I somehow carried them
along with me and left them in some horrifyingly conspicuous place
where someone was sure to find them? I drove myself half crazy imagining the cook or the gardener, anyone, everyone, finding my pants.
Knowing I was there in the house, *bleeding*. God!" She laughed softly.

"So. I was standing there, staring at the spot where they'd been,
when Aunt Kate came in to say, 'I've put them to soak in cold water
in your bathroom.' I was so embarrassed I didn't know what to do.
And obviously she saw that. I remember this so well. She smiled at
me and said, 'I do my own, you know, darling. I can't see any reason
why I couldn't do yours.' And she went off back downstairs, leaving
me standing there. All I could think of was, 'She loves me. She loves
me very much.' She also suddenly made me feel very good about
being a woman. That someday I might even be like her. Which
seemed to me eminently desirable. Well"—she smiled again—"years
ago, I did my own. And I couldn't see any reason why I couldn't do
that for you. Because I love you. That's all."

Gene put her arm out and Del moved closer into the circle of it, to
hear Gene whisper, "Sometimes, things you say, do, make me want to
cry. I cry too easily when I'm tired or feeling ill. I'm going to cry."

"Do you feel ill?"

"A little. But it's not important. You have to go away, have a holiday. It's important."

"I do like the *idea* of a trip. I don't honestly think it would be
good—either for him or me—to go with Leonard."

"What happened to your aunt?"

"She died. That next summer. She and one of the lovers. In a car
crash."

"That's so sad."

"It was," Del agreed. "I think of her quite often. More and more
often as I get older. God! It's strange the things that keep happening.
Strange, strange."

"Martin?"

"I feel happy and sad with him. Very happy. Almost frighteningly
happy. And sad because of it. I'm afraid to trust my feelings.
Especially with Martin. He's seen so much of the bad. Surgery three
times. God knows how many trips to that office. I can't help feeling

he has to think I'm the worst sort of fool." I'm frightened something will happen to him. Because of me. Or to both of us.

"Surgery?" Gene said.

Del nodded.

"What did *he* do to you?"

"You don't want to hear all that. Certainly not now."

"No, I do. You must want to tell."

"I thought I'd be able to tell Martin, talk to him about it. Because he'd seen so much. The damage, you know. But I couldn't. Not really. What surprised me was that he seemed to know such a lot, understand without my having to put it all into words. But I did—I do—want to talk about it, finally. He can't understand why I stayed so long, going on and on with all that. Sometimes, I wonder if I really understand it myself. I had the worst sort of need to make it all come right in the end. I refused to believe that I couldn't, in some way, illustrate to Lawrence that we could love each other, live together without … The hardest thing I've ever had to learn was that loving someone won't change him. But I thought it would. I believed that it could."

"Go on."

"I hate the way it makes me sound."

"Close your eyes and tell me."

"No, that's hiding. I've done so much of that. I'm tired of it, want to stop. All of it." She looked into Gene's dark eyes, hoping that the image and fondness Gene contained for her behind those eyes wouldn't suddenly be wiped out, destroyed by the things she had to tell. "It's all so complicated," she said, stroking Gene's cheek. Thinking, Please don't hate me, please don't. "Complicated. Having to do with hurting in order to experience any sort of pleasure. Like someone performing experiments on insects, butterflies. Trying to see if a moth could fly with one wing, or a grasshopper could make it on one leg. He had that sort of curiosity. At the beginning, a lot of the things that happened were accidents. Times when he was so involved with the results of his little 'experiments,' he completely forgot I was real, alive, capable of feeling pain. Accidents." She wet her lips and took hold of Gene's hand. Her own hands very cold. Gene's very warm. "One of the first times … I really do believe it was an accident. He was making love to me. And I was very excited. Tremendously. I moved suddenly when he didn't expect me to. He didn't intend …

didn't realize. Neither did I for a moment. His teeth … it took several seconds for the pain to register. And then I pushed him away, got up, went into the bathroom. Looked down, saw the blood, and fainted. A small tear, perhaps half an inch. Amazing that something so small could hurt quite so much. When I came around, he was standing there looking at me. Angrily apologetic. He couldn't believe I was making such a fuss over nothing. I remember shaking and shaking. As if I'd never stop. And how could I explain to him how much it hurt?

"Then there was the abortion. Very simple. If I didn't have it, he'd leave. He didn't want a child, swore he wouldn't share me with a child. And the child was all I'd ever hoped for. Wanting it so much. But wanting him just that much more. My God! I loved him so much. That was its own torture, loving him as much as I did. So, I had it done. And it wasn't right. Rebecca called for an ambulance.

"Martin was furious, livid. Not with me so much as with Lawrence for instigating the whole thing and with the so-called doctor who'd done it. Shall I stop?"

"No."

"You're sure? It seems I shouldn't be telling you these things."

"It's a good time for telling."

"Well … all right. After that. No, after the second round of surgery, when it was safe because there wasn't any possibility of my ever becoming pregnant, all sorts of ideas began surfacing, things happening. Some things that started out as amusing, even fun. Because his attention was wonderful and I was getting such a lot of it. And then, it starting turning into a nightmare. He couldn't perform. In the ways he had before. Couldn't. And I felt terrible. Guilty. Sorry for him. Concerned.

"He fixed on the idea of bondage. A captive. Someone who could neither retaliate nor defend herself. And that became a matter of course for quite a long time. I told myself it was something he needed, had to have in order to express his feelings. It was all endless justification. Making excuses for him because he couldn't seem to offer any for himself. And if he didn't feel the need for reasons, I did. I began withdrawing. Wanting him to find some other route to self-expression because I was becoming increasingly more frightened.

"He decided to capitalize on that. Accusing me of destroying his ability to perform because I refused to allow him to forget about the abortion, the results of all that. It wasn't true. Not in the sense that I constantly threw it in his face. I suppose it was true simply because I was there, walking around in front of him, living proof.

"So. There were his trips. Other women. Allusions to other women. And, finally, contrivances, embellishments. Because he'd reached a point where he couldn't perform at all with me. He sometimes could, apparently, with the other women. But not with me. And it made him angrier and angrier. And determined to punish me for creating all his problems in the first place. Convoluted madness.

"He'd trick me. Because I wanted to believe so desperately I half the time allowed myself to be persuaded into believing this time would be the time it would all be all right. And he'd make promises, lies having to do with wanting me to have some sort of satisfaction even if he couldn't. He'd convince me, lead me along. And then ... *use* ... things that ... hurt.

"So." She cleared her throat. "I was trapped. And the more trapped I felt, the more potent he seemed to become. Until he was all right again. As if he'd taken everything he needed out of me and regained his powers, his sexuality, as a result. He destroyed mine and got his own back. Then came more 'accidents.' And more things that hurt. Things I couldn't believe I'd survive. But I did. There was no control left. If I said anything or did anything, he'd have me certified, committed. And I actually believed him. My husband could legally wheel and deal me straight into an institution. Even though he was the one who was mad.

"The worst part of it is that he finally had me programmed. Like some pathetic white mouse. I knew the program, knew the signals. And if I went along and performed, it might save me some pain. I don't know. Anyway, he began getting rather bored with me. I'd become too passive. No fun any more. And he thought if he saw other women ... stoked my jealousy, it all might get back to the way it used to be. But I'd stopped caring. I was just afraid.

"That's about all, really. Except that I'm still afraid. I find I can react to someone, to Martin. And I can't help wondering if it won't all turn rotten and sick after a time. My brain tells me it couldn't happen with a man like Martin. But I can't stop being scared. I don't want to find myself ever again victimized by my needs. And an insane compulsion to prove myself equal to whatever's being dished up."

She closed her eyes for a moment, afraid to put the remainder of her thoughts into words. Putting words to the fear might cause it all to materialize.

"Go on holiday," Gene said. "You need it."

"That's what Martin said when I told him I was thinking of going."

"Did you tell him about Leonard?"

"Not specifically. Gene, don't hate me for that grubby story. I hate myself enough as it is. I couldn't bear it."

"I couldn't hate you."

"It's so damned sordid. I'm sorry."

"Never mind, never mind."

"Having you here has meant everything," Del said. "I've never been especially brave. But I've done a few things recently I actually have felt good about. The biggest thing was telling Lawrence he couldn't come back."

"But you're still afraid. You think there's more?"

"Let's not talk about it," Del said, sitting up very suddenly. "I'll go get you something to eat." She got up, then stopped. "If Grady calls, what do you want me to tell him?"

"Tell him to come."

Del smiled and went out.

Gene reached out to turn on the bedside lamp. It was dark in the room with the shades drawn. And the light seemed to help clarify her thoughts. She lit a cigarette, savoring the taste, her hand touching the edges of the bandage. Do I really understand? I think I do. Overwhelming contradictions. Del. Gentle, loving. But with a core of steel, refusing to break. The sort of woman that man—hadn't she seen him, felt the powerful negative forces?—would feel obliged to try to break. If for no other reason than the fact that Del had kept on loving him, despite his concerted efforts to kill or cripple her.

Projecting these thoughts, it seemed only logical that it all couldn't end this quietly, this undramatically. And she was suddenly afraid, seeing this. Would he try to do something more? But Del wasn't alone in the house. And there was Martin.

Rebecca came in carrying a tray. Del behind her bringing William.

Gene smiled and sat up.

"You're looking one whole lot better," Rebecca said, setting the tray down across Gene's lap. "Give me that cigarette." She held out her hand. "First you do your eating. And then you do your smoking."

Del sat down on the side of the bed. William's hand curled tight around her finger.

"Sure is one good baby," Rebecca observed. "Not one speck of trouble. Looks like his Daddy, eh?"

Gene said, "Yes," and picked up the mug of soup. For a moment feeling as if she might just fall over. The mention of Bill, that fist again in the belly. She held herself very tightly for several seconds, then tasted the soup. Good. She sipped at it, watching Del with William. Watching her kiss his fingers, then hold his hand to her cheek. Bending to kiss his forehead, then straightening with a contented sigh.

"Be happy," Gene said, causing Del to turn and look at her. "It isn't all that difficult."

"It sometimes feels as if it might be the simplest thing on earth. *Sometimes*. I'm afraid of being happy." Someone might come and smash it with an ax.

❋   ❋   ❋

When Grady called, Gene was sleeping again.

"What did she say?"

Del said, "She'd like to see you."

"Great! How's William?"

"Fine. Wonderful."

"You'll be around?" he asked.

"I'll be out this evening."

"Too bad. Next time, okay?"

She wanted to say, "If you hurt her, Grady, I'll destroy you." What she did say was, "I'll look forward to that," and hung up, then said good-bye to Rebecca and went back to the house to change for her evening out with Martin.

❋   ❋   ❋

Rebecca said, "She's still sleeping."

"Okay if I go in and wake her?"

"It's okay. But don't you go messing around, hear?"

He leaned forward and kissed her on the cheek. "I'm not the messing type."

"That case"—she smiled—"I'll be up to the house with Sally. The number's there beside the phone. Coffee just needs plugging in and there are some sandwiches in the fridge. See if you can't convince her to do a little eating."

He saluted and opened the bedroom door.

"Boy," he said very softly, "you sure to God are pretty." He closed the door and leaned against it. The faintest flush of color in her cheeks and that mass of thick, dark hair. Her throat. Bare. Somehow not as bad as he'd feared. But painful to look at. Evoking images of operating amphitheaters and gowned figures, masked faces. A white nightgown and full breasts. So appealing. He pushed away from the door and went to sit on the edge of the bed. No messing around. He wouldn't. But he could almost see and feel his hands on her breasts, on the curve of her shoulder. He got up and sat instead in the chair, lit a cigarette, and decided he'd just wait for her to wake up. Maybe grab a quick look at William and then come back.

He put the cigarette down well into the ashtray so there was no chance of its falling out and tiptoed to the door and out across the hall to see William. Asleep too. Little legs kicking out in some running dream. It made his chest feel huge, watching those little legs; made him smile, feeling fantastically happy.

He went back, retrieved his cigarette, and sat low in the chair watching her sleep.

❋   ❋   ❋

She opened her eyes, saw him sitting there, and felt a surge of pure pleasure at the sight of him.

"Could I just kiss you?" He smiled. "Without getting into big trouble or having Rebecca knock out my teeth?"

She smiled more widely and he came down out of the chair onto his knees on the floor and kissed her on the lips. A very sweet kiss that made something lift inside her.

"Hello, hello," he said. "You're the best-looking sleeper I've ever seen. I've been having a regular Disneyland fantasy-time sitting here, getting off on you sleeping."

"You're crazy."

"That's what you always say. I've got to get you a new writer."

"You *are*."

"How're you feeling?"

"Better. Just tired."

"I can understand that. Hospitals can really wipe you out. William's looking pretty hefty over there."

"Eight days old."

"There's a terrific song. D'you ever hear it? 'Jenny Rebecca,'" he sang, "'four days old, how do you like the world so far?' Knocked me out the first time I heard it. Streisand did it on her first or second album. I don't remember. Dynamite song. Just put me away."

"Sing it."

"Really?"

"Go on."

He sang it for her. He had a very pleasing, scratchy sort of singing voice.

"I love it."

"When you're up, I'll play for you. All kinds of things."

She lay back against the pillows.

"Two choices," he said. "Either we eat now and I brush your hair later. Or I brush your hair now and we eat later."

"Brush my hair?"

"Come on," he coaxed. "We'll both love it. Where's your hairbrush?"

"Bathroom."

He got the brush, then arranged her so she was leaning with her back against the side of his knee and began drawing the brush through her hair. He was right. She did love it. Something no one had done for her since childhood. Mornings when her mother had brushed her hair before weaving it into fat braids tied with pieces of string. So soothing it drew her close once more to sleep; down into a very serene state.

"I'm falling asleep."

"Okay, I'll stop and get the munchies."

He turned her around and eased her back against the pillows before going off to the kitchen to see what Rebecca had left.

While he was gone, she ran her hands over her hair dreamily. Thinking, How dear and funny he is. Doing all these things for me. Thought of him kissing her and contracted inside. Feeling it strongly. Incisions pulling in opposing directions. No pain at all now. But a certain residual caution. Favoring her body, treating it very carefully.

"Better grab what you can," he said, carrying in a plate of sandwiches and two mugs of coffee. "Because I'll tell you straight out, I'm starved. And these are very good-looking sandwiches. You want to start with the roast beef or the ham?"

"Roast beef."

"Right."

She took half a sandwich, bit into it. Watching him.

"Got a radio around anywhere?" he asked.

"Living room."

"Can't eat without music. Be right back." He carried his sandwich with him. A few moments, then the sound of something classical filling the living room, floating down the hall to her. "Like that?" He popped into the doorway.

She nodded.

"Eat faster," he said, resuming his seat, "or I'll beat you."

She took another bite, eating slowly. Feeling stuffed by the time she got to the last of the half she'd taken.

"More," he urged, holding the plate in front of her.

"Can't," she said, reaching for the coffee. "You eat them."

"Think you're kidding, huh? Watch them go!"

"Do you know that music?"

He listened for a moment, then said, "Stravinsky."

"That's wonderful. To know all that."

She smoked a cigarette, studying his face; enjoying the sight of him and pleased by his knowledge of music. It seemed a marvelous gift, to know a great deal about music.

"Is your family here?" she asked.

"Yup. Mummy, daddy, the old folks 'n' all. Older brother, older sister. Uncles, aunts, cousins. Get together a couple of times a year and we have to rent the Salvation Army hall. D'you ever hear Woody Allen years ago do that routine where he talked about how poor they were growing up? He had this great line about his father. They were so poor his father had a job as maître d' at the Salvation Army soup kitchen. Put me away!"

She laughed.

"Okay. So, we don't hire the hall. But they're nice, my people. My mother's into violin. She's first chair with the City Symphony. Dad's in electronics. He's got this very big ho-ho outfit on the lake. Factory, the whole number. My brother's on harp with the Symphony. And my sister's doing her number with social services for geriatrics. She's a shrink, actually. But she doesn't have a practice. Except on me. Because I turned rotten commercial instead of coming out pure like Sean and my mother. But I keep telling her three purists in one family ought to be enough to satisfy anyone, even a spaced-out shrink with no practice and a lot of superannuated surrogate grandparents. What about you?"

"My father and sister. Back in Illinois."

"You don't see them?"

"No."

"No show, huh?"

"Whatever that means, it sounds right."

"I love spending time with you," he said, reaching for the last of the sandwiches. "You know that? Aside from the fact that I get off just looking at you, you're so easy. You kind of go along with things. And that knocks me out. I love people who don't give you a whole load of crap, but who just go along; get inside of whatever's coming down and enjoy it. D'you know that, that you're easy?"

"Never thought about it."

"Well, you are. What was Willy's dad like?"

"Not yet, Grady."

"Too soon, huh?"

"Yes."

"Okay. Want to play cards? D'you play gin?"

"Yes."

"Great! We'll play for money or kisses. Which?"

"First see if you win." She smiled.

"Oh, I'll win!" He grinned happily. "I cheat."

Thirteen

I THOUGHT I'D TRY GOING AFTER A PATENT," ALEXANDER SAID. "DAD
and I were thinking we might get some interest from the telephone
company. But the only way we'll get into any of it is if you agree to
be a partner."

"But it's *yours*."

"Nope!" He shook his head determinedly. "You had the idea. And
that's the big part. Making it up wasn't all that hard. But ideas.
They're not so easy to come by. We'll get it all put down on paper, see
a patent attorney, and see how we go. But you're a partner or no go.
Dad had a talk with Mrs. Prewitt and she's going to arrange for us to
go see a lawyer."

"Me too?"

"You just have to sign the papers. We want you to have your fair
share, if there's any fair share to be had."

"All right." She smiled.

"It's working all right?"

"Fine."

"Okay. I'll be back to you." He got up, they shook hands, and he
left.

"He's a fair-minded man," Rebecca said quietly. "He wouldn't go
one step with this if you didn't agree."

"But really, Rebecca, it *is* his."

"Like he said, ideas count for a lot. You up to a little walk?"

"I think so."

"I'll get William ready. We'll take us a turn up and back the driveway." She went off to get the baby and Gene continued to sit for a
moment. Del would be leaving the day after tomorrow for three
weeks in England. In another week, Rebecca would drive her in for
her visit with Martin. And according to Martin, three weeks after
that, she'd be all back together again and ready for anything. Except

that she still felt so tired that she found it hard to imagine a point four weeks hence when she'd no longer feel so enervated, so permanently sleepy. But, of course, it would come.

And Grady had said, "After your big trip out next week, we're going out. To celebrate."

"Celebrate what?"

"Anything!" He'd laughed. "Whatever you like. Don't you feel like celebrating?"

"I'd love to go out."

"So, okay. That's a date. It's all settled. Naturally, you'll see me twenty or thirty times before then. But that is an official en-gagement, lady!"

"Okay."

Every day, sometimes for as little as half an hour, he drove all the way out from town, forty minutes each way, to spend some time with her. Then hurried back to the city to resume working.

"I'm a self-starter," he told her. "D'you know how incredible it is to get paid heavy-duty bread for something, something you love, I mean *love* to do? I can't leave it alone. I've got four commercials I'm doing. Two movie-movies. A TV flick. A couple of special-material numbers for this chick who's breaking in a new act. Terrific! I am also"—he paused significantly—"writing a little something for a friend of mine in my spare time. I'll play it for you next week. I can't wait to have you hear it. It's a trip I've been taking in my head, getting you up to the place so I can play for you."

Grady. It feels as if I care. But not the way I cared for Bill. He was so completely different. So sad often, and angry, too. It made me happy trying to make him happy. But Grady. He'd be happy trying to make *me* happy. It feels somehow disloyal of me to care about Grady. It shouldn't, though. I can't spend the rest of my life in a state of mourning. William needs more than that. I need more than that. And yet every time Grady comes close, Bill steps between us and blocks off the feelings, stops me, holds me back from the things I might say and do with Grady.

Does it ever end? It can't possibly be disloyal when Bill is dead and I'm here still alive and Grady's here and I need someone to hold me and want me and love me, I need more. Having more means letting Bill go, all the way go. Letting him move to some other place in my mind and feelings. A place where I could visit from time to time and say, "Look how our son is growing, how he looks like you." How did this happen? How did it come to this? It wasn't supposed to be this way. You were supposed to live at least another twenty years, be with me, be *with* me. I have to have someone. To brush my hair, perhaps. And smile at me. Make music.

"All set," Rebecca said.

Gene got up and walked to the door, still very caught up in the colliding thoughts. Remembering so many things, too many things.

"You okay?" Rebecca asked.

Gene turned to look at her. "Will be," she answered and stepped outside. At once lifted by the sunshine and the smell of fresh-cut grass, the sight of the trees and shrubbery, the flowers. She took a deep breath and held it, looking at the sky. Then smiled at Rebecca and fell into step alongside her as Rebecca pushed the carriage up the driveway.

"Fine day," Rebecca said, adjusting the carriage hood so the sun didn't fall directly into William's eyes. "Good for both of you to get some fresh air and sunshine. You know I swear this child smiled at me twice today."

Gene touched her on the arm, then wandered off across the lawn to look at the flowers. Mesmerized by the quiet hum of the air, bees hovering over the zinnias. Heat. Feeling the sun penetrating her shoulders and spine, drawing out all the impurities, leaving her feeling cleansed, even healthy.

When she turned, Rebecca had moved on up the driveway with the carriage. And Adele was coming down across the lawn, heading in Gene's direction. Gene stood watching her come, thinking, Mrs. Prewitt went away. There's nothing left of her. Gone, Mrs. Prewitt. Watching Del's body move, her hair lifting. Long legs and a very pretty sleeveless dress. A very pretty woman, smiling. Recognition, exhilaration. Gene went forward to meet her. Laughing as Del exclaimed, "Isn't this the most glorious day?" and they put their arms around each other, standing for a moment, breathing in each other's smiles. "You look so much better," Del said, touching the back of her hand to Gene's cheek before taking a step away.

"I am better," Gene said.

"Come walk with me," Del said, slipping her arm through Gene's.

"Are you anxious to be going?" Gene asked.

"Yes and no. I'm sure I'll enjoy myself once I get there."

"Have you heard from Lawrence?"

"No." Her expression changed. "It's so unlike him," she said. "I can't believe he'll simply let the divorce happen without making some last effort to keep the game going."

"Game?"

"Oh, it was." Del stopped, looking into Gene's eyes. "It was a game. What else could anyone call it?" She turned, looking down at the grass. "I hate the word masochism. It's such a stupid word, implying a great desire to be hurt, to experience pain. I never wanted to be hurt, or needed to be. I wanted him to *stop* hurting me and love me. I thought he could. Love. I thought all the rest of it was something he had to get out of his system before he could get down to caring. My mistake was believing there was caring in him. I was so hateful to you that day you came to make your offer on the gatehouse. I've been thinking about it all morning. Feeling awful about it. I'm sorry for it."

"Doesn't matter."

"I wish it had never happened."

"You sold me the house. That's what matters."

"What did you think of me that day?" Del asked, curious.

"I liked you."

"You did? How *could* you have liked me?"

"I just did. And I wanted the house. I think I'd have done almost anything to have it. And that was awful of me."

Del shook her head. "How did you get to be you?" she asked. "To be so tolerant?"

"I just am. Just trying to keep going."

"I suppose some things are simply indefinable," Del said thoughtfully. "But never mind." She smiled brilliantly. "As long as you're here."

A cloud cut off the sun at that moment and she shivered, thinking of Lawrence. His silence daily more intimidating. The sudden sensation someone was watching her and Gene. She turned and of course there was no one there.

"What?" Gene asked.

"Nothing." Del summoned a smile. "Come on, I'll show you the rose bowl. It's perfect this year. Elton's worked so hard on it. I'll have him cut you some roses."

✳   ✳   ✳

Martin was finding it hard to concentrate on what he was doing. Preoccupied with Del. Unable to think of much else but her. Wishing she wasn't going to go, yet knowing he hadn't any right to ask her not to or to try to move her in the direction of his preferences. It would be good for her to go. His brain knew that. But the rest of him wanted her to stay, to be near. And it made him impatient that he could be so childish. He reprimanded himself, thinking, Get on with the business at hand. Then thoughts of her arms, her mouth, her breasts, and felt his body heat rising rapidly. Get back to work!

The afternoon dragged, though, and he was anxious for the evening. Their last time together until she came home. Perhaps their last evening together, ever. Now why the hell did he think that? And why the hell did be feel so damned antsy, jittery? Wanting to call her every other minute to make sure everything was all right. For no real reason. Except there was a certain feeling in the air. And he told himself it was the heat outside, the air-conditioning in the office, the waiting room out there filled with women; one of the nurses out sick and Lasky picked this day of all goddamned days to take off. So that he and Rich had to double up and take the overload of Lasky's patients. Without even stopping for lunch. Food ordered in. And when he came out of one of the examining rooms there was an especially unappetizing lump of something wrapped in waxed paper sitting on top of his desk alongside a waxy container of something cold. Beads of condensation running down the sides of the cup, pooling on the wood.

He sat down, opened the waxed paper, looked at the sandwich inside, closed the waxed paper, and picked up the telephone.

Sally said, "She's walking outdoors with Miz Elliott. You want me to call her?"

"No. Just tell her I called. I'll see her later."

"Yessir."

"Thank you, Sally."

"Yessir."

He hung up, removed the lid from the drink container, looked at the brown liquid inside, replaced the lid. Thought about Lawrence Prewitt and his prostheses, all the rest of it, and clenched his fists instinctively, enraged. Christ! That someone like that was out there walking around, doing God knows what to whomever he felt like doing it all to. Doing it to Del. Unimaginable. Monstrous. He looked at the drink container, opened his hands, and buzzed Susan to come get rid of that whole mess.

"But you didn't eat," she protested.

"Fuck it!"

She looked at him sidelong, picked up the drink and sandwich, and went out, saying, "Mrs. Anderson's in Two. Thanks for the free lunch."

"Great! Thank you."

She looked back from the doorway, turned around, and took several steps into the office. "Something wrong?"

"Look in the waiting room and you tell me!"

"No. Something's *wrong*."

He sighed and slapped his hand on the top of the desk. "Nothing's wrong. I'm sorry, Sue."

"No sweat. You're sure, though?"

"Male menopause," he said dryly.

"No shit!" She turned and went out.

He laughed loudly and got up to go see Mrs. Anderson.

❉   ❉   ❉

Sally said, "The doctor called."

"Any message?"

"Nope. Just said to say he called and he'd see you later."

"All right. Thank you."

"Thought I'd go on out and have a look at that baby."

"Go on, by all means. I'm going to go up, shower."

"I'll be right back."

"Don't be silly. Take as long as you like. Rebecca's just out on the lawn there. Mrs. Elliott's gone in for her nap. There's not a thing happening. You might just as well keep Rebecca company. As a matter of fact, I think I'll take a nap myself. Will you wake me at—what time is it now, four?—five-thirty?"

"Okay."

Sally poured out two glasses of the Gallo Chablis she always kept cooling in the fridge and went out the back door. Del went on through to the front of the house and up the stairs. It was hot upstairs. The downstairs was always cool. But heat rises, she reminded herself as she did every day, every summer. And put on the air-conditioner in her bedroom, standing in front of it as she undressed, feeling the air from the machine beginning to cool; drying her. That hour outside with Gene. Perhaps she'd gotten a burn. She looked in the mirror. Her face did look a little pink. And the tops of her arms. How many years had it been since she'd sunbathed? She couldn't remember. Maybe she'd use the pool this year. And take a few brush-up tennis lessons. Martin played. It would be nice to play. How many years since she'd done that?

Liking the image of herself and Martin playing tennis, then afterward sitting in the shade, having a cool drink; laughing. He makes me feel better and better, healthier, saner, stronger. And that apartment. Awful. She turned to look at the room, imagining the two of them spending their nights together here. I think I would like that. I think I would.

Made sleepy by the heat, she opened the bathroom door, saw Lawrence sitting on the side of the tub. And, startled, cried out. Then held her hand over her mouth for a moment. Her heart gone crazy.

"What are you doing?" she asked, holding on to the door, trembling from the fright, the shock of seeing him there, smiling at her.

"Waiting for you," he said, dropping his cigarette into the bathtub, turning on the cold water for a moment to extinguish it. "You really have such a lot to talk about with your little friend down there." He straightened around. "Kept me waiting ages up here."

"How did you get in?"

"Now don't be stupid! I walked in. This is such a busy little household these days. Everybody on the hustle-bustle. I left the car on the main road and walked in. Your little buddy looks very nice without the belly."

"What do you want?" she asked, thinking if she pulled the door toward her she could lift her robe down from the hook on the back of the door, put it on.

"Nothing in particular. I just thought I'd come visit you."

"Lawrence, what do you *want*? I don't want you here. And I especially don't want you spying on me. My God! Sitting in here waiting for me. Like some sort of ghoul. Don't you think all this is a little creepy?" Be calm, stay in control. You can get out of this. He'll go away.

"I suppose, come to think of it"—he smiled—"it is a little on the creepy side. But then I couldn't exactly make myself at home in the living room, could I? Our good friend Elton might decide to take a machete to my face."

"What nonsense! You're talking about him as if he was some sort of ..." She couldn't think of an appropriate word and reached in back of the door. Nothing. Where was her robe?

"It's not there," he said.

"You took it?"

"Not exactly."

"Oh, for God's sake!" She turned and walked back into her bedroom, nervously pulling open the closet door. Stopping dead, her mouth opening, the air leaving her lungs in a rush. Her eyes straining, staring. A great heap of torn, slashed, ruined clothes on the closet floor. Terror. The blood pounding in her ears. "Oh my God!" she whispered, taking a step backward, colliding with something. Lawrence. She lashed out blindly, her only clear thought to get out of there, away from him. She shoved at him and tried to push past, but he grabbed her by the hair, his hand winding in, yanking back so that her body moved forward but her head went sideways. And then her body followed after her head and he had her.

"*What do you want?*" she cried, her eyes filling from the pain. It seemed he was pulling the hair right out of her scalp.

"Just a little get-together for old time's sake," he said.

She looked at his blank eyes and thought, I shouldn't have allowed myself to relax, to forget.

He put his hand on her breast. She jerked away. He brought her back with a hard, sharp twisting of his wrist. Saying, "Don't do that, Del!" in a voice so soft, so insanely soft as he closed his thumb and forefinger over her nipple and began to squeeze. Harder and harder. The pain excruciating, robbing her of her voice. A small whining sound emerging from her throat as his fingers closed together, tighter, tighter, a pleased expression creasing his face. Her stomach rising, knees going weak, eyes going out of focus. Until he stopped. And then the pain was worse. Spreading. And she was reciting one small prayer over and over inside her head. Please don't kill me Please don't, please don't kill me. Oh God! don't kill me please you're going to I know please don't don't I don't want to die, I knew it was wrong to find pleasure, take it, have anything for myself, wrong to hope, to be willing to believe there might be something for my life and now you'll kill me for it, God don't kill me.

His eyes narrowed slightly, his head dropped, his hand yanking her head to one side. His mouth at the base of her neck. Tongue running over the flesh there, making her skin crawl. Then his teeth sinking into her, biting down. She screamed. So hard her entire body vibrated with the effort of it, the blood flooding into her head, all the pain in the universe centered right there, right there; screaming.

That deadly quiet, softly menacing voice saying, "Shut up, Del. Or I'll kill you." Such a reasonable note to the tone of his voice. As if there were some sort of logic to the proceedings. You do this, Del, and then I'll do that.

Her mouth closing abruptly around the scream. Pain fanning out down her arm, through her chest, up into her throat. Nose running, eyes streaming. Watching him fearfully. Shivering, tensed for further pain. I don't want to die, don't hurt me anymore, just go away leave me alone please, oh *God*, please go away, somebody help me, somebody come, I don't want to die. Nothing I ever did was so wrong or so bad, not for this not to come to this, I'll die you'll kill me what should I do why doesn't somebody come ...

He produced a pair of scissors. From somewhere, nowhere. She didn't see where they came from. He simply lifted his hand and they were there. Effecting a flourish. "*Voilà!*" He smiled. His smile like kindling, setting her fear ablaze.

What he'd used on her clothes, she thought, her body desperate to escape, shrinking away from him. He held the scissors in front of her eyes, waving them slowly back and forth, grinning at her. So that she had to look, had to see, was compelled to admire their clean, perfect construction, the long, tapering blades. Her eyes hypnotically following the movements of the scissors. Then he raised his arm and she closed her eyes. I don't want to see, don't make me see. His hand tightening in her hair. The sound of the blades opening and closing, opening and closing. His hand grabbing at her hair. Grabbing here, then there. The scissors opening, then closing. And then she was released. He shoved her away, flinging his hand out into the air between them. Her hair floating, drifting, falling to the carpet. Her hair. They both watched. His hand releasing the scissors, letting them drop to the floor as they both stood transfixed by the sight of her hair drifting down.

She stood sobbing, a hollow ache in her stomach. Then, realizing the moment was hers, she ran. Got all the way to the door but he was right there behind her, grabbing her by both arms, whirling her around, dragging her back. Shaking her like a child's rattle so that her head snapped this way, that way, and she began screaming again, screaming. Her eyes searching out the scissors. On the floor, there.

"I told you to shut up!" he warned, his hand thundering into the side of her face, stunning her once more into silence. "You can't *ever* do what you're told!"

And then she was falling to the floor under him. His weight tremendous, her lungs feeling collapsed under all his weight. He was fumbling for something out of her sight, big forearm across her throat bearing down on her windpipe, making her gasp so she couldn't breathe, her eyes sliding sideways, picking out the gleam of the scissors. He was separating her head from the rest of her body. She couldn't breathe, thinking, I won't let you, you can't, don't, please, I don't want to die.

It hurt. More than anything he'd ever done, it hurt and she told herself not to resist, to go limp, go loose, open, let it happen, but still it hurt so horribly and he was strangling her, her arms flopping around like a beached fish without water, her body twitching trembling, she was dying all over, hurting. He was forcing the pain deeper, harder inside her. Her fingers inched toward the scissors touching the blade.

"What was that?" Sally said, looking around. "D'you hear that?"

"Probably just the gulls," Rebecca said placidly, wiping the baby's mouth. "They sure do make the worst noise." She looked up at several birds circling overhead. "They're a bit far from home."

"Probably looking for food. Less than two miles to the lake," Sally said distractedly, wondering if Rebecca was right, if it could've been the gulls. But no. It was something more. A feeling she couldn't shake, a sensation of something being wrong, out of tune. She heard it again and jumped up. "I heard it that time," she said, rushing back toward the house. "That's no gull." That's him. Found himself a way back into the house. Hurting her again when I thought we got shut of all that.

She wanted only to get him off, make him stop, make him go away, leave her alone. Hissing vile words at her, terrible, his forearm bearing down down across her throat, she had to make him stop, make him let her breathe. Tried to get a grip on the scissors but her strength was going.

Sally could hear them inside. But she was stopped by the closed door. What if it had only been the gulls? But it wasn't the damned gulls. Those weren't friendly sounds coming from behind that door. And no matter what happened, she was going to have to open that door, get rid of the crawly feeling. Put her hand on the knob, turned it. The door opening silently. Seeing. He was there right enough. Killing her. Del's eyes huge, face suffused with a bad purple color. And him saying he'd kill her.

Just for a moment, Sally couldn't think fast enough, didn't know what to do, how to get him off her. She took a step into the room and he heard her, his head twisting around, his face like murder, all contorted. And quicklike tried to move, but Sally kicked out blindly and he fell. Made this wild-animal sound and didn't move again. Neither of them did.

✳   ✳   ✳

Del thought for a moment he was going to let her go. Something happened, she didn't know what, couldn't see but it didn't matter, too late she lost it all, he was falling upon her again, so heavy, waves covering her head, filling her mouth, lost.

✳   ✳   ✳

Sally shouting incoherently into the telephone. He couldn't make much sense of what she was saying, shouted at her that he was on his way. Then slammed down the phone and tore out of the office.

She opened the door to him, pulling at him, crying, "I didn't know what to do so I called you. Upstairs, quick! Come upstairs!"

The two of them racing up the stairs. Stopping in the bedroom doorway. A long, long silence as his eyes looked and looked; his heartbeat so loud he had to turn to Sally to see if she was hearing it, too.

※   ※   ※   ※   ※

Fourteen

HE BROUGHT HER A RECORD.

"You've got to hear this," he said. "Let me put it on and then we'll sit outside and watch the sky while we listen to it."

In the kitchen, Rebecca slid the roast into the oven, wondering what had come over Sally. Rushing off that way. Probably nothing. Hearing things. She smiled over at William in the infant seat on the counter, sucking on his fist.

He opened all the windows, started the record going, then took Gene's hand and led her outside. To sit on the front step, listening to the music.

"What is it?" she asked, entranced by the fact of her hand in his.

"Dvorak. Romance in F."

"Beautiful."

She sat absorbing the music, thinking what a fine sense of giving he had. To come bringing music and present it to her with the sky. Her home at her back. Her child, and Rebecca, and everything familiar. A fine day, a glorious day. She'd napped and slept so soundly, so well.

"Funny," she said, noticing. "The gates are closed."

"They weren't when I got here. Somebody must've just closed them."

"Funny," she said again. The gates had never been closed before. Not in all the months she'd lived here. She looked up the length of the driveway to the house. Nothing unusual to see. Martin's car parked at the top of the drive. The door on the driver's side open. Did it mean something? The door open that way looked odd. As if he'd gone in intending to come directly out again. Or as if he'd left the car in such a hurry he hadn't had time to close the door. And if the gates were closed, when had Martin come in? Before or after?

"I like the way your nose gets all wrinkled right here when you're thinking hard," he said, touching her between the eyes. "What kind of heavy-duty brainwork's going on in there?"

She shrugged away her thoughts. "Nothing. Beautiful music." She smiled. "Thank you."

"Beautiful you. You're welcome."

Inside the gatehouse, the telephone rang. Then stopped. Rebecca had answered.

Grady put his arm around her shoulders, gratified when she leaned in against him, turning to look into his eyes.

"Do you have to hurry right back after dinner?" she asked, feeling closer to him every minute, every day. Drawn to his sense of humor, his generosity, his music. Wondering, though, if she mightn't be overendowing him with fine qualities because of her own needs.

"Nope. Have something exotic in mind?"

"No. I just hoped you'd stay for a bit."

"Thought you'd never ask."

Rebecca came to the door.

"Gene," she said, disposing with her usual "Miz Elliott" so that Gene was instantly on the alert, trying in a few seconds to read the extraordinary expression on Rebecca's face. "Go up to the house!"

Gene stood. Grady moved to get up, too, but Rebecca said, "You stay here!" To Gene, she said, "Go on! Go!" her body leaning forward, her urgency sending fear shooting through Gene, who stood a moment longer, then turned and went running off up the driveway. Turning once to look back at the gates, seeing Elton standing off to the side of them. Unable to see his face. She ran on, breathing hard through her mouth, very frightened. The open car door. The closed gates. Elton, a sentry. What did it mean? What?

The front door was wide open, too, and she came to a halt in the doorway wondering what to do, where to go. Then, looking up, saw Sally at the top of the stairs, beckoning to her. Gene ran up, asking, "What?" Out of breath, asking, "What's happened?"

"The police're coming," Sally said. "You go on in!"

"Where?"

"Guest room." Sally pointed.

She moved down the hallway and put her hand out to the wall for support, holding on, looking in. Seeing Martin on the far side of the bed, leaning over, talking in a low voice to Del. And Del, in a long-sleeved, high-necked nightgown, sitting with her knees drawn up, her arms wound tightly around her knees, staring straight ahead.

The sight of Del's face too terrible. And her hair.

Gene exhaled jaggedly, her fingers pressing into the wall as if it might reassuringly press back. Her throat hurting. Martin looked up, straightened, came across the room and led her back out into the hall to talk to her.

"Please, get her to talk, to cry! Anything, something!" he whispered. "She's been like that since I got here. See if you can snap her out of it. The police'll be here any minute. She's going to have to talk to them."

His hand on her arm directed her into the bedroom. Del's head turned very slowly. Following an instinct that told her something dreadful had taken place here, Gene went right up onto the bed, opening and closing her arms around Del, drawing Del's head against her breast, automatically rocking her. Her hand moving over the chopped-off hair. Some of it still long, some not more than an inch in length. Holding her secure, holding her tight; afraid to ask, afraid to find out. Noticing streaks of red in Del's hair, in her ear.

"What happened?" she asked Martin, who sat down exhaustedly on the far side of the bed, rubbing his face as if trying to reshape his features.

"Christ!" he said in a voice as wearied as his face. "Lawrence."

"What?"

"He'd have killed her. Damn near almost did."

Gene's arms closed tighter around Del in anticipation of what he was about to say.

"He's down the hall, in her room. Sally didn't know. She was scared witless, so she called me. Christ!" he said again. "I thought they were both dead." He shook his head, seeing it all anew. Lawrence sprawled across Del. The blood. The scissors in his throat. Her naked legs and one hand the only visible parts of her. The rest hidden by Lawrence's bulk. Telling Sally to call the police, then bending down to see ...

He'd had to get Lawrence off her once he'd established she was still alive. They'd understand that. He couldn't have left her there under the body. And then, having managed to ease Lawrence off to one side, the full impact, the horror. The blood all over her. Most of it Lawrence's. But not all. One of the worst moments of his life, having to remove the blood from her. Sitting now, thinking about it, he wanted to get rid of that thing, push it deep into the garbage, right to the bottom. But knew he couldn't. It was evidence. Christ! *Evidence.*

Gene stared at him. "He's *dead?*"

Martin nodded, then got up. "Try to get her to talk. I can't." He raised his hands, then dropped them. "She was defending herself. Sally saw, she's a witness. An accident. But she's going to have to explain."

There was the sound of a car pulling up in front of the house.

"Maybe," he said, "if I tell them she's in no condition to talk right now. Obviously, she's in no condition to talk. But they'll want ... Just try. Please." He turned and went out, down the hall.

Del's silence was becoming increasingly unbearable. Gene lifted her up to look at her. Del's eyes blank, her face utterly empty. Bruises all across the right side of her cheek and jaw. And what Gene now understood was blood. Spattered in her hair, her ear. Some still on her neck.

Drawing her back into her arms, she stroked Del's cheek, her hair, whispering, "Talk to me, tell me. Please!"

"I can't!" Del said at last. "Oh, God! Help me, it hurts. Inside. I feel dead."

"You're not dead."

She shook her head, eyes clinging to Gene's. "It hurt," she said in a dry, cracked voice. "Nothing. *Nothing* ever hurt more. I just wanted to make him stop. Just stop."

"But Martin said you'll be all right?"

"Martin doesn't *know*. Not about inside. How could Martin know? He won't *ever* know. But you do. You know, don't you?"

"He's trying to help," Gene said, despairing over the inadequacy of her words.

Del blinked, looked away. The searing pain inside her. Relentless. What was there left inside to damage? How could there be anything left after all the years? She blinked again. Hearing his voice again, feeling him fall. Dead. I killed him. She'd done that, but she didn't feel anything now, thinking it. Feeling nothing. Killed I killed him. Looking at Gene's throat. The scarf had come undone. She studied the scars, examining the words in her mind. *Killed. I. Killed. Him.* The scars had faded considerably since that first afternoon when Gene had bared her throat in order to have a home here.

"Martin gave me a shot," she said, unmoving inside Gene's arms. "It's making me dopey." I'm a killer I killed him, the scissors went into his neck and his life came out of his mouth, it was red his life. I don't feel anything. Only dizzy.

"You're going to be all right," Gene was saying.

Voices in the foyer downstairs.

"Over," Del repeated stupidly. "I'll go to prison."

"It was an *accident!*"

"But ... No."

"Sally saw. Everything will be all right."

What did Sally see?

She was finding it almost impossible to follow what was happening. Gene being asked to step outside. And some man. She thought he must be a policeman, coming into the room with Martin. The two of them looking at her. The stranger's mouth moving. Did she speak to him? She could hear the echo of voices, could feel her own mouth moving.

"I've given her a sedative."

"Just a few quick questions."

"I don't think she's up to it."

"I'll make it fast."

A moment of complete panic as Martin came over, began unfastening her nightgown. What? What was he doing? Her arms too heavy to lift. Her mouth filled with chalk, wanting to say, stop what are you doing, don't do this, not in front of him. Her eyes fixing on the man with the notebook, trying to retain the name she'd been given, to remember the name that belonged to him. She'd been told. Hadn't they told her? Mouth so dry, hands so cold. I'll go to prison. Isn't this the beginning, how it gets done? The telephone ringing, ringing. Footsteps, voices. She wanted Gene back in the room, needing her there to understand. Why was this happening? Am I dead after all? Is this hell? Is this hell, with Martin opening my nightgown exposing my breasts to the eyes of this stranger?

She could feel herself crying, feel her throat working, chest heaving. But her eyes were so dry, unmoving. The detective leaning closer, looking, saying something she couldn't make sense of, could only feel the violation. Martin's voice static in her ear, his hand under her breast static, the stranger's eyes on her breast, her neck. How could Martin do this to her?

How, when she'd trusted him? She closed her eyes, her frozen hands clenched. And when she opened her eyes again, Gene was back, holding her. But was it real? Was it safe to trust what she thought she was seeing?

She blinked, then again. Her eyes beginning to feel freer, more able to move. Feeling it all welling up, up from her chest, down from behind her eyes, shaking her so that she had to make some effort to hold on. Her hands fastening onto Gene. Gene soft. Gene real. Gene you care. Gene no one ever cared that much but you do. I don't want to die but it's so close still so close. Will they take me away, put me in a prison, say I murdered him? She opened her mouth to speak and the force of it shocked her, taking her utterly by surprise. A cry that came from the deepest, most critically injured part of herself. And then the tears. So that she was able to close her eyes and let them slide out, away, carrying so much torment with them. Crying and crying, on and on; her body a symphony of pain. Pain going numb, going dull, going distant. Martin's magic medicine spreading through her system cooling the heat of her nerve ends, depriving the pain of its thrust and, inside, the wound defused. Her thoughts scattering, thinning; diffused.

"Yes yes yes," Gene crooned, rocking her, murmuring an ancient chant, words and motions that came from something primal and knowing; willing Del to sleep. "Sleep yes yes it's all over now sleep."

While footsteps came down the hall. People crowding into Del's bedroom down the hall. Gene lay with Del inside her arms, hearing the many sounds. Voices. The arrival of the ambulance. The smell of cigar smoke from the hall where men stood, talking. Martin's voice. Sally's. Questions. Elton. A glimpse of Sally quietly but firmly closing the guest room door, cutting the voices in half. And then somehow Del's drugged sleep becoming her own.

A long time, the shadows growing thin across the floor and the light turning, changing, deepening; a breeze rising, the rustling branches outside, summer scents and serenity. Cars, engines starting, going.

Martin sat in the chair in the corner, looking at the two women asleep on the bed. Thinking—admittedly abstractedly—that reality was something that definitely changed from moment to moment, its perspectives constantly altered by one's own. Reality, a few minutes ago, had been explanations and a capsulized version of Del's medical history. His giving of evidence. And then listening to Sally tell what she'd seen, tell of what she'd heard and seen for a lot of years. Sad and sickening what Sally had seen and heard. He was awed by the woman's loyalty, her fierce and somehow surprising loyalty to this woman on the bed, asleep in the arms of another woman.

But now, here in this silence, was another reality. Misleadingly serene and silent. But there's been a death, he thought. An accidental death, Detective Hockley had agreed. Very definitely agreed. Yet traces of skepticism continued to lurk in the corners of the man's eyes, in the still-unasked questions that would come later. Martin's head ached. He saw a slight movement. Gene's hand. Signaling to him.

She got up unsteadily and they moved out into the hallway, where from some instinct neither of them sought to question, they came together; holding each other for several moments before separating, allowing room for the words.

"They'll be back in the morning to talk to her again, get a more complete statement."

"What will happen?"

"I don't know," he said tiredly. "All I do know is the press is going to have a field day."

"They're going to arrest her?"

"Of course not! There's no question of that," he said fiercely. "No question!"

"She kept saying over and over that she'd killed him. But it was an accident."

"It was an accident."

She let out her breath, then drew it in again sharply. Remembering to ask. "What did he do to her?"

"What?" He couldn't think as clearly as he'd have liked.

"I couldn't make sense of what she said. About hurting so terribly."

His expression softened. "A prosthesis. Did you know about all that business? Had she told you?"

She shook her head, the word meaningless to her.

He explained. She held her hand over her mouth, her stomach leaping wildly, threatening to overturn itself.

"Go home," he said kindly. "Get some rest. I'll be here."

"Yes," she whispered, and left the house, the long shadows. Walking woodenly down the driveway in the last of the evening sun to see Grady standing, waiting for her. Looking deeply worried. Walking straight into his arms with a terrible need to be held and comforted. Wanting not to have to deal with all the images—both real and imagined.

"Rebecca told me," he said, his hand in her hair. "Is she okay?"

"She will be." She has to be. I want her to be.

"Dinner's ready, but I don't suppose you're in the mood to eat?"

"No. But I will. I want to be well, strong."

"Scary seeing the unmarked cars come rolling in. Elton manning the gates. The ambulance. Car from the coroner's office. You were gone so long. I was starting to quietly freak out."

❉   ❉   ❉

They ate. Grady putting the Dvorak on again for distraction. She forced herself away from thoughts about Del, about how it must have been. Rebecca spending the night at the big house in case she was needed. The two of them cleared the table then walked outside to stand listening to the night. Looking at the gates. High and impenetrable in the darkness. Looking at the house. The lights flanking the front door like two eyes staring into the night.

"Stay with me tonight," she said. "I need you here."

"Okay."

"I can't make love to you, Grady."

"I know."

"But I need you here."

❉   ❉   ❉

She climbed into bed in her nightgown and lay waiting for him to come close to her. Wondering if this was a cruelty she was inflicting on him, a kindness he was performing for her. He came down beside her and she went close to him asking, "Am I being selfish?" and he said, "No. Don't be crazy! No."

"I love her, Grady. She's my mother my sister my daughter my friend. What he *did to* her." She closed her eyes, shivering. "He cut off her hair, beat her, *bit* her. Did the most monstrous things to her. Had been doing it all for years. It hurts me. Because she's right. I *do* know. But I can't absorb it all. Please hold me."

"Are you lovers?" he asked, not sure how he'd feel if she said they were. All at once terribly confused. Not sure if what she was saying was simply what she was saying, or if there were ambiguities here that he was too unsubtle to catch.

"No," she answered. But was that true? Are we lovers? What are lovers? "We just love."

"You know I love you," he said.

"I think I know that."

"Is there a possibility?"

"I'm not sure. I think there could be. It's still too soon. I don't know anymore what I need. Except to have you here now. Thank you for staying."

"Don't thank me for something I wanted to do."

"Thank you for wanting to, then."

"Are you trying to tell me something?"

"No. Just that I don't take any of this for granted."

"I know that, lady. Don't you think I know that?" He smiled in the semi-darkness.

"I don't know what I know." Her tone plaintive. "I thought I did. But I don't."

He ran his fingers over her throat, then lowered his head and kissed her there. The gesture told her everything she'd ever need to know about him. She felt tremendously comforted, reassured.

He lifted his head to look at her. She brought him down again to kiss him more. Feeling the contractions. His kiss was soft, light. They looked at each other again. Almost eight months since Bill's death, since she'd held and kissed him, taken him in, deep in, as far as it could be accomplished in in.

Grady's hands on her breasts. She quivered, making a small sound. He kissed her breasts round and round and round, making her ache inside. His hands taking the nightgown away, moving on her hips, across her belly, down her thighs. All of her responding, wanting to give. Thinking, this isn't fair of me, not fair, I can't take, just take, giving nothing.

"I do want you," she said, savoring the feel of his skin warm under her hands. "I do."

"You're so soft." He sighed. "So soft."

Perversely, she thought of Del at that moment and began to cry.

"It's okay," he whispered. "It's okay." He stroked her, lulling her, taking her past the tears. She curled into him, kissed him lingeringly, then slept. Deep and hard. Without dreams.

He left a note saying, Call you later. Love, G.

She went to get William his bottle and was sitting with the baby on the front step when Rebecca came down and sat beside her.

"God forgive me," she said, "but that man deserved to die. Nobody could blame her. Could they? They won't blame her, will they?"

"Martin says no."

"That's what I thought. Sally said to tell you Del's up now, asking for you to come."

Gene gave her William and went inside to dress. The police would be coming back this morning. To ask their questions. Take statements. Could they blame Del? No no.

❊   ❊   ❊

"They'll be here in an hour. I want you to do something for me. Will you do something for me?"

"All right."

"Get the scissors. There's a pair in the bathroom. Fix it for me. I can't. Please? Cut the rest off." She had to close her eyes for a moment, dizzy again. Seeing the gleam of the scissors on the floor, feeling her hand crawling toward them.

"I'll try," Gene said.

She was very nervous doing it, her hands shaking. But Del said, "I *need* you to do it. I know you can make it look better. It has to look better. I can't stand seeing myself. Later, I'll have it fixed properly. But now. You understand, don't you?"

"I understand."

She did the best she could. Then brushed the loose hair from Del's shoulders, stopped by the teeth marks. Very distinct. Blue at the interior, red-inflamed at the perimeters. Del stood up cupping her breast, looking down at it. Her nipple had turned dark purple. Threads of red were snaking their way up her breast.

"Did you ever read that book by Carson McCullers?" she asked Gene. "It was made into a very bad movie. With very well-known people. Elizabeth Taylor. I can't remember the name of it. What was it? I can't remember. But there was a woman. With an odd husband. She cut off her nipples with gardening shears."

Gene grimaced.

"Thank you." She ran her hand over her hair. "It feels better. I'm sure it looks better. Come talk to me while I have a bath." She turned, her eyes for the first time revealing emotion. "Don't leave me!" she begged, standing with her arms wrapped around herself. "Just for a while. Please?"

"I won't leave you," Gene promised, wondering if it was possible for someone to shrink overnight. Del seemed impossibly frail, thin; her hipbones jutting, her ribcage prominent. And the scars.

"I keep on feeling so scared. I forget for a few minutes. Then I remember and I'm scared all over again. Martin says I'm lucky. Not seriously hurt. I'm lucky," she repeated, her eyes going distant.

"But you *are* lucky."

"How can you hurt something that isn't there? That's what I don't understand. How can it hurt as much as it does?"

"Don't talk that way. You're very much there."

"Martin says much the same thing." She looked down at her bare feet. "Amazing. Do you know what Martin did?" She looked up again.

"What?"

"He cried. I've never seen a man cry before. Sat and held my hand and cried. It made me feel so strange, so sad, seeing him cry. Why can't I get connected? I feel so cut off from me, from everything. As if Lawrence had put some of me over here and some over there and no matter how hard I try, I can't bring all of me together. I *killed* him."

"It was an accident," Gene said with as much firmness as she could muster. Placing her hands on Del's arms for added emphasis. Forcing the message into her eyes. Willing it to penetrate into her brain. "An accident. No one could possibly blame you for defending yourself."

"He had his arm across my throat," she said, almost absentmindedly, touching her throat. "And I thought about you, that I'd never see you again. He kept telling me I'd spoiled it all. Why did I have to spoil it all for him? I don't know what I did, what I spoiled. What did I do? Telling me he wanted me to die. I'm cold. It looks so lovely and warm outside. Is it?"

"I'll start the bath for you."

Del's hand closed on Gene's arm, stopping her. "Am I ugly? I feel so ugly."

"You're not ugly. Your hair will grow back. You'll be fine. You're not ugly. All this will heal and you'll be fine again."

"I keep trying to tell myself that. But ... *I killed him*. It's over, and I'm alive when he wanted me to be dead, and I can't think of reasons for all this happening. How did it happen? I'll never understand. How could he blame me when he was the one who did it all? I didn't mean to kill him, just ... I couldn't get him *off*."

She lay back, letting the water cover her, feeling the heat eating the pain out, swallowing it in big bites, taking it. More of Martin's medication, working along with the heat and the rhythmic flow of her thoughts. Looking at herself, finding the sight of her own body unrecognizable.

"Strange," she said. "This morning has been so strange." Her voice unrecognizable, too. "Martin made quite a lot of calls. He canceled my reservations, let Leonard know I wouldn't be there. Called my brothers. Emery's in Rome with Lowee and the children. Clark was just leaving with Meg to meet them there. They're terribly sorry they can't come, be with me. Then Martin came back to the guest room and sat down beside me and was quiet for quite some time. And that was strange because the feeling I had was that he seemed to belong here, in the house, on the bed beside me. Just as it was strange not to have him with me in the bed in the night. He slept downstairs. On the sofa.

"And the telephone keeps ringing. And Sally lied, said the morning paper didn't come. But it always comes. She doesn't want me to see, to read what they've written about it. Have you seen?"

"No."

"I want to wake up, find none of this happened. I feel so strange. Shaky. Strange. Martin crying. I think that was the strangest thing of all. Seeing a man cry. I can't describe to you how distorted everything seems. If I can't wake up, perhaps I can go back to sleep, dream it away. Make it all go away. Somewhere. *Oh Jesus God!* It's coming again!" She gripped the side of the tub, her eyes squeezed shut, shuddering. "Happening over and over. Hurting, hurting. He keeps throwing me down, cutting off my hair. Pushing it. His eyes. God! His eyes! All those other times I could close my eyes, accept it. It was just something huge, something hard I could bear, my body could accept it. But this time, this time there was nothing, no help, nothing, dry and it hurt. Oh God! It hurt so much. I just wanted to try to get him off but something happened I didn't see, and he ... It was like he tripped and fell so suddenly.

"What I'll do, what I'm going to do, I'll tell them—Martin says, you say, everyone says accident. Tell. And after he wants to take me away somewhere for a while. Ten days perhaps, he'd like it to be longer, it's hurting again so much! But he can't take any more time than that right now, as it is he's throwing the whole office into chaos, but imagine he's willing to do that for me. I am going"—she opened her eyes, the shuddering slowly diminishing—"I am going to tell the truth, tell. All of it. And after, go away. Somewhere. With Martin, let him help me. Put all the pieces back. He says we'll lie in the sun and get high and make love. He says. He says I can do it, have to. Go away and make love in the sun, it won't hurt. But it will, it does. Hurts, and I know it'll keep on hurting but I'll do it. That's what I'll do. Because I need someone in my life to care about my life and whether or not I hurt inside. Help me! I do. Hurt inside. And he does care. He does. I might even love him. I think I could. If I thought I knew how, what it was, love. God, I want to love someone and not have it hurt. The way I love you. And your baby. And anyone you love because I do love you and there's no pain." Her hand closed around Gene's. "I did kill him. If he hadn't fallen that way, if that hadn't happened, I'd still have used the scissors." Her fingers dug into Gene's hand. "Last year he would have killed me. I'd have let him. But this year, I couldn't. I'm not making any sense, I know I know. It all has to do with you, Gene. Caring. I couldn't let him kill me. Has to do with Martin, too. I couldn't just let it happen. But I never wanted him to die."

Fifteen

IT FELT LIKE A TRIAL. AS IF HER WORDS AND ACTIONS—EACH AND EVERY one of them—were being judged. And the telephone ringing nonstop was such a distraction. She looked again at the detective. A man in his late forties. With lines of fatigue around his eyes and mouth. Hair carefully combed up from just above his ear to cover the bald place on top. A large belly. Thick-soled black shoes. And a name she simply couldn't remember.

"Dr. Ingram," he was saying, "has given us copies of your medical record. He's been very complete." He looked over at Martin. Does he suspect Martin of something? she wondered. "And, of course, your housekeeper has been most helpful. Now, if you'd be so kind, we'll go upstairs, go over it all step by step, and then I'll be on my way." He moved toward the doorway and she gripped Martin's arm, whispering, "I don't remember his name."

"Hockley. Come on now, Del. Let's get it over and done with."

The need to cry was overwhelming. She whispered, "I feel so ashamed, so ... Hockley?"

"That's right."

"You removed your clothes in here. Is that correct?"

"Yes."

"Why here? Why not in the bathroom?"

"Because it was cooler here. I'd just turned on the air conditioner."

"Did you know he was in the house?"

"No. I ... No."

"Okay. So then you came through here, into the bathroom."

"I opened the door. He was there, sitting on the side of the tub."

"And what did you do?"

"I was startled. I don't know what I did."

"Did you say something? What did you say? What did he say?"

"I don't remember. I think I asked him what he was doing here. I was frightened."

"Then what?"

"He said ... some things. I wanted to get my robe from the hook on the back of the door. But I couldn't."

"Why?"

"Because he was there. I didn't ..."

"What?"

"Didn't want him to know I was afraid."

"And then?"

"He said some more things. I reached for my robe but it wasn't there. No no. He *said* it wasn't there. And I wondered how he knew that. I asked him did he take it and he said he hadn't exactly taken it."

"Go on."

"I wanted to get away from him, put something on, some clothes. I came back here into the bedroom, opened the closet door. Everything was like this, the way ... it is."

"What did he do then?"

"Pulled me. By the hair. Not letting me go."

"Where did this happen?"

"Here. I think. Here."

"Okay. Go on."

"We ... struggled. And then he ... he ... hurt me"

"Where?"

"My breast. Then here, my neck. I screamed and he told me to shut up or he'd kill me."

"He said, 'Shut up or I'll kill you?'"

"Yes. That."

"What did you do?"

"I stopped screaming."

"And?"

"He had the scissors. Waved them back and forth in front of my eyes. Then he started cutting my hair. I could hear it."

"You didn't see?"

"I had my eyes closed."

"I see."

"I tried to get out of the room then. Ran. To the door."

"Go on."

"He came. After me. I screamed again and he ... hit me. Saying again he'd kill me. We fell. No. He threw me down, fell on me, his arm across here choking me. I couldn't breathe. And he ... he ... I can't!"

"Just take your time, go slowly, and tell me what happened next."

"Oh God! I ... he ... his knees ... forced my legs open. And uh ... reached, I couldn't see what he was doing. Then he did it, pushed it into me."

"What?"

"The stick."

"What?"

"I ... I called it that."

"He'd used it before?"

"Martin ... ?"

"Tell him, Del. Go ahead, tell him."

"Yes. Before."

"You consented previously?"

"No! Never! I..."

"You what?"

"I had no choice. I couldn't ... Sometimes he tied me ... to his bed. But he ... *prepared*. I ... it wasn't so painful... so terrible."

"Precisely how did he 'prepare?'"

"Oh, *please* ..."

"Look, Mrs. Prewitt, I know its unpleasant and difficult for you, but it's important. What had he done to prepare those other times?"

"Oil. Or something. Something. I don't know."

"But this time he didn't."

"No."

"Okay. Let's go on now."

"I couldn't breathe. His arm on my throat. I saw the scissors on the floor, reached for them. I wanted to get him off, make him stop. That's all. Just make him stop. I couldn't breathe. I knew he was killing me."

"What happened next?"

"I don't know. Something. I had the scissors in my hand. But the way he was holding me ... Then something ... It was as if he'd tripped. He fell. On the scissors. His eyes. And his mouth opened. Blood came out."

"And then?"

"I don't remember."

"What's the next thing you do remember?"

"Martin. Dr. Ingram. Making me smell something."

"You undertook to remove her from beneath the body, Doctor. Is that correct?"

"Yes."

"Before or after you determined she was alive or dead?"

"After."

"What did you do next?"

"I removed the prosthesis."

"It was still inside her at that point?"

"Yes."

"I see."

"I removed it. Then attempted to clean her up somewhat in order to determine the extent of her injuries."

"Before or after you telephoned for the police?"

"Sally telephoned while I was doing it."

"Okay. Now, wait a minute, I just want to make sure I've got this down correctly. According to my notes, you said Mrs. Prewitt sustained a vaginal tear."

"That's correct."

"How serious?"

"Fairly serious."

"And this tear was, in your opinion, a direct result of the attack?"

"Most definitely."

"Requiring what sort of treatment?"

"Several sutures. Sally assisted."

"How many exactly?"

"Five or six."

"Okay. Just one more question, Mrs. Prewitt. Which hand did you use, your left or your right?"

"The right, I think. Yes. The right."

"A couple of other questions, just for the record. Proceedings were underway, I understand, for a divorce."

"Yes."

"And you both agreed to this divorce?"

"Yes."

"Had he ever attempted a reconciliation?"

"No."

"He hadn't come here previously to talk to you?"

"Once. One evening he was here. Surprising me. The way he did ... this time. Once."

"I see."

"Please. *Please!* Years and years I had to listen to him tell me all about his women, I listened. There was nothing else I could do. He was all I wanted then. Just to be with him, have children. Not a career or anything else, just to be with him. But he made me get rid of the baby, made me do it and he wasn't even there. Came back after it was all over, angry with me because we couldn't, I couldn't make love after the surgery."

"Mrs. Prewitt, you don't have to ..."

"He took everything away, everything. And then, then he wanted to take me, take my life away, too, and I couldn't let him. All the pain and hurting, the operations, promises he made to everyone and never kept. I kept all the promises but I didn't mean to kill him, it's just that he wanted to kill me and I didn't promise that. I was always frightened, always so afraid to take any pleasure in anything because pleasure wasn't ever a part of it, of us. I couldn't let it happen. It was my *life* and I haven't anything else left. There isn't anything else."

She stopped abruptly, looking at her hand on Hockley's sleeve, forcing herself to let go. Aware of the silence in the room, the ticking of the clock on the bedside table.

"We'll let you know when the body's released," the detective said, taking a step toward the door.

"Am I going to be charged with something?"

"No, Mrs. Prewitt."

"I didn't intend to kill him."

"I understand that." He took another step, then turned back. "I wish you well, Mrs. Prewitt. I'm sorry I had to drag you through it again. But I don't write the procedures. We'll be in touch. About releasing the body."

She stood at the window, looking at the cars parked outside the fence. Hearing the detective exchanging a few last words with Sally. Then the front door opening, closing. She saw him emerge at the front of the house, stopping to talk with the other officer who'd accompanied him. Wondering why she'd been so convinced she'd be punished for the loss of Lawrence's life. Having pictured herself closed in behind high gates, wire mesh, steel bars.

But that's the way it's always been, she thought. Living behind gates, enclosed by the impenetrable mesh of my obsessions. And his. I called it freedom, marriage, even love for a time.

"You had to tell him everything?" she asked, watching the two men climb into their car.

"I had to, Del."

"Everything."

"I had no choice in the matter." His voice was very quiet.

"Everything," she repeated, feeling doomed. So shameful to have public declarations made about her private life, private body.

"I'm sorry," he said. "But it was important that they know none of what happened was for the first time."

"Was there some doubt about my innocence?"

"Not really. Certainly not in view of what Sally witnessed."

"Did he ask about you and me?"

"No."

"I'm surprised. I thought he probably had."

"He didn't."

"Will you be able to stay with me now?"

"Of course, I will. Are you asking me to stay with you?"

"But if you do ... Won't they ... ?"

"I'd like to give you another shot, Del. You're so overwrought, upset."

"I've put you right into the middle of all this. I'm deeply sorry for that."

"You haven't done anything to me," he said reasonably. "All this has to do with what *Lawrence* did to *you*."

"But I feel so guilty." She turned finally to look at him. Her eyes large with confusion, shock.

"There's no need for you to feel that way. No need at all."

She turned back to the window asking, "What are they all doing down there? As if they're waiting for something."

"I'm going down the hall to get my bag. I'll be right back. Okay?"

"Yes. Okay."

Elton opening the gates to allow the detectives to go through. Two men attempting to break past Elton and get up the driveway to the house. Alexander running down the drive. Father and son forcefully ejecting the intruders, then once more locking the gates. Walking away from the people clustered there. What did they want?

Jesus God! The shame of it. The sick shame of it. That sad gray man writing it all down in his little notebook. And the stick taken away with him. They had it all, everything.

"Del?"

She looked around to see Martin preparing a syringe.

She removed her dress—Sally's dress—and stood waiting.

"I feel like an addict."

"Don't be an idiot!" he said sharply. "There's nothing here you could become addicted to."

"I have an astonishing capacity for addictions of one sort and another."

"You're feeling sorry for yourself."

"No," she said truthfully. "I'm feeling terrified. And I don't know why. You'll stay with me?" she asked as he held her arm steady, stabbing the needle in.

"For a little while. Then I've got a few things to do. But I'll be back later," he added quickly.

"Do you *want* to be here?"

His eyes met hers for a moment, then shifted as be withdrew the needle, dabbed her arm with a bit of damp cotton.

"Do you, Martin?"

"I want to be here." He set down the syringe and lowered her slip to examine her breast. "I'll give you a couple more antibiotic capsules. I don't like the look of this. How's the pain?"

For some reason his professionalism, his tone set her to trembling, feeling chilled. "The pain is splendid," she answered, searching his eyes for someone she thought she knew.

He touched her face lightly with his fingertips, then tilted her head to the side in order to examine the burgeoning infection at the base of her neck. Seeing her for these moments as a series of damaged parts. Then, raising his head, seeing her mouth, her eyes, shaken by the reality of her totality. Not just parts requiring his ministrations. He put his arms around her, cradling her head to his shoulder.

"I'm sorry," he said. "I didn't mean to do that to you."

"I know, I know."

"In a week or so, you and I are going to get on a plane and go somewhere. The two of us are going to have a fine, quiet time together;

resting, talking, putting this whole nightmare in back of us. I'll make love to you and you'll be fine, just fine. I wish we could make love right now. Do you understand what I'm saying?"

"Yes. No. I can't think."

"You know you understand my meaning."

"You had to give it to him, didn't you?"

"Give what to whom?"

"*It.* To that detective."

"Yes." He sighed. "I had to."

"I'm so ashamed."

"Del, it's all right. It wasn't your fault. None of it."

"But it *was.* Wasn't it? Somehow?"

"*It wasn't your fault!*"

❋　　　　　　❋　　　　　　❋

She couldn't stay away from the window. Turning back again and again. They were always out there. She wondered if it was the same group or a changing one. Why didn't they go? Their presence intimidated her, made her feel like a freak, or an animal. Something deformed, aberrant. She kept going back to look.

"What do they want?" she whispered, huddling close to Martin, frightened by the faces that came and went, in and out of focus, as the Rolls moved through the gates.

"Sensation," he answered, wondering if she was going to give way to all the pressures, if she'd simply shatter beneath them. "Once the funeral's out of the way, things'll quiet down, get back to normal." They want to see a killer, he thought. It's what they want you to be.

She sat away from him once they were through the gates and nervously lit a cigarette.

"What are you thinking?" he asked, touching her arm.

"Nothing. I'm afraid. Just afraid."

"But it's over now, Del. There's nothing to be afraid of."

"Yes there is," she said evenly. "It hasn't ended yet."

❋　　　　　　❋　　　　　　❋

The senior Mrs. Prewitt and her daughter, DeeDee, had just arrived and were standing in the foyer of the funeral home. Seeing them,

Del's fear seemed to grow suddenly into a substance she could taste in her mouth, could feel coating her entire body. The two women turned. Mrs. Prewitt—a frightening image of Lawrence as an elderly woman—whirled around, advancing on Del, lumbering across the space between them. Her eyes glittering with hatred, sorrow, rage. Del watched her approach, feeling herself ready for what she sensed was coming; feeling, too, an unanticipated sympathy for the woman. The mother who'd lost her son. How could she, being only his mother and never the bearer of his secrets, know what her son had really been? If only there didn't have to be this great distance of misunderstanding between them. If they could just sit somewhere together quietly and talk about him. She opened her mouth to speak as the older woman's arm swung out, her hand flashing through the air— diamonds glinting—colliding with the side of Del's face. The impact stunning so that Del nearly lost her balance.

"*Mother!*" DeeDee rushing over. A victim of divided loyalties. Wanting to apologize to Del, to her mother, to anyone, everyone. Saying, "She doesn't, didn't mean ... I'm sorry, Adele. Truly." Taking her mother's arm, leading her hurriedly away into the chapel. Mrs. Prewitt's sobs of outrage the only sounds in the place.

Watching DeeDee getting Mrs. Prewitt settled down there in one of the front pews, Del asked herself, What am I doing here? I shouldn't be here. There's no reason for me to be here.

"I think I'd like to leave," she said in an undertone, aware all at once of Martin's arm protectively encircling her and the group of shocked faces all frozen, waiting and watching to see what her reaction was going to be.

"Is that really what you'd like?" he asked, matching her quiet voice. "You want to leave?"

He felt so tired, so completely played out. Days and nights of trauma. He curbed a sudden impulse to say, Do whatever the hell you want. Saying instead, "Look, I know this is no picnic. It's ugly and unpleasant as hell. If you want to stay, we'll stay. You want to go, we'll go. But let's move out of the way here so the rest of the people can get past us. We're creating a traffic jam."

She nodded and allowed him to steer her to one side of the foyer where she lit a cigarette. Two tears crept out from beneath her dark glasses and made their way slowly down her face. She stood very still, smoking her cigarette; the tears the only indication of her humiliation.

Silenced for the moment by a kind of delayed reaction to what had just happened, he stood before her watching the tears move with maddening slowness down her cheeks. Absorbing her, experiencing some sort of delayed reaction to her. Finding her all at once impressive; oddly, starkly, beautiful despite her thinness. Furious with himself for his prior impatience. Because now, being objective, he was forced to admit she was displaying awesome courage and dignity. And right then, realizing so many things, he understood that he'd already committed himself and that there'd be no turning back. Because despite her present indecisiveness and fearful state, something inside him responded to the look of her, the remembered feel of her, the sound of her throaty voice, the receding memory of her laughter. *Are you going to kiss me? Start here.* He wanted to hurry her away from there, take her somewhere warm and safe and free of old terrors, new humiliations.

"If you want to go," he said again, "we'll go. Don't suffer through this. There's really no point to it, unless you *make* a point of it."

She tried to think, to decide. Unaware of the people who approached her to offer their sympathies. She lit another cigarette, her hands trembling.

A group of press people attempted to get close to her, but Elton suddenly materialized. A uniformed wall self-erected between her and them. Elton wasn't going to allow any further incidents.

"I had hoped," she said finally, "that Emery might make it. He said he'd try. I suppose the plane must be late."

"He still might get here."

"We can sit at the back," she said, having decided. "In the last pew."

"Whatever you say." He took her arm, she put out her barely-smoked cigarette, and they moved inside.

Beneath the dark glasses, her eyes moved over the faces of the people assembled, returning again and again to the closed coffin up front. Wishing she could somehow see inside, be certain Lawrence was actually in there. She had the irrational feeling that he might suddenly pop out from behind the draperies to sneer at her.

The words of the service went right past her, failing to connect. All meaningless. Mrs. Prewitt in the front, noisily weeping. None of it seemed real.

The instant the last word was spoken, she signaled to Martin. "I can't do any more than this," she whispered as they hurried out to the car.

"You didn't really have to do this much," he said, caught up in the feeling of unreality. The man they'd eulogized in there having no apparent connection to the man he'd met, to the damage the man he'd met had done.

✳   ✳   ✳

"You've got to eat something." Martin said, placing two more antibiotic capsules in the palm of her hand.

"When will you be back?"

"I don't know. Let me call you later. Eat something! I mean it."

He kissed her good-bye and left. She went into the bathroom to take the capsules, then went down the hall to her bedroom. Opening the door to stand looking at the dried bloodstains on the carpet. Wanting to scream. All of it rushing back at her, making her heart pump too fast and her lungs contract. She slammed the door and ran down the stairs to the kitchen. Stopping at the sight of Sally and Rebecca standing by the stove talking, William, in his infant seat, on the kitchen table.

"Did anyone call?" she asked breathlessly, the sound of rushing water in her ears.

"Nobody."

"What about the new number?"

"Day after tomorrow's the soonest they said they could change it."

"And you called the carpet people?"

"Tomorrow." Sally walked over, took a cup down from the cupboard, filled it with coffee. "Take this," she said, giving the cup to Del. "I'll bring you up a tray."

"I'm not hungry."

"I know that. It's what you say. I'll bring you up something to eat."

"I'll be going," Rebecca said.

"You needn't go," Del said, setting the cup down on the counter. "I'm going to go up. Get out of this dress. Lie down."

I'm going mad, and you both think so, too.

"Go on up," Sally said, already taking things out of the refrigerator. "I'll bring the tray right up."

"All right. Stay, Rebecca. Please. Stay." She turned and went back down the hall.

✳   ✳   ✳

"What did you see? What happened?"

"I saw what he was doing. That food's getting cold!"

"But what did you do? Did you do anything?"

"I kicked him at the back of his knee. Hard as I could. He saw me. I didn't want him getting up coming after me. So I just kicked at whatever I could reach."

"That's why he fell."

"Come on, eat up. It's all over now. There's no sense in going over and over it."

She ate part of the egg and a slice of toast, then vomited.

Feeling chilled, her stomach aching, she lay down with the comforter to sleep. The telephone rang and she answered automatically. To hear a whispering voice. Obscenities and raspy breathing. She threw down the receiver, staring at the telephone with her heart once more pumping too fast. Got up and went into the bathroom to vomit again.

"I'm going mad," she said aloud, returning to the bed to wrap the comforter around herself. She lit a cigarette sitting back against the pillows, wanting to sleep but afraid to try.

The door opened.

"It's time for William's nap," Gene said, carrying the baby over, sitting down with him on the side of the bed, watching Del crush out her cigarette in the ashtray. "Sally said you were going to lie down. And I thought you might like to nap with a friend." Gene smiled coaxingly.

"You want to leave him here?"

"Would you mind?"

"No ... I ..."

"Good. Have a good nap. Sally and I are going to make bread." She went out smiling, her face feeling unnaturally stiff.

Eyes heavy-lidded, William lay contentedly across her lap, ready for sleep. Smelling of milk and baby powder and an indefinable sweetness. She lifted him, rearranged the comforter, then lay down with him in the circle of her arm. Entranced by the flawless texture of his skin, the length of his eyelashes, the strength of his tiny hand wrapped around her finger. His cheek smooth, silken beneath her lips, against her cheek. His warmth and roundness, his small, compact body fitting so perfectly into hers.

So effortless, so simple. His eyes closing, breathing deepening, and he was asleep. She watched his sleeping face until her eyes could no longer focus. He was too warm, too close. Feeling herself relaxing for the first time in so long. The muscles in her jaw, in her arms and legs, in her stomach; all of her going loose.

Downstairs, Sally said, "I just made a fresh pot. Let me get you a cup."

"Thank you."

"How'd you think of doing that, leaving the baby with her?" Sally asked, lifting the receiver off the hook, opening the cutlery drawer, dropping the receiver in, and then closing the drawer.

"I couldn't think of anything else," Gene admitted.

❊   ❊   ❊

She awakened to see William's face an inch or two from her own. His eyes wide open, his mouth opening and closing, making sucking sounds.

"Such a funny face." She smiled, shifting slightly, realizing the wetness on her arm was William's. "You need to be changed."

She picked him up, and her dress, and carried him down to the kitchen where Gene and Sally were setting the dough to rise a second time.

"He's wet." She smiled at them, feeling foolish.

"I brought along a spare." Gene took the baby.

Del gave him up and stood groggily blinking into the late afternoon sunshine streaming in through the kitchen windows. Breathing in the yeasty smell of the bread, feeling warm.

"You're making bread," she said. Then smiled at the obvious.

"You're hungry," Sally declared victoriously. "I'll fix you a sandwich. Something light so's you don't spoil your dinner. I've got a nice lamb roast."

"There's a peculiar noise in here."

"Oh that! I took the phone off the hook. Guess I can put it back now." She opened the cutlery drawer and replaced the receiver. Then turned at the sound of Del's laughter, feeling her own mouth curving in response. Everything was going to be okay after all.

Sixteen

THE EVENING AFTER DEL AND MARTIN LEFT, GENE WENT OUT TO DIN-
ner with Grady. And after, to his place. A huge open loft with mas-
sive plants and track-lighting and large pillows on the floor. She sat
on a stack of pillows by the window looking out at the city while
Grady played music that made her dream. Played and played for her
while she looked at the lights and breathed in the night air and
thought about Del and Martin gone away together, hoping they were
being peaceful together, happy together. Wanting so much for Del to
find contentment, to find herself again.

Thinking about making love with Grady in another week or so.
They would. It was what she wanted. Weeks of conscientious absti-
nence. Resisting each other night after night. Something deep and
thoughtful and fine-feeling growing between them. Thinking how
he'd kissed her throat that night. Thinking about Bill. The sorrow
dulled down to something small but permanent, indelible. Yet fading
daily, nightly. Wondering if it would be that way for Del. The memories like ribbons blown away by the wind.

She turned from the view of the city to smile at Grady, holding her
hands clasped in front of her mouth in smiling silence, paying
homage to his music and the notes he'd written, a theme for her.

❉   ❉   ❉

Del stood on the balcony outside their room. Smoking a cigarette,
feeling the heaviness of the air, breathing in the thick perfume of
exotic, night-blooming flowers. Drawing the smoke deep into her
lungs, trying to shake off the horror; appalled by her body's refusal to
be loved when everything inside her craved the attention he was
offering so lavishly. She stood, listening to Martin moving about
inside the darkened room, wondering if anything would ever be right

again. It seemed so unfair—primarily to him—to find herself so completely frozen inside night after night.

"Want to get dressed and go for a walk?" he asked, coming out onto the balcony.

"I'm sorry," she said, looking down at the lights along the path. "Perhaps this was a mistake."

"It wasn't a mistake," he said, wanting to touch her but not sure that it wouldn't just serve to set her off again. "You needed to get away, so did I. Give yourself a chance."

"I thought I was."

"There's a name for it," he offered quietly.

"There's a name for everything," she said tonelessly.

"The first time we made love, you told me you were no good at it. I remember your stressing the 'if.' 'If' I could get inside you, then you probably wouldn't come. I'm aware this isn't the first time it's happened."

"Oh God! Please, don't be a doctor."

"Sorry. I *am* a doctor. I can't help being what I am any more than you can."

"At the last, with him, it was most of the time."

"It's psychological. Your brain says it's going to hurt so your body refuses to let it happen. It's called vaginismus. Not all that uncommon, just not talked about a great deal. Women don't like to admit things like that. Just the way men don't like to admit they can't get it up."

"I'm not consciously refusing you."

"I'm not saying you are. There's no accusation being made, Del. I'm trying to tell you I understand. I know there's a reason. I'm not pressuring you. I'm not trying to do anything, really."

She stubbed out her cigarette, then faced him, holding her hands tightly together.

"I'm all right. And then I get scared. I can't help it."

"Scared of me?"

She shook her head. "Not of you. You've been so good, so kind. It's just that I'm still in pieces. And I can't bring it all together so that I can make love to you. I've got to be enough myself so that I can let myself go and make love to you. I'm not saying it properly. I sound like an idiot."

"Why're you being so hard on yourself? Let's forget it for now.

Would you like to do something? It's still early. We could go down to the bar for a drink, or take a walk along the beach. We don't have to stay here having a confrontation."

"I want to stay here, though," she said, unlacing her fingers, "having a confrontation. That's what's so awful about it. I *want* you." She smiled with some effort, her nerve endings still screaming with fear.

"Oh, Del." He smiled. "Sometimes you scare the hell out of me. And every single damned time I've got you pegged to pull some typically female blame-placing ploy, you throw out the truth and I've got to stand by and watch you try to deal with it all single-handedly. We're *both* in this. Is it safe to put my arms around you?"

She nodded.

"Let's just lie down, talk awhile, and then go to sleep. Okay? We've got five more days and nights to play with. There's no great rush. Anyway, I don't give up all that easily."

"The rush is in me," she said, calmed by the strength of his arms and his eternal reasonableness.

She couldn't shake the feeling that it was wrong to lie down in his arms, all filled with wanting, yet unable to satisfy any of it.

"Would you like me to?" she asked, slipping her hand between his thighs.

"Sure I'd like you to." He caught her hand, stopping her. "But don't."

"Why not?"

"Because it's just too one-sided. I can't"

"Are you angry with me? I'll understand if you are."

"D'you want to know something?"

"What?"

"I love you. Do you know that? I *love* you. Unless you can be right there with me, it's just no good. I don't need it that badly."

"Maybe we should smoke some of your grass ..."

"Not that, not now. That's cheating."

"Wasn't it cheating the first time?"

"It definitely was not. It was just another something, like an extra drink. That was different."

"Okay." She gave up.

"Look, going through that whole business, I kept wanting to walk away. That's the truth. I kept asking myself what the hell was I doing. But every time I looked at you, thought about you, I knew I couldn't just walk away from it. You don't bore me. I don't know. There's nothing insincere about you. I like your legs."

It made her laugh.

"Let's stop now and just go to sleep," he said, easing her closer.

She closed her eyes, remembering how he'd talked about mutuality. It existed. If she could just allow it to happen.

❋   ❋   ❋

In the morning, after a late breakfast, they walked down to the beach.

"It seems silly to stay at the pool when the beach is right here, don't you think?"

"Don't like pools all that much anyway," he said, taking her hand. "I think I'll try to swim off some of that breakfast."

"I used to like to cook." She pushed her sunglasses back up her nose. "I stopped after a time. What was I going to say? I forgot."

"Sorry, I can't help you there. I flunked mind-reading."

She laughed. "I remember. I enjoy watching you eat. It's marvelous to see someone eat who has the kind of appetite you do."

"So now you're thinking you might take up cooking again."

"I might." What will we do, you and I? Is it going to be occasional evenings and sometimes on weekends? Why can't I seem to see the two of us together in the house? Or am I afraid of that, too?

"How's this?" he asked, dropping her beach bag on the sand.

"Fine." She glanced down the beach. A few people here and there. Some children at the far end.

"Coming in?"

"Not yet. You go ahead."

He threw down his beach jacket and pounded off across the sand into the water. She lit a cigarette, watching him, finding it extraordinary that they were here, in this place, together. The waiter assumed they were married. Greeting them as Doctor and Missus every time they went in for a meal. Not an unnatural assumption. Two people; one male, one female, of a certain age. Together. But we're not married. We don't even make love. One male, willing. One female, unable. Eight nights of trying and failing.

She looked again down the beach, noticing the children were getting closer. Native children. A girl and boy of seven or eight. She let her eyes return to Martin who was swimming parallel to the beach.

The sun was very strong. She looked at her watch. Not yet eleven. Unstrapped the watch and dropped it into the bag, reaching at the same time for her suntan oil. Stopping suddenly, stricken by the fact that Lawrence was dead and she was still alive. Alive, on a beach, with another man. One who said he loved her. A man I want, she thought, too aware of the knotting inside. I look at you and undergo all the symptoms of desire. But my body refuses to allow you in, refuses to heed my messages that insist you have access.

The children were perhaps a hundred feet away, playing in the water, their laughter reaching out to envelope her as Martin came up, threw down his towel, and stretched out on his back, exhaling loudly.

"I'm out of shape," he said, catching his breath. "I'm really out of shape."

"I think you're ..." She looked at his chest, his legs. "I love looking at you." Her hands itched to touch him.

He smiled, shielding his eyes from the sun. "You enjoy watching me eat. You love looking at me. Take it easy. A little flattery goes a very long way."

"It isn't flattery. It's the truth. I love you." She said it and the knotting inside grew worse.

"You think it's going to cost, but somehow it never does," he said softly. "Isn't that how it feels, saying it?"

"Exactly how it feels."

"Me too. But having managed to get it said in the first place, now I feel kind of power drunk. Or something. I want to keep on saying it to you. I love you, Del." His fingers circled her wrist. "Scrawny, malnourished crone that you are. With that godawful bathing suit. No, don't tell me! I know. The incisions."

"That's right. You surprise me knowing the things you know."

"After lunch, were going shopping for some halfway docent bathing suits. That thing's for someone about seventy with varicose veins and flab."

She leaned over to kiss him, tasting the sea salt on his lips.

"Why don't you come into the water with me?" he said, his hand traveling up and down her arm. "I want you so goddamned much."

The children were closer now, their laughter wrong-sounding. She raised her head and saw that they were throwing something up and down in the water. Hearing a peculiar mewling noise. She stared, trying to see what it was. Saw and jumped up.

Martin sat up asking, "What?"

She didn't hear. She was watching the children holding the puppy down under the water.

"*Stop that!*" she shouted, running. Her knees rubbery, a pounding in her head. Knowing the puppy was drowning. Its pathetic cries cutting into her. Running toward the two children who stood, blank-faced, watching her approach. Their laughter gone. "What are you *doing?*" she cried, almost in tears, coming to a stop on the sand in front of them. The little girl holding the puppy. The animal quivering, whining. "You're killing that puppy!" she accused. "Is it yours? Does it belong to you?"

"We just find it down the beach there," the boy said. "Don't belong to nobody. We asked."

"Why are you doing that to it?" she demanded, angrier than she'd ever been in her life. "It's terrified! Look at it!"

Both children turned sobered faces toward the dog.

"We set it free," the boy said, taking the puppy from the girl, setting it down on the sand where it sat shuddering, squealing.

"No!" she said, wondering what she was doing. "Pick it up and bring it here!" Her voice had gone peculiar and she was shaking. She hurried back to where her things were, bending to snatch up her towel. "Have you got any money with you?" she asked a bewildered Martin.

"Never mind," she said, stooping again to open her bag. "I've got some." She pulled a five-dollar bill from her wallet, then whirled around to face the children. "Take this!" she ordered, pushing the bill at the boy, wrapping the towel around the puppy, holding it in her arms. "All right?" she challenged them.

"Yeah, okay!" the boy said, taking the girl by the arm, the two of them running off.

"What are you doing, Del?" he asked quietly as she knelt on the sand wrapping the puppy securely, warmly in the towel.

"I don't know," she answered frantically, shaking so much she could barely function. "They were killing it! I had to do something. Look at the poor thing! It's shaking so hard." She lifted the puppy into her arms, feeling its sides heaving as it labored to breathe. Clutching it to her breasts, sobbing. Knowing people were watching, not caring. "We've got to find a vet," she said. "Have him looked after. He's sick."

"Okay. Let's go get changed. You go ahead. It takes you longer. Give me the puppy and I'll find out about a vet at the office while you're doing that."

She looked at him suspiciously.

"Come on! I'm not going to throw him back in. You go on and I'll bring all this stuff."

"You think I'm crazy!" She sniffed, getting to her feet.

"Sure do. But you'll notice I'm not arguing."

She took the room key and ran off. Small brown puppy shivering in Martin's arms, no longer whining.

✳   ✳   ✳

"Why're you bothering?" the vet asked. "This puppy's got fleas, worms ... belly all distended from the worms. Easier for everyone to just put him down, forget him."

"*No!*" Del cried. "Don't you have medicine for the worms? And flea collars? Shots. I don't want him put down. I want him made well. If you can't do it, there must be someone on the island who will."

"Okay." He smiled. "Don't go vexing yourself. No other vet on this island in any case. Leave him with me a few days. I'll give him shots. But what'll you do when it comes time for you to leave?"

That stopped her. She hadn't thought that far.

"We'll take him with us," Martin said. "Right?"

Relief flooding through her. "That's right. We'll take him home."

"You'll be needing some kind of carrying box. And papers. I can see to it, if you're really intent on taking him."

"Yes, yes. See to it. Please."

"It's okay," the vet said placatingly. "I'm gonna see to it."

"Whatever it costs!" she said wildly. "It doesn't matter."

The vet laughed. "I wouldn't never want to fight with you, woman! Don't fret yourself about this poor old pup. We'll get him fixed up."

✳   ✳   ✳

They were bumping their way back along the road out of town in the mini-Moke when she said, "Stop for a minute, will you?"

"Another animal in need of saving?" He grinned, pulling off the road, putting the car into neutral.

"I'm going to start crying again," she warned him. "So just grin and bear it. I'm going to smoke another cigarette, too."

"Be my guest."

"You thought I was crazy," she said thickly, wiping at her eyes with the back of her hand. "I suppose I was behaving like a madwoman. But you didn't say it, or stop me. You went along." She looked at his mouth, then at his eyes. "I don't even like dogs." She laughed, sniffing back the tears. "But I couldn't let that happen. It was so little and so scared. Martin." She stopped, her throat closing. She looked away. "Lawrence wouldn't have done what you did, wouldn't have supported me the way you did. He'd have made me feel like a fool, threatening to have me put away. He'd have created a scene. And then, later on, he'd have taken me up to the bedroom to punish me for my transgressions.

"You asked me once why I stayed, put up with all that. I was a virgin with Lawrence. How was I to know that every other man wouldn't be just the same as he was? Oh, logically, objectively, I knew that couldn't possibly be the case. But so many convenient lies get told through the years. I wanted to win when the only possible outcome was to lose.

"I don't know why I did that about the puppy. Now that it's all over, I can't believe I created such a scene."

"I can," he said, his hand on the back of her neck. "I was there."

He moved his hand away. Her neck felt suddenly cold.

"Yes, you were. I feel so ... odd now."

His hand on her shoulder now. "We missed lunch. Hungry?"

"Are you?"

"Ate way the hell too much breakfast." He smiled. "No."

"I'm trying to think what to name it."

"How about B.P.?"

"What's that?"

"British Petroleum. There's a station just up the road there."

She laughed. His hand closed around hers. "That's awful!"

"Okay. So call him B.P. for best pup. I happen to like B.P. and that fellow's half mine."

"How so?"

"Territorial imperatives."

"I don't know what that means. But all right."

His hand tightening around hers. Her breath catching in her throat, breasts feeling suddenly heavy, swollen.

"Let's go back," she whispered, looking at his mouth.

❊   ❊   ❊

"Don't look that way!" he said softly, his hands on her face.

"What way?"

"As if I'm going to hold you under water until you're ready to burst, then sell you to some nutty woman for five Yankee dollars."

"There's something I want to ask you."

"Ask me anything," he said, his thumb pressing lightly into her nipple.

"Could you conceive of living in the house with me?"

"Isn't that what I've been doing these past weeks?"

"I suppose it is. But you know what I mean."

"I know what you mean and yes I could."

"It's just that we've got a partnership now. In B.P."

"We certainly do." He opened his mouth over her breast. Her hands twitched, her thighs unlocked.

"I was trying to … I keep forgetting what I'm trying to say."

He lifted his head. "Stop trying for the moment."

She could scarcely breathe for the heat. Her body on fire. Her throat, pulsing. "I want to kiss you," she whispered, drawing his mouth down to hers. Willing the parts of her self to come together. So hungry, made hungrier by his tongue coaxing hers to respond. Her breathing as labored as the puppy's had been. Her hands opening over his shoulders.

His hand slid up the length of her inner thigh and she went tight. Telling herself, No! Let it happen. Forcing herself to allow him to touch her. Dry like a bundle of old newspapers in an attic, crumbling at the touch of human hands. Belly trembling as he pressed kisses on her navel, moving down.

"Love your long beautiful legs." He smiled, then eased her thighs open and put his mouth on her.

She couldn't feel it, he'd give up surely, getting no response, get tired and give up a hopeless cause. But then he did something with his hands, something that made her feel naked as she'd never felt before. Naked and exposed. And his tongue striking that nakedness drew a startled cry from her throat, caused her hips to roll, insides twisting. As if he'd peeled away her flesh and was making love to her exposed nerve endings. She clenched her fists against the pleasure, unable to fight it; moving steadily toward completion.

But then he stopped and lay down upon her, his mouth on her neck, his legs between hers. She started to say something but he whispered, "Sshhh," rocking gently against her, his hands in her hair. "Sshhh." His mouth on hers. Fingers stroking her arm, then his weight was gone, hands on her breasts. Gone. Hands sliding down down, the pressure building inside, the delicate stabbing of his tongue making her want to scream, taking her closer and closer, deeper and deeper into the growing need. He stopped again. Her body instantly cold, deprived. Words crowding into her mouth but no, "Sshhh," turning her over onto her belly, atop her again, rocking rocking his hands locked over her breasts. Some new variation on an ascent into terror? Beginning to feel a familiar fear. You wouldn't do that to me, would you? God! Don't, I'm frightened. Turning again and she allowed her hands to lay claim to him, her fingers whispering the words, she might distract him if she did this, if she caressed him, explored the dimensions of his capacities, sealed her mouth with his body. He twisted, held her open, refusing to be distracted, returning her to a state of needing; his tongue a weapon. She cried out. He stopped again. She began to cry. Blindly reaching to lead him in, fill the emptiness. Shoving aside the pain. Stiffening but determined to go past fear past pain past suspicion. Relaxing then around him, kissing him small kisses, whispering, "I want you I love you it's all right all right. Oh God! It's all right. I'm so close if you don't move at all just hold me very tight, tighter, I'll come oh! I'm going to hold me hard as you can oh please harder, tighter please oh God! I was so afraid so afraid."

❋   ❋   ❋

Sunday evening. Grady spread a blanket on the lawn at the rear of the gatehouse, plonking William down, then lying propped on his elbows, making the baby gurgle with pleasure. Laughing. Telling William, "I've got a case on your mamma, kiddo. D'you think she can hear us?"

"She can hear you." Gene laughed.

"Oh hell!"

"I do, too, you know," she said.

"You do too what?

"Have a case on you."

"Dynamite! We'll have a great time."

She smiled.

The car pulled into the driveway and Gene got to her feet as the door opened and Del climbed out. Darkly tanned, widely smiling. Her teeth very white behind the smile. Her hair cropped like a small boy's. Looking rounder, healthier. Walking carefully as if the package of her self was something she'd just been given and she was being very protective of it. On the far side, Martin got out of the car with B.P.

"I brought you a suitcase full of presents," Del said, taking hold of Gene's hands.

"Thank you. How are you? Was it good? You look so well. So well."

"Mostly good. It's hard learning someone else's language. It does feel like that—like a new language."

"And everything was all right?"

"Eventually. He does care about me and about the things I care about. It takes some getting used to. Breaking all the old bad habits, learning new good ones. I missed you. And William. Did you miss me?"

"You know I did."

Martin was talking to Grady, who was standing holding William and looking over every few seconds as if he expected the two women might suddenly dematerialize in front of him.

"You'll both have dinner with us here," Gene asked, "won't you? Such a cute puppy."

"My alter ego. His name is B.P. You're not wearing a scarf."

"No."

Del's hold on her hand tightened. Then she let go, saying, "When I was twelve years old, you were six. Now, I'm forty and it feels like my thirteenth birthday. Strange going into new times, new feelings. When you were six years old, did you have an imaginary friend? I did. And she was like you." She laughed, then turned, looking around. "It's all so green. Familiar. I wasn't sure about the house, about coming back. But I am now."

On impulse, a little giddily, she kissed everyone in turn. Then, saying, "May I?" to Gene and receiving Gene's go ahead, lifted William

out of Grady's arms and, still smiling, walked off across the lawn.
Home.

✳   ✳   ✳

✳   ✳   ✳

About the Author
Charlotte Vale Allen was born in Toronto Canada and lived for three years in England before moving to the United States in 1966. After working as a singer and cabaret/review performer, she began writing full-time with the publication of her first novel LOVE LIFE in 1976. The mother of an adult daughter, she has lived in Connecticut since 1970.

✳   ✳   ✳

Get in Touch
If you would like to comment on this book, or you would like to be added to the author's mailing list in order to receive notification of forthcoming books, please write to:

Charlotte Vale Allen
c/o Island Nation Press LLC
144 Rowayton Woods Drive
Norwalk, CT 06854

✳   ✳   ✳

Visit the author's website at:
http://www.charlottevaleallen.com

Printed in the United States
17909LVS00004B/202-210